THE HAUNTING OF ADRIAN YATES

THE HAUNTING OF ADRIAN YATES

MARKUS HARWOOD-JONES

METONYMY PRESS

MONTREAL, QUEBEC

The Haunting of Adrian Yates

ISBN (print): 9781998898008
ISBN (EPUB): 9781998898015
ISBN (PDF): 9781998898107

This is a work of fiction. Names, characters, events, and incidents are either the products of the author's imagination or used in a fictitious manner. Any resemblance to actual persons, living or dead, or actual events is purely coincidental.

Metonymy Press
PO Box 143 BP Saint Dominique
Montreal QC H2S 3K6 CANADA

Printed in Canada by Imprimerie Gauvin
First edition
First printing - 2023

Cover illustration and design by Keet Geniza
Edited by H Felix Chau Bradley
Author photo by Katia Taylor

Library and Archives Canada Cataloguing in Publication

Title: The haunting of Adrian Yates / Markus Harwood-Jones.
Names: Harwood-Jones, Markus, 1991- author.
Identifiers: Canadiana (print) 20230533280 | Canadiana (ebook) 20230533299 |
ISBN 9781998898008
   (softcover) | ISBN 9781998898107 (PDF) | ISBN 9781998898015 (EPUB)
Classification: LCC PS8615.A775 H38 2023 | DDC jC813/.6—dc23

Dépôt légal, Bibliothèque et Archives nationales du Québec, 2023.

For River

PROLOGUE

efore Adrian Yates knew his own name, he knew the graveyard. The subtle bend of its grass, left to run long and yellow in summertime. The gaunt, twisted trunk of its solitary oak tree, arms forever tangled in the iron fence. Uneven rows of slick, mossy stones; his favourites were the ones without names. Some had their letters worn by alternating seasons, ice storms and acid rain. Others buried here were simply too poor to afford a stonemason's hand, remembered instead as *Mother*, *Son*, or *Beloved*. Then, there were those like Adrian. Those whose heartfelt names might never have made it to their own lips, much less to another's ears. Those who hid in closets and knock-twice bars, in poems tucked under pillowcases. Laid to rest by unsuspecting spouses and children, they remained unknown to anyone—even themselves.

With a rough scrubber and kitchen scissors for the

weeds, Adrian would walk along the narrow lines of dirt. He never quite knew what he was looking for, until he found it. An obscured date, perhaps. A patch of dandelions, reaching towards the sun. A tug in his chest would tell him who needed attention. Adrian would then sink into the mud to begin his work. He wiped away their loneliness, one stone at a time.

While sprucing up their cracks or trimming back weeds, Adrian told them stories, secrets, gossip. He spoke about the drudgery of high school, his unengaging teachers, the petty conflicts of his classmates. He'd share snippets of his parents' arguments at home or speculate on the staying power of his best friend's latest hobby. When the weather turned and the ground hardened, he came with library books and read his favourite passages aloud while sipping hot tea from a thermos. The graves listened well and shared their lessons, too. On the best days, they would remind him: it's not so bad to go without a name; sometimes it makes you more interesting.

In time, Adrian did learn his name. It inched out along the margins of his notebooks, in the fog on the bathroom mirror. He held it tight, cultivating a secret sense of familiarity. He carried it throughout the day, tucked in his back pocket. When at home, in the privacy of his own room, he'd slip it out of hiding and pick off any stray bits of lint before taking it to bed. It became his friend, his confidant. Yet, his name grew restless. Unsatisfied with living in obscurity, it began to writhe and pulse and plot its escape.

On an autumn evening, when sunset shadows ran

long across the city streets, Adrian's fathers were marathoning a sitcom. It was some old-person thing, cancelled ages back and then reposted online by a niche yet determined fan base. Dad sat with a bowl of popcorn balanced on his lap, picking out crispy bits that had burned in the microwave. In turn, Pop snacked on the charred cast-offs while offering well-worn critiques of continuity errors and romantic clichés. It was a practiced dance and they ran through its steps without haste or fatigue. Adrian was their singular audience. He occasionally added to the banter while prepping food in what passed for a kitchen in their pocket-size apartment.

As Adrian peeled back the cardboard cover of a microwave meal, he held his name under his tongue. Its presence added a pleasant zest to an otherwise dreary dinner. Pop paused his commentary to pick a popcorn kernel from the back of his gums. When Adrian opened his mouth to fill in the gap in conversation, his name jumped at its chance. It scurried along his soft palate, dodged clenching teeth and leaped like a bird too young to fly. Adrian tried to catch it, but too late. The remnants of his secret ran between his fingers like egg yolk and landed with a squelch.

In the silence that followed, Adrian tested his ability to rewind time. He watched his fathers carefully, uncertain if they'd noticed the gooey mess now splattered across the kitchen floor. Dad gave a short thumbs up, saying, "Sure thing, kiddo." Pop grunted agreement and dug around for the remote. The microwave chimed, announcing the pre-packaged food had gone from frozen to burnt. Adrian rushed back to his room but his appetite failed to follow. Entombed beneath a pile of blankets, he could still hear the television's laugh track.

Despite its lacklustre welcome, Adrian's name became a repeat house guest. Dad made space around the coffee table, letting it nibble on the crumbs of their daily small talk. Pop would invoke it when reminding Adrian to wash the dishes or take out the trash. The first few times, Adrian winced. Not because his name felt wrong. Rather, it was too right, too real. Even when whispered, his name felt like a shout. The slightest hiccup was a passing glance on exposed skin. Every pause held with it the weight of the world's judgement. His fathers' efforts were just that— effort. Their awkward adjustments weighed on Adrian's narrow shoulders. Staring at the stucco ceiling night after night, he listened intently to their muffled chatter. He was waiting for a slip-up, a complaint. When none came, Adrian became all the more wary. No doubt they were stewing in unspoken resentment. What other explanation was there?

It wasn't until his sixteenth birthday that Adrian learned the truth. His name appeared again, this time in Dad's slanted handwriting, scribbled on a dollar-store card that Pop probably picked up on his way home from work. It was the mundanity of it all, the way it sat so quietly alongside a plate of (only slightly burnt) homemade brownies. His fathers hardly even seemed to notice its presence as they fiddled with a pack of matches, taking turns at failing to light the birthday candles. That's when Adrian saw his name for what it had always been. Like the mould between the shower tiles or the pigeons nesting on anti-roosting spikes across the street, it was just a fact of life. Persistent, if nothing else, it had moved in, unpacked its suitcases, and made itself known as a member of the family.

Zoomer was absolutely thrilled when she found out. They had been walking home together after school, her laughter trailing behind them like mist. Adrian smiled along, his name riding in the folds of his oversized hoodie. It hissed and whined, desperate to see the light of day. He gripped it in his fists, muffling the protest. But Zoomer must have heard it anyway. She asked him outright, while kicking at a frozen puddle. Caught by surprise, Adrian couldn't think of a lie fast enough and accidentally told the truth instead. Yes, he'd been carrying a new name. "Well then," said Zoomer, "let it out already."

Not here. Where the cars drove too fast and neighbour kids raced their bikes down the broken sidewalk. Where old men permanently sat on rusty patios of daytime bars, smoking pack after pack even on the coldest winter days. No, if he was going to share his name, it had to be some-where else. Someplace private.

So, Adrian led Zoomer to the graveyard.

A small plot, it had no good reason to be so quiet. The fence-posts were wide set and rusty, an ineffective bar-ricade to local noise and traffic. Yet when they stepped through the gate, the city's clamour bent to the rustling of unraked leaves, the crunch of fallen twigs. The sprawl-ing vines of forgotten planters had already gone to bed for the season, their stems withered and brown. Staunchly rooted alongside the rows of graves were a couple maple trees, several cottonwoods, and a lonely old oak. The stones themselves kept their secrets, silently welcoming Adrian's return. As with so many things in life, the grave-yard needed no reason to be what it was; it simply knew no other way to be.

The cemetery trees rattled, branches bare. Adrian huddled with Zoomer below the empty canopy, unfurled his fists and let her peer inside. He cradled his name like a broken-winged butterfly. Zoomer marvelled at this new delight, and a second later snatched it up like a hungry cat. She toyed with it, rhyming and singing with it, dancing around gravestones and back out into the street. By the time they arrived back at their shared apartment complex, she had worn his name through. It was as if she'd never known him any other way.

Though Zoomer was sworn to secrecy, word began to spread. Adrian's name whispered itself into the ears of his teachers and classmates. Soon, other pieces of Adrian began to emerge. Over winter break, he met a new reflec-tion. On his way out of the shower, it had tapped on his shoulder and drawn attention to Pop's beard trimmer that sat charging beside the bathroom sink. The clippers were warm running behind his ears, down his neck. Bits of black hair scattered across the bathroom tile while steam dripped down the mirror. In the end, Dad had to come in with kitchen scissors to help tidy up the back.

There were still days he woke up numb. Nights when

his thoughts raced across the popcorn ceiling and his eyes refused to shut. However, on the day his binder arrived in the mail and Zoomer insisted they bake a celebratory cake, Adrian was able to roll up his shirtsleeves to mix the icing. The cuts along his wrists had faded into bumpy scars. They were replaced by nicks earned with the shaving kit Pop bought him at a Boxing Day sale. Though his peach fuzz hardly needed pruning, Adrian enjoyed the lather on cheeks and the sharp scent of aftershave.

On a wet weekend in early spring, Zoomer showed Adrian how to sneak onto public transit. Stealing their way downtown, they fished out fresh looks from a second-hand shop. His favourite find was a pair of high-tops. Adrian had been walking a little taller lately, and all his old shoes had become too tight. These ones beckoned to him, with their worn insoles and busted laces, their frayed lining and sides the colour of fresh pine on a chilly morning. They were perfect. More than perfect, they were *his*. When Adrian got home that night, he pulled out a Sharpie and signed each tongue, treasuring the joy of writing his name.

Adrian's visits to the graveyard became sparse. He had lost some commonality with the nameless ones who rested there. He still kept an eye on the place from his bedroom window, up on the fourteenth floor. It was less formidable from an aerial perspective. When standing among the rows of graves, the grounds seemed to sprawl out in all directions. Seen from above, the patchwork lot looked more like a temporary oversight. A forgotten stretch of grass and stones, large enough to hold a couple retail stores or a pay-per-hour parking lot. Plastic bags and fast-food cups were frequently stuck between its fence-post teeth. It slumped between walls of glass and concrete, the cause of frequent traffic jams as drivers struggled around its uneven intersections.

The whole neighbourhood was on stolen time. Everyone seemed to think so, especially Pop. The sparks of "revitalization projects" had already snaked across downtown like fire through dry leaves, leaving ash and unfinished condos in their wake. The city's eye would soon look towards their strip of tacky corner stores and block apartments; its mouth would open wide and draw them in, promising higher property values and nicer restaurants. The cemetery would be swallowed, along with everything else. Some zealous young developer would rebrand it as "untapped real estate" and all of Adrian's old friends would get paved over, turned into the foundations of an overpriced café or weed dispensary.

But not yet.

Weeds sprouted through the sidewalk cracks. Porch planters and balcony gardens shot up with fresh sprouts. The graveyard's cottonwoods became laden with downy seeds that filled the breeze. The city never held still; parts were always dying off, getting eaten up and then regurgitated as something entirely new. It turned out, Adrian was the same. The night his name had first escaped, he'd lost his footing in the world and never quite regained it.

When walking to school or making a midnight run to the 7-Eleven, Adrian would go out of his way to pass that old iron gate. When craving a pinch of peace, he could still go walk those unkempt paths, talk with the crumbling graves, and admire the monoliths. It was comforting to know, in the face of so much upheaval, some things could remain.

ONE

The upstairs neighbour was practicing his trumpet again. Despite hours of rehearsal, he had improved little. He actually seemed to be getting worse. Adrian had been the unwilling audience of a muted concert over the last three months. It was broken into parts—first a clarinet, followed by a trombone, then a brief but brutal stint with a violin. The aspiring musician's quest for his ideal instrument left Adrian restless and struggling for sleep.

Even without the ceiling symphony, Adrian's world was too noisy. Impatient drivers, wailing sirens, city busses and their squealing brakes. By day, the sharp hammer of new construction and endless roadwork. At sundown, the cacophony lessened only slightly. From a barrage to a thrumming pulse, the city's heartbeat never fully stopped. Dad loved it, of course. He said that buzz was better than any white-noise machine, in contrast to the drafty farm-house on the East Coast where he'd grown up. Adrian had to take Dad at his word; born and raised downtown, he could hardly recall a single quiet night any time in the last sixteen years.

The neighbour hit another sour note. Adrian gritted his teeth.

Sitting up in bed, Adrian rested his head against the thin wall that separated his room from the living space. The television's muffled tones leaked from the other side, doling out the worst news of the day. Pop must have fallen asleep on the couch again. He always said that he got his best rest that way, bathed in a medley of global tragedies, political pundits, and repetitive commercial breaks. The TV had been on a lot more since Pop started working over-nights. That was when the whole apartment began to feel unstuck in time.

Pop had begun to roam the halls at odd hours. Often, the only evidence of his presence were the drips of cof-fee on the carpet. In contrast, Dad normally went to bed early and woke up late. Yet, he too could never seem to shake the bags from under his eyes. Even nights like this one, when they both had the evening off, neither had much energy for idle conversation.

The weighty summer heat didn't help. With the air conditioning always on the brink of breakdown, his fathers kept the curtains drawn to stave off the heat. With the looming lack of structure of schooldays or even the sun's rise and set, Adrian's circadian rhythm drifted.

Hours would blur together into an endless grey. Unable to sleep, he'd burn through library books and cellphone data. Tonight, he'd run out of both.

Adrian kicked his sheets, sticky with sweat. He flipped his pillow to get the cool side, then flipped it again. He lay on his back, perfectly still, and counted down from one hundred. Eyes pinched shut, he visualized himself drifting down a gentle stream. When he peeked at his phone, hardly fifteen minutes had passed. All the techniques for battling insomnia that he'd read about online were clearly worthless. So, if sleep wouldn't come, he'd have to go out and find it.

An orange glow flickered along the bottom of his fathers' bedroom door, and from within came the frantic clacks of a laptop keyboard. Dad was working on his latest "big idea"—a novel about his childhood, chasing sheep over hills of red clay. Or was it a sci-fi spec script, a space opera about planet-hopping cats? Adrian couldn't keep track of the myriad yarns that Dad constantly spun, unspooled, and spun again.

Adrian's egress was swift. He knew just how to tilt his bedroom door-handle, which furniture and floorboards would rat him out if he looked at them the wrong way. Pop was in his usual spot, head lolled into a couch cushion. Blue light danced across his face as some car commercial played for the dozenth time tonight. He snorted in his sleep but did not wake, not even when the shoe rack whined to Adrian about the lateness of the hour. As for his sneakers, Adrian coaxed their loose soles down to squeaking only once.

Laces set, they slipped with him out into the hall.

One of the two elevators in the complex had been broken through winter and into spring. The superintendent showed little interest in changing course for the summer. The remaining lift was left to service the entire building, making the wait so long, Adrian speculated that he could walk up to the penthouse, down to basement, and return to the fourteenth floor with time to spare. Instead, he opted for the heavy, metal door that sat at the far end of the hallway. Black paint pronounced it an exit to the AIRS.

The *S* and *T* had faded so completely, Adrian briefly wondered if the builders had written it like that on purpose. Maybe they'd been trying to save on paint. He grasped its silver handle and the door sighed itself open. Adrian began the long trek down. The slap of his sneakers resonated through the concrete stairwell, all the way to the ground floor.

By June, the city's sidewalks remained warm well after sunset. Light pollution mixed with heat painted an endless orange sheen across the sky. A paltry breeze brushed Adrian's cheek and offered little relief. At the curb, Pop's voice whispered in the back of his mind: *Downtown drivers have no love for pedestrians—they'll run you over up, down, and sideways, then say it's your fault for not wearing a neon vest.* Even though the streets were relatively quiet, he scooted down the road to use the crosswalk. From there, his shoes knew the way.

A wrought-iron fence shimmered beneath the gaze of flickering street lights, patches of corrosion glittering crimson. Adrian knocked a tuneless melody along the bars as he came to the graveyard's only entrance. The archway's bars were decorated with spiralling patterns, intricately carved details lost to years of ice and rain. Tall doors had once gated the property but they too had rusted, the memory of them marked by broken hinges on either side. The gate was permanently open, a yawning maw through which anyone might enter.

Adrian trailed a hand along the cool iron. A sudden sting made him jerk back, fist drawn into his chest. His finger gleamed in the darkness, a droplet of fresh blood. Something had pricked him. Upon closer inspection, he discovered the tendrils of a rosebush. It had crept aside from a nearby headstone, entwining with the gate. Whoever had planted this memorial had not returned to prune it. Wiping off his hand on his jeans, Adrian stepped into the graveyard.

Soft dirt crunched beneath his sneakers. The long grass sighed as it bent in the breeze. Cottonwood seedlings misted the ground, the very last of the season. A nighttime songbird warbled its pleasant tune. Adrian walked along the centremost path, a natural route carved through generations. Though not that many mourners came around, nowadays.

The graveyard was a hanger-on, a leftover from a bygone era. Adrian had never witnessed a funeral procession there, nor were there any years marked among the gravestones beginning with the number 2. In the haphazard hands of a largely absent caretaker, its thick weeds and half-buried headstones invited few outsiders, as was Adrian's preference. The graveyard was one place he could remain uninterrupted. From the outside, it was unassuming. Yet once in, the rows upon rows seemed to stretch into forever. Adrian was certain he could stay there for ages and never grow tired.

The small, empty eyes of carved angels watched as Adrian slipped between the graves with ease. He paused occasionally, taking in familiar names and epigraphs, crumbling etchings of flowers and family crests. A few had framed photos, their faded faces locked behind cracked glass. While saying hello to his old friends, Adrian tried to ignore the regret pooling in his stomach. It had been three months since his last visit, which itself had been brief—a mere stop on his way downtown to meet up with Zoomer. He wasn't a good neighbour, not like he used to be. Stepping lightly, he drifted from the path.

Towards the back of the lot, the old oak tree beckoned to Adrian with a crook of its branches. Riddled in fist-size knots, its gnarled trunk was so wide that Adrian could not fit his arms around it—and he'd tried. The whole thing leaned with effort, as though a giant's hand was pushing it down towards the earth. Its low-hanging leaves tickled the tops of nearby headstones. The smallest grave among them was almost disappeared, lost beneath years of unraked leaves and dirt. Adrian crouched to get a better look.

Headlights pierced through the fence. Wincing, Adrian stumbled backwards. The corner of his sneaker was caught and began to rip loose. He shouted, landing hard on his

backside. Adrian groaned as he rolled over onto his stomach. After a moment to catch his breath, he untangled himself from the tree's heavy roots.

Palms caked with splinters and dirt, he found the
busted shoe salvageable. A good thing, too, since he
couldn't afford to replace it. Pulling a handkerchief from
his pocket, Adrian cleaned off his sneaker, then himself.
The cloth's grey paisley pattern was frayed at the edges. It
had been that way long before it had been gifted to him—
that is, if one could count a bequeathment as a present.

A small stack of identical hankies had been left to him
by his grandfather. Pop was always going on about how
they were so much more environmentally friendly. Dad
loved to point out that such things were also vectors of
disease, an invitation for germs to party in your pocket.
Adrian didn't care much either way. He just liked the feeling of carrying around a piece of old Pop-Pop.

Crumpling the handkerchief, Adrian's attention drifted
back towards the gravestone. *Sorel Carter.* The birth and
death dates were obscured, eaten away by at least a decade's
worth of decay. Adrian had not thought to bring his cleaning supplies. He scrubbed the stone with his handkerchief
instead and managed to reveal a few carved details. *Born
19*-something-something. *Aged 17 years. Beloved Son.*

Adrian picked at the patches of moss and tidied things
as best he could. He liked the name of this one, muttering
it to himself as he worked. "Sorel." He relished the taste
of it, the way it rolled around on his tongue. He resolved
to return and tend to Sorel again, next time with proper

equipment. It was about time he got back in the habit. The stone was worn but not cracked; with a little love, it could almost look new.

Resting a palm against the gravestone, as one might hold the shoulder of a friend, Adrian observed a moment of silence. Eyes closed, he listened to the rustling of the leaves, the muted tones of passing traffic. A chill crawled up his arms, through his chest, and around the back of his neck. It bristled along Adrian's hairline and turned to a pinch in his nose, so sharp and sudden that he nearly cried out. The feeling passed just as quickly and when he blinked, all was as it had been. He was in the cemetery, kneeling at a grave. He released his breath.

"You missed a spot."

Adrian yelped and turned, knocking against the gravestone. Pain ricocheted up his arm. He winced, a fresh bruise forming on his elbow.

A figure loomed over him, pale and lanky. It leaned, tilting its head to one side and revealing a grin of uneven teeth. When Adrian blinked, it seemed to change. Or maybe he'd just been too panicked to see clearly. It was just a teenager. No more than a year older than himself, Adrian would guess.

The stranger's white collared shirt was missing a few buttons. The knees of his corduroys were almost worn through. They were a stark contrast—Adrian had a round face and thick black hair cut short on either side. The other boy was all sharp angles and pinched lines, a mop of ginger curls. His skin possessed an eerie sheen, glistening even in shadow.

Adrian brushed off his jeans, his face burning with embarrassment. It was unusual to meet someone else at the cemetery, sure. But that was hardly cause for a screaming fit. He fought with his voice to keep it steady as he asked, "Who're you?"

"I think you know." The stranger's cheeks were hinted with freckles. Smiling impossibly wide, he silently extended an arm. Adrian willed himself not to step back. He wouldn't be intimidated by this weirdo.

Palm open, the boy's long fingers were lit by the glow of a nearby street lamp. Except, no, that wasn't quite right. Where his skin touched the light, it fell translucent. He offered Adrian an unfinished sketch of a handshake.

"What?" Sorel laughed. "You've never seen a ghost before?"

Two

irrors. It's all got to be mirrors." Adrian paced, searching the cemetery grounds. "That's how they do it." He grabbed at a nearby gravestone, studying its cracks for hidden cameras or fishing wire. Finding neither, he moved on to interrogate nearby bushes and shrubs.

Padding after him, the tips of Sorel's shoes did not quite touch the ground. "Who's 'they'?"

"Them! They!" Adrian threw up his arms. "You know what I mean."

"Do I?" Sorel's voice was warm, if a bit squeaky, and never in the same place twice. His words echoed, as if coming down a long hallway.

"Of course you do," Adrian snapped at the boy who was definitely *not* a ghost. "Magicians or whatever, they use mirrors all the time. It's, like, an optical illusion thing."

21

He pawed the smooth surface of a tall stone monument that marked the graveyard's midway point. "It could be a projector maybe. But then, where's the speaker?"

"It's got to be here somewhere." Sorel's wry grin flickered beneath the glow of a street light. "Keep looking."

"This isn't funny!" Adrian spun on his heel and marched back towards the oak tree. "You could really freak someone out like this." He searched for machinery hidden in the gnarled bark but came away with sticky hands, having only found a patch of sap. He scrubbed the tacky substance against his jeans. "Alright," he laughed harshly. "You win. Consider me pranked. Let me guess, you're filming all this for some crappy YouTube channel—don't I have to sign a waiver or something?"

"And this is exactly why I don't show myself off to the living." Sorel ran a hand through his shaggy, ginger bangs. "I put in all this effort just to get accused of parlour tricks."

Adrian waited for the reveal, for the act to drop. If Sorel was messing with him, he was seriously dedicated to it. Hovering in place, picking at his nails, he acted like this was all just so mundane. As if *Adrian* was the one being willfully obtuse. His insistence on existing, impossible as he was, began to make Adrian light-headed. Everything started spinning and Adrian's stomach lurched, like he'd been walking up a flight of stairs and missed a step. He slumped against the tree. This has to be a dream, he told himself. A super vivid, super freaky dream.

Maybe he'd fallen asleep after all. Adrian wracked his mind for tips he'd read online, ways to check if you're really awake. He pulled out his phone and looked at the time, expecting the numbers to be all wobbly and illegible. But the screen's brightness glared back at him with absolute clarity. It was just after three o'clock in the morning.

"Well, shit," he mumbled. "I'm gonna be tired tomorrow."

While Adrian had his existential crisis, Sorel knelt next to the small grave that bore his name. A faded handkerchief lay in the grass, dropped in the moment of panic. He reached for it, but the fabric slipped through his fingers. Jaw set, Sorel tried again. And again. On the third attempt, he managed to pinch the corner of the cloth and gently lift it. It floated through the air, a tiny flag. He smugly held up his achievement to Adrian, asking, "Could an optical illusion do this?"

No sooner had Sorel posed the question did the cloth fall through his fingers once more. This time, it refused to be caught. It fluttered back onto the ground, immobile as before. Breath in his throat, Adrian's race to rationalize this moment came to a screeching halt. He crawled from the tree's base and collected the handkerchief for himself, finding the fabric unnaturally cold.

"I guess not," he had to admit. "But that makes you a—what?" He giggled at the raw absurdity of such an idea. "A spirit? Maybe a poltergeist?"

"You could say that." Sorel tucked a fist under his chin. "But I'd rather you just call me by name."

◆◆◆

The longer Adrian sat in the graveyard, the less troubled he was by Sorel's continued presence. Back against the oak tree, fingers fiddling in the long grass, he studied his new acquaintance. Steadily, he grew accustomed to the way Sorel's face turned transparent when caught in the headlights of passing cars. As the conversation moved from expressions of shock to casual banter, the tinny echo of Sorel's words became less ominous—rather, it was fairly pleasant. Adrian's own voice began to sound odd in comparison, all flat and heavy.

A fraction of Adrian's rational mind still clung to the idea that this all was some elaborate trick or a drawn-out nightmare. But aside from a couple teasing comments, Sorel didn't seem to care. Adrian's belief, or lack thereof, did not change the fact of him. Over everything else, his confidence in himself was far more convincing than any well-reasoned argument or paranormal party trick. Sorel was dead, just as much as Adrian was alive. And they were sitting together, chatting like they'd just met up for a Tinder date.

"Got any siblings?" Adrian absent-mindedly plucked at the petals of sleeping flowers. "Or, did you have any?"

"A sister." Sorel fiddled with buttons on his shirtsleeve. One was loose, hanging by a thread. Yet no matter how hard he pulled, the stitch would not break. "She hasn't been around in a while, though. Nobody has."

"Oh. I'm sorry." Adrian bit down on the inside of his cheeks. What was he thinking, asking a dead guy about his family? "That's gotta be lonely."

"Sometimes." Sorel leaned against his own grave, elbow clipping through the stone. "But then you started coming by."

"You've seen me?" Hugging his legs, Adrian buried his face against his knees to hide any of the warmth rising on his cheeks.

"Sure I have." He said it like they both should know. "Mostly in the afternoons, sometimes late at night."

Adrian squeezed his legs to his chest. He knew he should be freaked by the idea of someone watching him—a ghost, no less. But there was something flattering about the idea. "I didn't realize."

"I know," Sorel nodded. "I didn't want to give you the heebie-jeebies, so I just let you do your thing." His attention drifted and Adrian followed his gaze across the cemetery, studying the quiet rows of uneven stones. "At first, I thought you knew someone here. I saw you tidy up some old geezer's spot. But then you went a different way the next time, and the time after that." As Sorel spoke, Adrian could see a shadow of himself weaving through the graveyard, kneeling to tug stray weeds and scrubbing off bits of bird crap. "I always hoped you'd make your way to mine, one of these days. Took you longer than I expected."

A lump of guilt slid down the back of Adrian's throat. "I'm sorry," was all he could think to say. "I guess I got kind of busy lately."

"Don't be too hard on yourself. I know how life is." Sorel tucked a curl behind his ear. A moment later, it came loose and drifted back into place. "Or, I used to."

In the distance, a siren wailed.

"So, what's it like?" asked Adrian. "Being..."

"Dead?" Sorel tapped his shoes. They were a pair of old, leather wing-tips and looked about a size too big. The heels were worn, curved up at the back. "It's not so bad," he decided. "Kind of boring sometimes, but time passes differently on this side."

"Like, faster?" asked Adrian.

When Sorel shook his head, his hair faded at the tips like it was made of smoke. "More like, smoother. All the little bits cut down and the corners shaved off." He moved a hand through the air, tracing his meaning. "You grok me?"

"Grok?" Adrian laughed. He'd only ever heard his dad use that phrase. "I don't. I do not grok you. But thanks for trying anyway." He ran his hands through a patch of budding clovers and plucked the pair longest among them, weaving their stems together. "Sorel, I'm sorry for not believing you, about the whole ghost thing. You've got to admit, though, it's all pretty unreal."

"Says you." Sorel stuck his out tongue, revealing streaks of blue and purple where it should have been fleshy and pink. "Back in my day, we were a lot less cynical about encounters with the unknown."

"And when exactly was *your* day?" Adrian smirked, folding in another flower.

"Dates and numbers kind of lose their meaning when you're on this side." Sorel knocked the ground of his own grave. "Especially when you're stuck in a six-foot pit."

"Okay but, are we talking horse-and-buggy times?" Adrian held up his clover chain to check its length. "Or boom boxes and cassette tapes?"

"I don't like to dwell on the past." Sorel shrugged.

"That's sort of ironic," Adrian snorted. "Don't you think?"

Sorel didn't answer, he just looked towards the graveyard's arch. The shining face of a gibbous moon cast it a cool blue while the city streets beyond ran amber and grey. When he finally did speak, Adrian had to strain to hear it—like he was catching pieces of a conversation, pressed against a closed door.

"I can remember some things," Sorel whispered. "My mother. Not her face but the way she smelled, like vinegar and soap. And our home, how my sister grew herbs on the windowsill. Always planted too early, they'd wilt in the frost." He scowled at the skyline. "And I remember how things used to look around here. Before all the towers and noise and people." A passing car spilled its headlights through the fence, and for a second, Sorel was not there at all. When he reappeared, he rubbed his eyes like he'd been caught in a camera flash. "Everything is so loud these days."

"I know what you mean." Adrian plucked another handful of clovers, looping their stems and securing each blossom into its place. "That's why I like it down here, at the graveyard. It's the one place in the world I can just be left alone." He chuckled. "Or, so I *thought*."

"Sorry about that." Sorel was grinning again, a lopsided smile that showed off the gap in his front teeth. "Voyeurism kind of comes with the territory."

Adrian started on another witty reply but was interrupted by a buzzing in his pocket. Digging out his phone, he blinked at the cracked screen and adjusted its brightness. Two missed calls, four messages waiting. "Shit!" he cursed under his breath. "Sorry, Sorel, but I should—"

But when he looked up, no one was there.

He walked around the graveyard twice, just to be certain. Adrian found no sign of Sorel anywhere. Pink and gold danced on the horizon, sunrise playing across the glass of downtown towers. Adrian dusted off the dirt from his clothes. He lingered for a moment and set his clover chain on Sorel's gravestone. "Hope I get to see you around."

THREE

"here the hell were you last night?" Zoomer chewed on the straw of their shared Slurpee cup. "I called you like a hundred times."

Adrian gnawed on a handful of rock-hard gummy candies. "Guess I slept through it."

"Don't give me that crap." Zoomer made a face, her tongue dyed bright blue. When she smiled, he could spot the tooth she had cracked on a lip ring last winter during her zinester-DIY-punk phase. "We both know you're basically a vampire."

She had a point. If it wasn't for school, Adrian would probably be full-on nocturnal during most months of the year. In the summer, he slept through the days with blinds drawn; it was the easiest way to avoid the worst of the city's rolling heat waves. By the time he was up and out of bed, the city had usually cooled. Everything just felt better in the night's navy-orange glow.

"You trying to kill me then, dragging me out into the daylight?" He nudged Zoomer with his elbow.

The midday sun glared down like a great, burning eye. There wasn't even any smog today to help take the edge off. The pair sat at the edge of a neighbourhood parking lot, its bubbling pavement barely shaded by a line of stick-thin trees. Adrian wiped the sweat from his brow with his even sweatier hands. "I can't believe you talked me into doing a Sev run in this heat."

Except, he could believe it. It was almost impossible to say no to Zoomer. She had a way about her, an ability to shape the world through raw force of will. It was a remarkable quality, though not always the most convenient. It also counted in her favour that Adrian had no other friends in their shared apartment complex. Adrian's fathers said he'd always "struggled to socialize." Though Zoomer insisted most people their age were vapid, self-involved, and worst of all *boring*—she encouraged Adrian to take his exclusion from their meaningless cliques as a point of pride. He wasn't quite convinced of her perspective, but it was still nice to have someone in his corner.

On their first encounter, Adrian had been certain that Zoomer was a pawn of one such popular group, setting him up for a prank. One afternoon in the laundry room, she just started chatting with him like they were already old buddies. Out of pure curiosity, Adrian had played along. Two years into their friendship, he still sometimes wondered if she was just messing with him.

Her name, the de facto title of their generation, didn't help matters. It seemed like a prank in itself, but she never offered another option nor gave any indication that it was a joke. Still, Adrian figured, there was no way someone would actually name their baby "Zoomer," let alone choose it for themselves ... right? Despite all his second-guessing, Adrian hadn't put up a fuss about it. Zoomer's own granny even referred to her that way, without a hint of sarcasm. So, he decided to just accept it. After all, for people like them, names tended to have their own force of will. Zoomer was just Zoomer, simple as that.

"It's not so bad. You just run hot." Zoomer pulled her thick curls into a bun, exposing a fresh undercut. She tilted the Slurpee in Adrian's direction. Only a few dregs of luke-warm syrup remained at the bottom of their shared cup. He declined the offer with a wave of his hand. "Anyway, what I was gonna tell you last night," she said, chewing on her straw, "is somebody forgot to reset the washers after they took out the change! I did, like, five loads of laundry, totally free."

"Oh, yeah." Adrian popped a sour cherry gummy into his mouth and chewed it over, looking off across the parking lot. "Sweet."

"Yeah, totally sweet," Zoomer huffed. "Then, I got naked and ran through the whole building. Plus, I rigged the elevator to only play 'Baby, I'm an Anarchist' on repeat."

"Wow." Adrian's tongue worked out a patch of gelatin

caught between his teeth. His attention drifted a few blocks down, in the direction of the graveyard. The memory of last night still buzzing in the back of his mind. "Really cool."

"Okay, that's it!" Zoomer pinched Adrian's arm, a hard twist for emphasis.

"Ow!" Adrian inhaled sharply and pulled back, rubbing his shoulder. "What the hell was that for?"

"Checking to see if you'd downgraded from vampire to zombie." She clicked her tongue. "Seriously, what the hell is going on?"

"You could've just asked," he pouted. Of course, there was no point in dragging things out. From the moment he got home last night, he knew it was just a matter of time until he told her. "I think I met a ghost."

Mid-sip, Zoomer sputtered and smacked her chest. "Are you serious?!"

"No joke." Adrian crossed an *X* over his heart. "I needed some air last night, so I went down to the graveyard—"

"Without me? You promised I could come next time!" Zoomer crumpled the Slurpee cup and tossed it aside. Adrian shot her a look and she groaned, snatching her trash back off the ground. "I wasn't gonna leave it there," she mumbled and got up to stuff the cup into a nearby garbage bin. "So you gonna tell me what happened or what?"

The sky's solitary cloud began to move off and sunlight gleamed brighter than ever, baking the pavement. Adrian winced and sheltered his eyes. "Like I was saying, I was down in the yard. And there was, like, this guy—"

"A real guy?" Zoomer plopped down at his side again. "Or like, a ghost-guy?"

Adrian sighed. "Do you want to hear the story or not?"

"No, yeah, definitely." Zoomer tucked in her legs and mimed a zipper across her mouth.

"Alright then," Adrian muttered. "He said his name was Sorel. He was buried in that cemetery, so I guess he haunts it now. I saw his grave."

"But was it like a ghost-ghost?" Zoomer scrunched up her nose, showing off the shine of her home-pierced septum ring, and stared him down. "Or a shadow person or grey lady or—?"

"I don't know." Adrian rolled his shoulders. Beads of perspiration formed down his back. Wearing a binder in the summer was always a damp affair. "He seemed pretty real, except for the being-dead thing."

"Mhm." Zoomer chewed on her nails, chipping their fresh black polish. "Dude, are you messing with me right now?"

"No!" Adrian insisted. "At least, I'm not trying to." He picked at the laces of his high-tops. The sole on his left shoe was still cracked—but maybe that happened someplace else and he'd just forgotten. "I don't know. It was probably just a dream or something."

"Absolutely not!" Zoomer gave him a firm poke. "You are not gonna rationalize away the only cool thing that's ever happened around here!" She tugged open the worn straps of her saddle bag and dumped its contents. Amid the wads of Kleenex and ketchup packets were a lighter, some scrunchies, a tightly bound pack of tarot cards, and a bottle of spironolactone. With one last shove, a pocket-size book joined the array: *Wytchcraft and Magik: A Practical Guide.*

"What is all this?" asked Adrian.

"It's my birthright!" Zoomer grinned. She picked up the book and started flipping through. The pages were covered in highlighter and notes. "I'm from a long line of witches. Didn't you know that?"

"I thought your gran was Catholic," Adrian pointed out. He'd seen the gaudy portraits of Virgin Mary displayed on every wall of that one-bedroom unit.

"You can be both!" Zoomer shot back. "Don't be so binary."

"Right. My mistake." Adrian rolled his eyes. This wasn't the first time Zoomer had revealed some new special interest on which she was suddenly an expert. He'd seen her go through her playwright phase, during which she'd spent her days and nights whipping together a dozen different scripts. Most of them were still unfinished, floating in a cloud somewhere. Then last spring, she had decided she was a professional vlogger and started filming every waking minute of her life for a week straight. That lasted until she had to reset her browser, lost all her passwords, and couldn't get back into her channel.

Of all her big ideas, the most time-consuming might have been when Zoomer tried to start a business flipping thrifted clothes. The plan was to scrounge as many second-hand items as possible, match them together to make a bunch of unique outfits, and then ship out the looks to monthly subscribers. Of course, she had insisted on bringing Adrian along as she spent hours sorting through the bins at Value Village. The whole project wasn't a bad idea, really. Until she realized that VV Boutique had upped all its prices ever since bougie teenagers decided to go all sustainable and vintage. The major price hikes on even the ugliest bell-bottoms left few funds for her website and shipping costs.

"Back when I lived out in the country, with my sister, I used to see weird stuff all the time." Zoomer scribbled something in the margins of her book. "Spirits, fae, you name it." She chewed on the back of her pencil, decimating any rubber left. "I always figured that the city was way too loud and bright for them to visit. Totally toxic for contact with the beyond."

The sun made its steady pursuit across the sky. Adrian leaned back, grasping for a pinch of shade. "Did your gran buy you all this stuff?"

"Oh, no way." Zoomer held up the book and cards for Adrian to see. "This WitchTokker I follow was having this giveaway and I got second prize! Can you believe it? All I had to do was like a couple of her videos, follow her on TikTok and Insta, and tag like fifteen friends!" She reached down her black tank top and revealed a cloudy grey crystal hanging around her neck. "This even came with it!"

Adrian looked sideways at the necklace. "Is that plastic?"

"It's sodalite!" Zoomer snapped back.

"What's that, crystallized Pepsi?" Adrian giggled, until the smile slipped from Zoomer's face. "Sorry. Bad joke. I guess I'm kinda tired."

"No shit." Zoomer flipped to another chapter of her book. "Its no wonder you're wiped—peering into the veil can be very taxing."

"For sure," Adrian mumbled. "Taxing. Yep."

"Well, I hope you're not totally out of spoons." Zoomer flashed her cracked tooth again and started to shove everything back into her purse. "Because tonight, we're gonna have ourselves a séance!"

FOUR

"Oh, spirits of the cemetery, trapped on this mortal coil, we call on your presence under this full moon!" Zoomer's hands were raised above her head. Her voice shook with gravitas as she rocked back and forth. "Make yourself known!"

Adrian opened one eye. "There's no way that's a full moon." He scratched his legs, sitting in a particularly itchy patch of the graveyard's yellow grass. "Three-quarters, at best."

"Shush." Zoomer wrinkled her nose. "It's *waning* from full, which still counts."

The shabby corners of Pop-Pop's handkerchief fluttered in the breeze. It was spread between them like a tiny picnic blanket and held in place by several crystals. Each stone had a very specific set of properties, explained by

Zoomer and promptly forgotten by Adrian. She had also set down a water bottle, a butter knife, and a set of tarot cards. In the centre was a melted candle, and Zoomer had nearly burned off her fingertips trying to light its stubby wick; eventually, she declared that the *intention* to light a flame was all that really mattered anyway.

It had taken a week to manage a trip to the graveyard, mainly because Zoomer had insisted that they go at midnight. On their first attempt to meet up, Pop had come home at the exact moment Adrian was lacing up his sneakers. He was clearly skeptical that Adrian was "just trying to break them in"—if his shoes were any more broken, they'd fall to pieces. Thankfully, Pop was too tired to really put up a fuss about it. The whole affair freaked out Adrian though, and he decided to lay low at home for a couple nights. Zoomer had then slept through their second try and, on the third one, found her granny sitting at the front door like a sentinel. How had she known about their plan? Neither had the foggiest idea.

All this fumbling meant they had missed the full moon but Zoomer gave no sign of concern. She sat across from Adrian muttering a chant, certain that this was going to be it. They were going to catch themselves a ghost.

"Psst," she hissed at Adrian. "I said no peeking!"

"How can you tell if I'm peeking, if you're not peeking?" Adrian crossed his arms.

Zoomer huffed. She reached into the depths of her patchwork denim vest to reveal a palm-size flashlight. "Oh, you who haunts this grave," she started up again,

"I call you in to this circle to speak with us, through this medium!" She carefully loosened the edge of the flashlight, causing the beam to flicker.

"Isn't that cheating?" Adrian pointed out.

"I saw some ghost hunters do it on YouTube." Zoomer shrugged. "This way just makes it easier for the spirits. Trust me." Adrian opened his mouth to argue but she shot him a look. "Do you want my help with this or not?"

"Not really..." Adrian mumbled.

If Zoomer heard him, she didn't acknowledge it. Instead, she waved with excitement at the flashlight as it started to flicker rapidly. "Look, it's happening," she hissed. "Are you here with us now, spirit? If yes, please turn off the flashlight."

The bulb fluttered, then went dark. Zoomer wiggled with excitement. "It's working!" She grinned. "Okay. Okay. Is this— Are you the ghost who met my friend here last night?" The two stared at the unlit bulb between them. After a few seconds of silence, Adrian slumped his shoulders. This whole thing was kind of ridiculous.

Just as he was about to suggest they call it off and go back to Zoomer's place for Netflix or something, the light came back on. The beam was stronger than ever, completely steady. A chill ran up Adrian's spine. "Yes! Thank you, spirit!" Zoomer clapped. "Now, tell us, what is your name?"

"That's not really a yes-or-no question," spoke a familiar voice from the air between them. Adrian jumped, accidentally scattering the careful arrangement of crystals.

The open water bottle fell sideways, spilling out onto the dry grass. Sorel materialized a second later, kneeling beside their small circle. His hand was on the flashlight's cap. "Sorry about that," he snickered. "I didn't mean to scare you."

Adrian's heart thudded in his chest. His binder was twisted, hampering his breath. He blinked a few times and rubbed his face, waiting for Sorel to disappear. When that didn't work, he whispered to Zoomer, "You seeing this right now?"

The whites of Zoomer's eyes sparkled in the moonlight. She was slack-jawed, speechless for possibly the first time since she and Adrian had met. Sorel hovered a ways back from the remnants of their séance. "You know, if you wanted to talk, you could've just said hi."

"Well, hi." The words were dry in Adrian's mouth. He stood and pulled at the bottom of his shirt to straighten out his layers. "What're you doing here?"

"Where else would I be?" Hands stuffed into the pockets of his corduroy trousers, Sorel paced in the direction of his grave. "It's not like I can go too far."

Adrian's heart rate was beginning to slow, the fragments of his thoughts shifting back into sentences. "How am I supposed to know that? It's not like I know the rules for, like, haunting or whatever."

"What, they don't have a how-to-haunt book in the library?" Sorel played with a curl of his shoulder-length hair. "Or did you just skip the homework and go straight to summoning?"

A smile danced across Adrian's face. "Tough talk, for a dead guy." As soon as he said it, Adrian clapped his hand over his face. "Sorry," he mumbled through his fingers. "I don't know if that's, like, rude or something."

"It's okay." Sorel's gaze drifted past Adrian, towards the rusty fence that enclosed the yard. "You're not wrong." The wisps of his ginger hair flickered briefly beneath the street lights. "Truth is, I sometimes forget what living people know about. And I guess I'm out of touch with what life is like on that side, too." He chuckled. "It doesn't help that I can't really get out much."

"So, you really can't leave the graveyard?" asked Adrian, stepping after him. "Like, at all?"

"Kind of a bum rap, right?" Sorel smirked. His eyes glimmered, flecked with the memory of a hazel pattern. He held Adrian's gaze, who found he couldn't look away.

Suddenly, a bright flash struck them both. Adrian tripped back, blinking spots. "What the hell?!" As his vision readjusted, he saw Zoomer was holding up her phone. "What are you doing?!"

"Making history!" Zoomer squealed and she snapped several more photos. Sorel shrank back and tried to cover his face, but his hands turned translucent in the phone's spotlight.

"Dude, stop," Adrian snapped at Zoomer. He stumbled towards her and pawed at the phone. "Cut it out!"

"You stop it!" Zoomer lifted her phone out of Adrian's reach, the camera's focus strictly on Sorel. "This is way too major *not* to document!" She sidestepped Adrian's clumsy grasping and closed in on her target.

Sorel gave a wordless wail and covered his face with both arms. A second later, he fell upwards and was gone. "Sorel!" Adrian shouted and reached out after him, grasping at the empty air. He spun towards Zoomer and demanded, "Why would you do that?!"

"Why would you not?" Zoomer turned her back to him and began to review the footage. Adrian grabbed at the cell a couple times but she easily pushed him off until all he could do was stand there fuming. "Come on, you can't *seriously* be mad," she snickered. "Think of the implications—we just discovered there's life after death!" She waved her phone in the air like a beacon. "Once I get this online, we're gonna be famous!"

There was a sudden spark and Zoomer yipped, dropping her phone. It scattered aside and landed, sizzling, on the ground. A sulphuric odour tinged the air. Sorel reappeared, wiping his hands. "I'd hardly call showing up on my doorstep a 'discovery.'"

"Did you seriously just—" Zoomer gaped at her phone, a smoking brick among the weeds. She knelt beside it, the cracked glass a dark mirror of her shocked expression. "Oh my god! I'm gonna literally *kill* you!"

"A little late on that one," Sorel laughed. He glanced at Adrian to share in the joke but got no reply. Zoomer was on the brink of tears, lips quivering. Adrian had seen her like this only a few times before. Once, when she was kicked out of class for being too "disruptive" for the third time in one week. And again, when she had discovered

Adrian was skipping second-period gym after he'd been teased for his new name during roll-call. That face wasn't a cry, it was a countdown clock.

He had to move, quickly.

Adrian stooped to grab the phone, still hot to the touch. He took Zoomer by the arm and pulled her aside. "Hey, hey, it's okay," he whispered, careful to put himself between her and Sorel. "We can totally fix it. Didn't you do, like, a phone-repair course a couple weeks ago?"

"Yeah," she sniffled. "Maybe." Zoomer grabbed her phone back, testing out the buttons. The screen briefly lit, only to go dead once more. "Files might be messed up though."

"Good," Sorel sneered. He hovered closer to Adrian, speaking from the side of his mouth. "Is that good?"

"It means the pictures and stuff will be gone," Adrian hissed back.

"Dammit!" Zoomer smacked the phone with her palm, trying to will the device back to life. It stayed dark. "Seriously?!" She shook the phone at Sorel. "Do you have any idea how expensive these things are? And this phone has, like, all my pictures from back home! If I can't get those back I'm—you're gonna be—"

"A dead man?" Sorel crossed his arms.

"Zoomer, come on." Adrian put a hand on her shoulder. "Maybe we can go to your place and check it out?"

Jaw clenched, she shrugged him off. "Yeah, whatever," she muttered, and shot Sorel one last dirty look before stomping back towards the gate.

Adrian held back until she was out of earshot. "Sorry about that," he said to Sorel, under his breath.

"It's okay." Sorel exhaled, drifting back down to stand at Adrian's side. "Thanks, anyway. For coming back."

"Of course," said Adrian. It was the closest he'd ever been to Sorel. A tingling sensation rose between them, a kind of magnetic pull. Adrian eyed Sorel's nervous fingers as they fiddled with the collar of his shirt.

Zoomer huffed and kicked at some dirt by the gate, making a show of how much she *wasn't* going to wait around.

"You should go," said Sorel.

Adrian nodded. "See you soon, though."

"You better." Sorel waved and vanished once again. The space he left behind was charged, the way the air gets static before a storm. Adrian waited one more second before he jogged back towards Zoomer. Even faced with her wickedest scowl, he was unable to suppress his own blushing smile.

FIVE

he dishwater was a dark storm, swirling in the sink. Adrian grasped a sponge, bits of its yellow fuzz floating among rainbow-slick waters beside coffee-stained mugs and bent fork prongs. He massaged circles on the surface of a dinnerplate, avoiding nicking his thumb on its familiar chipped edge.

The apartment thermostat was kept low in winters, at Pop's unspoken demand. Adrian had learned to savour soaking his chilly fingers in the soapy basin. This habit brought comfort even on hot summer nights. A few steps away, Dad lingered beside the kitchen stove with a wooden spoon in one hand and his phone in the other. On a front element, a pot's water struggled to boil under noodles put in too soon.

"How's the feed?" asked Adrian. "Anything good?"

Dad giggled and double-tapped the screen. "You know it." He set aside his spoon to type something. "I'll send it to you."

Adrian rolled his eyes. The very fact that a meme had arrived on Dad's page was proof that it was passé. His forwards were always reposts of reposts, low-resolution screenshots riddled with puns and old-people jokes. Adrian didn't even bother to pick up his phone as it rattled on the countertop. Not until it lit up again—and again.

A series of texts rolled in, all from *Granny Z.* Tilting his head to scan the message preview, Adrian wiped his hands on a dish-towel. Why would Zoomer's gran be texting him? Better question, how? The last time he went over to visit, she still only vaguely understood the difference between her smartphone and the TV remote.

The pasta water was now bubbling at a steady pace. A couple stray noodles leaped over the edge to sizzle on the stovetop. "Looks about ready." Adrian prodded at his dad before slipping towards the hall.

"Mhm," Dad muttered, not looking up. "I got it."

Tugging his door shut, Adrian fell onto the bed with phone in hand. He scanned the latest round of texts.

Granny Z: turns out those YouTubers are total liars

Granny Z: 😵 😵 😵 😵

Granny Z: fixing a phone is like, impossible

Granny Z: you need like, tiny screwdrivers and crap

Granny Z: anyway. looks like I'm stuck borrowing this phone forever. old one's totally busted 😔

Adrian chuckled to himself, tapping out a reply.

Adrian: Wow Gran. You're really getting good with emojis. I'm impressed!

Granny Z: ha fucking ha

Granny Z: this is totally your ghost boyfriend's fault btw

Adrian flinched at the bite of that last text. He ran through all the directions their argument could take. On the one hand, Zoomer had crossed a line trying to sneak a photo like that. Sorel was just trying to set his boundaries. Not to mention, she could have tried to clue Adrian in on her whole master plan. There must have been a reason no one else had ever gotten a clear shot of a spirit like that—what if there was some kind of ghost-law about living people snagging documentation of their existence? The last thing they needed was to end up on an afterlife edition of *Judge Judy*.

At the same time, Adrian did feel pretty bad. It wasn't just a phone that got wrecked, it was a piece of Zoomer's home. She rarely talked about her life before the apartment complex but Adrian knew she used to live with her parents, and a sister too. Then one day, that all ended and she moved in with her gran instead. In their years of friendship, Adrian had never seen her folks come by for so much as an afternoon visit. He sometimes wondered what the story was there, but Zoomer always tensed up when he broached the question. If he prodded, she'd find a reason to end the conversation, and then it'd be days before she'd answer a text or call. After a while, he learned to let it be. Adrian had watched his fathers run their circular arguments into the ground and his main takeaway was that sometimes, it's better not to push someone's buttons—he'd keep in his lane, politely ignoring the glaring gaps in Zoomer's life story. Maybe one day she would open up. Or maybe she wouldn't, and that would be that.

Adrian: That sucks.

Granny Z: more than sucks

The text chat fell quiet. Adrian waited. A few times, Zoomer started to type and then deleted. Whatever her untold saga, Adrian knew she held on to those memories of her life before. Her broken phone was one more chip in the link between then and now. If nothing else, he could sympathize with her loss.

After a while, Adrian broke their electronic silence.

Adrian: I really am sorry about you losing all that stuff.

Adrian: But dude, you know you can't just take people's pictures without asking.

Adrian: I'm pretty sure ghosts still expect you to get consent. 👀

A small checkmark appeared beside his last text. Zoomer had read the message. Still, no reply. Adrian tossed his phone aside and sat up on his bed. From his window, he spied that island of sparse trees and yellow grass between the oceans of concrete. He watched for any sign of Sorel pacing the grounds, any movement at all. Headlights drifted past, illuminating only the long shadows of gravestones and tangled branches.

An incoming message buzzed. Adrian tried to ignore the knot of anxiety in his gut as he reached over to read Zoomer's latest text.

Granny Z: I get that

Granny Z: just wish he'd asked me to delete the pics before going all paranormal activity

Adrian's skin prickled, like a cold breath had brushed the back of his neck. He snapped his head towards the window, half expecting to see Sorel peering back. But there was nothing, just the faint reflection of his own room against the city skyline. Pulling at his comforter, Adrian snuggled under the blanket. More messages were coming through.

Granny Z: he's damn lucky he's hot tbh

Granny Z: for a dead guy

Granny Z: otherwise, trust. it would have been go time

Adrian scoffed. Leave it to Zoomer to think even a ghost could be cute. Musing over his next message, Adrian considered her point. Sorel did have a certain flair about him. His captivating eyes still sparkled in Adrian's mind. But he wasn't about to admit that.

Adrian: lol

Granny Z: don't you lol me. you two had major vibes

Granny Z: 😤😭😭😤

Granny Z: that's u

Adrian scowled at the phone screen. Zoomer always could read him, usually even better than he could himself. It was time for a change of subject.

Adrian: Congrats btw, your first séance was a total success! 🎉

Granny Z: ty. guess it was more like a gay-ance

Granny Z: géance?

Granny Z: whatever you get the joke

Adrian: I think it's pronounced gayancé.

Granny Z: lol stfu

A laugh tickled Adrian's throat. It was all just so *silly*! Their night at the graveyard, his encounters with Sorel—everything! It was purely unreal. Giggling to himself, Adrian started to type out another reply.

The sharp ring of a fire alarm broke his train of thought. Adrian winced and covered his ears, stumbling out of bed. He hurried into the hall. Smoke billowed from the kitchen.

Dad was jumping back and forth, waving a plastic cutting board and trying to fill a glass of water at the same time. On the stovetop, the pot of pasta puffed like a chimney. "Adrian!" Dad looked back over his shoulder, not at all cloaking the panic on his face. "Stay back, okay? I've got this!"

"What the hell is going on?" Pop stood hardly a foot onto the threshold, keys still in hand. He dropped his work bag and ran towards the kitchen, grabbing the glass from Dad seconds before its water hit the pot. "What do you think you're doing?!" he hollered over the blaring alarm.

"Fixing it!" Dad's voice cracked as he shouted back.

Pop didn't reply, just snatched the lid off the counter and slammed it onto the pot. Using a dishrag, he moved the whole thing off the stove and into the sink. The smouldering pasta eventually burned itself out. "If that was an oil fire, you could've burned the damn house down."

"It *wasn't* though." Dad stomped off to pry open the closest window. Fresh air filtered in through its limited, two-inch gap—a safety feature for all high-rise apartments in the complex. The smoke began to clear, trails of their ruined dinner snaking out into the evening sky. "I had it totally under control."

"That's not how it looked to me." Pop began to putter around the kitchen, scrubbing the scorch marks off the stovetop. "Guess we're going without dinner tonight."

"We'll just have to order in." Dad was already scrolling through a delivery app.

"With whose credit card?" Pop sneered. "Or did you ask your publisher for another advance?"

"Hey, not necessary." Dad glanced towards Adrian and dropped his voice. "We said we weren't going to *do this* in front of him anymore."

"Do whatever you want." Adrian spun on his heel and marched back towards his bedroom. "I'm out of here." He slammed the door, a touch harder than he'd intended. But he wasn't about to go apologize.

The stink of burnt food and tense words lingered throughout the apartment. Adrian sighed, leaned against his dresser, and took out his phone. Zoomer had finally texted back.

Granny Z: so. when are we going again??

Adrian: asap.

SIX

After a day of baking in the summer heat, the cemetery dirt was cracked and dry. Yet, it remained cold to the touch. The sun hadn't even set all that long ago but as Adrian ran his fingers through the grass, he half expected to find frost at its tips. He sat at the base of the oak tree, and Zoomer hunched over a few steps away. She was sitting directly on Sorel's plot, nibbling on her thumbnail, bits of black polish blending into her dark lipstick. "What about Ouija boards?" she asked. "Are those real?"

"How would I know?" Sorel sat cross-legged, a couple inches off the ground, elbows propped against his bony knees. "I never messed around with that stuff."

"He might not even have ever seen one before," Adrian pointed out. "It's not like Amazon ships to cemeteries."

Zoomer bit off a chunk of her nail and spat it on the

ground. "You don't know that."

"Why would you get a talking-board from a rainfor-est?" asked Sorel. Adrian began to explain that he was talking about an online store, but it occurred to him he'd have to try and explain what the internet was first. Zoomer snickered at the whole clumsy affair.

A welcome breeze ran through the graveyard trees, rustling their full and waxy leaves. As Zoomer resumed her interrogation of Sorel's otherworldly knowledge, Adrian sighed and let his eyes rest for a moment. After everything that had happened during their first encounter, he'd been uncertain if he could coax her back to the grave-yard. Even more so, there was no promise Sorel would appear to them again. Yet Zoomer's curiosity outweighed her frustration. In fact, it was her suggestion they revisit the yard. And when they did so, there was Sorel, manifest-ing the moment Adrian passed beneath the iron archway. He had waited for them.

Sorel's apology was awkward, mainly because he still had little grasp over what had happened. He didn't under-stand the device nor how he'd managed to break it, but he could tell Zoomer's phone was precious to her. Crossing his heart, Sorel promised that he'd had no idea what would happen when he tried to grab it. It was on instinct, an acci-dent, nothing more. Zoomer accepted that explanation. However, she did make a habit of leaving her new-to-her phone at home.

As for Adrian, he was accustomed to sidestepping conflict. After years of navigating Dad and Pop's various disputes, he was almost proud of his ability to defuse tension and redirect hurt feelings. He knew how to keep his opinions to himself and look for reconciliatory opportunities. It took a few more visits before Zoomer and Sorel could relax into each other's company again but Adrian could see the hurt was healing. Beneath the heavy-lidded gaze of a crescent moon, tonight they were sealing their truce with a dusty bottle of whiskey. Zoomer had pilfered it from her granny's not-so-secret stash.

Truth, Dare, Drink was undoubtedly one of Zoomer's favourite games. She frequently badgered Adrian into playing, but it wasn't quite the same with only two people. Besides, he wasn't much a fan of alcohol—not since last fall, when Zoomer had talked him into crashing a classmate's house party. Adrian had learned the hard way that vodka coolers have more alcohol per litre than most cans of beer. That night, he'd fallen asleep cuddled up to Zoomer's toilet. The next day, he'd woken in a twisted-up binder, sneakers inexplicably missing their laces. He'd since learned to mime his shots.

"I'm mostly surprised you still play with those things." Sorel tapped his chin, still considering the Ouija question. "They were old news, even back in my day." The cap of the whiskey bottle sat at his feet, a makeshift shot glass. Zoomer insisted he participate though none of them were quite certain how his spectral body would react to raw liquor. He'd happily taken all his truths and dares so far.

"I think one time, I was curious about them." The more Sorel thought on the question, the less tangible he became.

Even his words trailed off like wisps of candle smoke. "I brought up the idea to ... my mom? But it was a no go. I don't think she ever bought into that paranormal stuff."

"That's ironic." Zoomer snorted.

"Hm?" Sorel blinked, like he'd just remembered she was still there. "Oh, yeah. I guess so." He hesitantly laughed along with her. "I'm pretty sure Mom was the no-nonsense type. She didn't even want me watching *Star Trek*."

"Oh!" Adrian perked up. "Were you a fan of the original series? Or, wait, is it—you *are* a fan?" He stumbled over his words. "Sorry, um, I didn't mean to—"

"Ugh!" Zoomer threw her head back as she groaned. "This is like watching someone try to figure out the singular 'they' for the first time. Absolutely brutal."

"I think I was, yeah." Sorel wound his jaw, chewing out the memory. "I used to go down ... down the street I think. Or maybe it was on the next block?" He tilted forward, peering eastward of the graveyard. "There used to be a hardware store down that way. And this guy—what was his name? I know I went to school with his sister." A crease of concentration formed across his brow. "I used to go by after class sometimes. He'd let me hang in the back of the store." Sorel's words began to crackle like a radio losing signal. "He was so nice. Really sweet to me." His presence flickered, like he'd stepped into the hazy gaze of a street light. "We'd watch *Trek* and just talk and smoke and..."

"Oh, come on!" Zoomer waved her hand at the space where Sorel had been sitting. "Just when he was getting to the good part!"

A second later, Sorel reappeared. "Sorry about that." He rubbed his eyes. "What was I saying?"

"You were telling us all about that cute boy you used to know!" Zoomer squirmed, inching closer. "Don't leave us hanging now—just how *much* trouble did you get up to in that back room?"

"Zoomer..." Adrian buried his face in his hands. Why did she *always* have to go there?

"Oh, um." Sorel shrank into himself. He drifted backwards, lifting further off the ground. "We didn't— I don't think he—"

"Can we just get back to the game?" Adrian clapped, shutting down this train wreck of a conversation. "Zoomer, truth or dare!"

"But Sorel hasn't answered *my* 'truth' yet!" Zoomer whined. "If he's not giving me a straight answer on Ouija boards, he's gotta do his shot!"

Adrian shook his head. Zoomer was stubborn, if nothing else. "How about we just bring a board next time?" he suggested. "Then we can find out together."

"Ugh." Zoomer huffed. "I guess that works." She turned aside and began to fiddle with her hair.

"Sounds like fun." Sorel nodded along. "And I think it's my turn now, so Zoomer, I dare you to—"

"You didn't even ask!" Zoomer drew her curls into a bun and whipped out a velvet scrunchie. "Did you not have this game back in ye olden times or whatever? You've got to say 'truth or dare.'"

"Fine." Sorel pursed his lips. "Truth or dare?"

Zoomer fussed with her up-do and knotted it tight. "Dare, obviously."

"Well, now I gotta think of an even better one." Sorel gave a lopsided grin and started to look around for a task. Zoomer began to weigh in, rattling off her own mischievous ideas for graveyard dares.

Tacit peace restored to their trio, Adrian let his own attention drift aside and upwards. He gazed at the grey apartment block a few streets over, counting floors until he found his bedroom window. He knew it by the orange glow of his salt lamp, left on indefinitely. Though he was too far to see it clearly, he imagined the rainbow flag strung up on his bedroom ceiling, his zine collection and bits of unfinished drawings all hung with twine. He ran through a mental list of all the little pieces of himself collected there, the things that made that box in the sky his home.

"How about I dare you to go pull off that nasty stuff someone strung up on the fence," Sorel suggested. "You see what I'm talking about?"

"Oh yeah. Ick." Zoomer faked a gag. "Looks like someone tried to yarn bomb that fence-post—that stuff gets so gnarly after a couple months."

"If that means it gets gross, yes it really does," Sorel shuddered. "Been bugging me for ages. Makes me itch, like a Band-Aid I just want to rip off."

The window just left of Adrian's bedroom was flecked with shadows and blue light. Probably the shopping channel. Pop had taken a break from the news this week, preferring to take cheap shots at the endless peddling of what he called "mass-marketed crap." Though, if Dad happened to be around, there was a decent chance at least one of those "crap products" would appear in the mailbox the following week. Adrian narrowed his eyes, searching for movement—was there even a chance that both his fathers were still awake, perhaps even enjoying a quiet night together?

The harder he tried to look for them, the more his vision blurred. Adrian winced, reminded of the headaches he got sitting at the back of class. For the last couple months, Dad had been promising to book him in to see an optometrist. First he wanted to find one within walking distance, then he cancelled that appointment because he found a cheaper place across town. Except the affordable one had a complicated booking system and Dad promptly lost his password for it. He was always doing that—putting things off, missing all the fine details. Rubbing his temples, Adrian asked himself, was it really a wonder Pop lost his temper sometimes?

"Well, okay, I can do that." Zoomer shuffled to her feet. "That's not, like, a super hard dare."

As she approached the fence, Sorel shivered and pulled even further back. "Says you." He twitched as she began to untangle the wad of yarn. "I can't even get close to that thing."

"What, this stuff?" Zoomer held up the unspooled mess. "It's not so bad. Just kinda mildewy."

"No, the fence." Sorel pulled at his shirt collar. "Can't you feel it? All sharp and terrible—any time I get too close, I feel like I'm gonna ralph."

"Damn." Zoomer tossed the last of the yarn-mess over the fence. "So, you really are stuck here inside the fence? That's gotta get old."

"You're telling me," Sorel shuddered as Zoomer came back to the circle. She grabbed the whiskey bottle and knocked back a swig. "Hey, I thought you only had to do that when you *don't* do the dare."

"Yeah, well—" Zoomer hacked and smacked her chest, wrestling the drink. "If we keep that pace, we'll still be sober by sunrise."

The living-room window went dark. Adrian's wavering hope was quickly snuffed out. Dad had probably gotten fed up with Pop sleeping on the couch and turned off the TV, trying to get him to come to bed. Which, of course, Pop wouldn't do. As he put it, if he was up, he was up. Pretty soon, Pop would be microwaving a midnight coffee and on his phone, seeing if he could snag an extra shift. Which meant the apartment would be that much emptier by the time Adrian got home.

Annoying as he was sometimes, at least Dad stuck around long enough to mess things up. Pop seemed to practically live at work these days. And if he couldn't go in, he'd roam the house in search of something to complain about. The leaky tap in the bathroom, the rings on the coffee table—everything was always broken, and always somebody else's fault.

Adrian stared at the square of their apartment, watching it blend in with all the other empty windows on the block. How silly he had been, thinking his fathers could be up there and happy together. They were too caught up in their own worlds and petty conflicts. Had they even noticed he was gone? Unlikely.

Times like this, he never wanted to go home.

"Dude? Buddy?" Zoomer snapped her fingers. "*Hel-lo?*"

"Hm?" Adrian turned away from the living-room window. Still, its after-image was burned in his mind like a camera flash. "Sorry, what?"

"We were asking if you'd like to go next?" Sorel told him. "For the game?"

"Oh, yeah." Adrian tucked his arms around himself, suddenly feeling a chill. "Sure."

"Something up?" Zoomer asked. "You've been real quiet tonight, even for you."

"It's whatever." He pinched the bridge of his nose, nursing the growing headache. "Let's just play the game already."

"Fine." Zoomer nudged the whiskey towards him. "Truth or dare?"

"Dare," Adrian answered without hesitation.

"Cop-out." Zoomer lay back in the long grass, her arms behind her head. After a moment to think it over, she decided, "Alright. I *dare* you to tell me what's making you such a grouch."

"I'm not a grouch," Adrian frowned. "Everything is fine."

Sorel sucked his teeth. "Come on now. Even I know 'fine' never really means fine."

Scowling, Adrian pulled at a handful of the graveyard's

long grass. He contemplated telling them the brutal truth. Those quiet yet persistent thoughts that swore the world would be better off if he never went home, never went anywhere, ever again. At least if he was gone, his fathers wouldn't have to pretend like they cared about each other anymore.

No, he couldn't say that. Not out loud. That would only make the thoughts louder, more real. Instead, he settled on a gentler version of the truth.

"Alright, if you're not gonna drop it," Adrian said, unclenching his fists, "my dads had another blow-up the other night and it's been all extra tense at home ever since."

"They're fighting again?" Zoomer fiddled with her septum piercing. "I thought they were in, like, couples counselling or something."

"I think they had to stop when Pop lost his benefits, or maybe it's just not working anymore." Adrian kicked out a leg and lay on his back, too. "They don't really tell me anything. Even when, like, I'm right there, you know?"

Zoomer nodded. "So rude."

"*So* rude!" Adrian threw his arms into the open air. "It's like, I'm seeing all this shit happen—you could at least pretend to care about what I think! But they're so caught up in each other, sometimes I'm like, would they even notice if I left for good?"

His question echoed off nearby headstones. The silence of the graveyard was thick but the city's noise had begun to creep in. Stiff winds howled through the gaps in the city's broad towers, filtering down between the fence-posts. In the distance, a car alarm went off. A dog wouldn't stop barking, even as it was told to shut up. Adrian turned his face aside and peered towards a nearby alley, where raccoons hissed and bickered over the cast-offs of a fast-food restaurant. His headache was growing worse.

"I used to ask myself the same thing." When Sorel spoke, the world quieted again. The car alarm stopped. The raccoons scurried into the shadows. "All the time, I wondered, would anyone *really* miss me if I was gone?" Lying on his side, Sorel traced invisible shapes in the dry cemetery dirt. Adrian watched him, carefully. "And yeah, some didn't. But some really did. Most were kind of a mixed bag." Sorel glanced up and caught Adrian staring. "For what it's worth, I wish I hadn't been in such a rush to find out."

The two held each other's eyes for a moment. Adrian could feel Sorel peering deeper. It was like he could see through him, *into* him—a witness to something buried so deep, Adrian himself had not been ready to touch it. Strangest of all, his piercing gaze did not hurt. In fact, there was a faint pleasure to it. A thrill, a flutter that rose in Adrian's chest. He had been seen.

"Well, this has been an absolute bummer of a truth." Zoomer sat up, giving one last twist to her nose ring. "I want a do-over."

"A do-over?" Adrian scoffed and propped himself up. "Are you serious?"

"Deadly so." Her eyes flashed between Adrian and Sorel.

"I don't love the way you said that," Sorel muttered.

Zoomer paid no mind. "While you two were getting all macabre or whatever, I thought up a proper dare. Something *fun*." She set her sights on Adrian. "Do you remember what you dared me to do, last year, at Paula C's Halloween party?"

"Not really," Adrian admitted. "Just that I ended up yartzing in her fancy heated toilet."

"Try to think on it." Zoomer pulled on a stray curl and let it snap back into place. "We were in that tacky-ass basement…"

"Right!" The memory began to take shape in Adrian's mind. "With all those animal heads on the walls. So creepy."

"And…?" She gave him an encouraging nod. "You found that old ship in a bottle and I said we should play—"

"OH!" Adrian smacked his cheeks. "Oh no, Zoomer, we can't. That's too far."

"Come on," Zoomer groaned. "Don't be a party pooper."

"What? What is it?" Sorel looked between them for answers.

"You're the worst." Adrian glared. Zoomer had fully backed him into a corner. She knew he wouldn't leave Sorel out of the loop. "At the party, we played spin the bottle," said Adrian. Sorel blankly stared back at him. "So, she's saying, we should, you know…" He tapped his fingers together, miming the meeting of two mouths.

"I dare you two to kiss!" Zoomer clapped her hands in excitement.

"Oh!" Sorel's face shimmered, an approximation of a blush. "Um."

"Obviously, we're not going to," Adrian quickly reassured him.

"Obviously," Sorel reiterated. "Not, if you don't want to ... with me."

"It's not that!" Adrian quickly tried to explain. "I didn't mean to—it's just, would it even be possible?"

Sorel shrugged. "Beats me."

"One way to find out!" Zoomer wore a wicked grin and poked at the whiskey bottle. "Or you could take the shot."

Adrian sneaked a glance at the bottle and bristled. His stomach twisted, warped with a medley of thrill and dread. He turned to face Sorel directly. "Well, I guess we could try it. If you're okay with that?"

Sorel nodded faintly. "Why not?"

Moving closer, Adrian struggled to look Sorel in the eye. Instead, he studied the back of Sorel's hands. Thin, blue veins glimmered beneath the surface of his skin. Scattered freckles ran up his arm. Sorel's collarbone peeked through the unbuttoned neck of his pressed, white shirt. Adrian examined the bend of his shoulders, the strong line of his jaw, the graceful tip of his aquiline nose; with each freshly catalogued detail, his own heart beat faster. A buzzing sensation rose between them—a magnetic pull. The longer they sat in silence, the more undeniable it became.

Sorel tucked a lock of ginger hair behind his ear, but it wouldn't stay put. "I can't exactly take you out to dinner first," he laughed, awkwardly. "Should I at least hold your hand?"

"Is that what people do?" asked Adrian. "It's been a

while since—"

"Same." Sorel chuckled. Adrian cracked a smile, too.

Leaning towards one another, the thread between became woven and taut. The meeting of their lips turned from a question to an inevitability. Adrian briefly wondered, *Will his lips be cold?*

A motorcycle engine ripped through the night. Its high beams roared past the graveyard and cast them all in brilliant light. Sorel vanished and Adrian, already too far to pull back, fell forward. He landed, face-first, in the hard dirt.

Zoomer let out an uproarious laugh. "Oh my god!"

"I'm sorry, I'm sorry!" Sorel reappeared. He rained down apologies, hovering a few feet above where he'd last sat.

"It's fine." Adrian rolled over. "I'm fine."

"That was too good!" Zoomer was gripping her sides. "Do it again!"

"Yeah, right," Adrian grumbled. "You already got doubles." He grabbed at the whiskey bottle, and with just a moment of hesitation, knocked back a shot. Instantly, he began to hack loudly. The sharp liquor burned his throat.

"Alright, alright." Zoomer caught her breath. "You've got to admit that was funny, though!" She snapped a pair of finger guns at Adrian. "And I bet it took your mind off the drama on the home front, didn't it?"

Still coughing, Adrian had to admit she was right. "Just a little, yeah." He winced and glanced at Sorel to share a quiet smile. "Who's up next?" he asked, tongue raw and tingling with an aftertaste of burnt cinnamon.

SEVEN

The windows of the family car were perpetually filthy. No matter how many times Dad used the squeegee at the local gas station, they always drove away with more streaks than when they'd arrived. Adrian had become accustomed to his back-seat view, peering out at the world through layers of grime and occasional bird crap. Even on sunny afternoons, like today, the city streets were dingy and smudged.

The check-engine light flashed every few minutes. "Damn thing." Pop smacked the dusty dashboard. "Keeps turning back on."

"Must be on the fritz," said Dad, doing a crossword puzzle on his phone in the passenger seat. "We just got it serviced a few weeks back."

"More like a few months," Adrian grumbled.

"Same thing." Dad looked back and motioned to the stack of papers in Adrian's lap. "You got enough of those? We could always stop at the library if you need to print more."

"Yep," Adrian answered bluntly. They'd already had this conversation three times before leaving the apartment.

"You'll need two for every business on the block," Pop added in. "One for management, and a second for if they lose the first."

"Hell yeah!" Dad's phone sang a small tune as he got the last question right. "Record time."

"On *easy* mode," teased Pop. Dad said something back but Adrian couldn't catch it. The engine whined as they steered around a large pothole.

The little car made its way downhill with only a few hiccups. They passed corner stores shoved up against narrow row houses, laundromats, and off-brand meat markets. Every few minutes, an empty lot. Blocky, white signs stood like crosses in a graveyard, tied to chain-link fences and the windows of abandoned storefronts. Their bold text promised more "developments" were on the way.

No matter how many times Dad tried to clean out the car, the back seat always smelled like old cereal and dried milk. The car jolted over a speed bump and Adrian's stomach jumped with it. He groaned, eyes aching from lack of sleep. He sneaked momentary naps during each blink. He longed to turn around and crawl back into bed; he should still be resting, regaining his strength for another late night at the cemetery. Studying the rows of coffee shops, he fantasized that Pop might pull over and order them all double espressos to go.

"You know," Adrian pointed out, "most places do their hiring online these days."

"All the more reason to go in person." Dad poked at his phone. "You'll stand out!"

"He's right," Pop nodded, slowing their approach as they hit downtown traffic. They inched along next to a dozen other grumbling cars, all while passing cyclists weaved through the congestion with ease. "This is how it's done, son."

"Uh-huh." Adrian crossed his arms and glared out the window. "And did you get your custodian job by dropping off a résumé?"

"When you're my age, you *know* people." Pop scowled as he struggled to change lanes. "You're still getting yourself out there. You've got to do the legwork, make the connections."

"So my real problem is that I'm a nobody," Adrian scoffed. "Thanks, Pop."

Dad tucked his phone away and leaned over the shoulder of his seat. "Can we cut it with the attitude, pal? Nobody wants to hire a Mopey Molly."

"A *what*?" Adrian smirked. "Did you just make that up?"

"I did not—it's totally a saying!" Dad turned to his partner. "Babe, back me up here!"

Pop kept his eyes on the road, grumbling something about a minivan up ahead. At the next stop light, they idled beside an old church. The chapel doors were nailed shut with a wooden plank. A billboard outside advertised the forthcoming SANCTUARY LOFTS. A similar sign was planted across the street, outside an old strip mall. It, too, was being hollowed out, making room for FORTY STORIES OF MODERN LIVING. Starting at prices Adrian doubted he'd ever earn in his lifetime.

"Damn condos," Pop growled. "Taking over the whole freaking city."

"Who's even buying those places?" Dad tensed his jaw. "With the market the way it is..."

"With the way it is, our place is next." Pop's knuckles braced against the steering wheel. "It'll be all too easy for some damn investor to come, kick us all out, and flip it into a pod hotel or some other nonsense. And then where will we end up?"

"Don't talk like that, babe," Dad tutted. "There's no need for pessimistic thinking."

"It's *factual* thinking," Pop snapped as he was cut off, yet again, this time by someone on an electric scooter.

Peering from the back seat, Adrian studied the billboards; the mock-ups of pristine white rooms with city-wide views, the perpetually smiling faces of prospective owners. Maybe Pop had a point. To hear him tell it, the city was destined to become a wasteland of skyboxes set at impossible prices, advertised indefinitely to a street-dwelling public who could only look up and wonder. If that was the world Adrian was set to inherit, what was the point of sticking around to meet it?

"Hey, look at that!" Dad tapped his finger on the driver's side window. "That new popcorn place still has a 'help wanted' sign."

"I thought you dropped a résumé off last week." Pop peered at Adrian's reflection in the rear-view mirror. "Did you call to follow up like I said?"

Adrian fidgeted with his seat belt. "I've been busy."

Pop opened his mouth to say more but Dad cleared his throat, jumping in to say, "I think I know what's going on here."

"What?" Adrian voice cracked. How could they know about Sorel—no, that didn't matter right now. More importantly, were they upset? Did they want to *meet* him? He wasn't sure which would be worse. "What're you—?"

"It's pretty damn clear to me, too." Pop finally got into the left lane, only to face a wall of construction pylons. He clicked on his turn signal yet again. "Adrian, your problem is that you just don't want to wake up before noon."

"Oh." Adrian slumped back into his seat. Of course this wasn't about Sorel or his nights away or anything faintly relevant.

"That wasn't how *I* was going to put it..." Dad's protest trailed off before it could even start.

"Your whole generation has some serious motivation issues. You know, some of us don't get to just sleep all day." Pop made it in to the next lane and pressed on the gas, barely beating an oncoming red light. "We wake up, put on our uniform, and contribute something to society."

Adrian sighed. He was all too familiar with this brand

of reprimand. "Pop, you work nights," he pointed out. "You *literally* sleep all day." That got a chuckle out of Dad. Pop was not so amused.

"Adrian, you—" Pop smacked the horn as another e-scooter weaved far too close, nearly clipping the driver's side mirror. "What's going on with you? You used to be so full of pep, you were bouncing off the walls!"

"Yeah, when I was, like, five." Shuffling his sneakers, Adrian kicked at the loose tissues and fast-food boxes on the car floor. "Almost like time has passed between then and now."

"There's no need to get smart with us," said Dad.

"I wasn't—" Adrian let out an exasperated sigh, crossed his arms and sulked against the window. "Whatever. I *do* work. There's just not many gigs right now."

Dad gave him a sorry look. "Buddy, let's be honest. Dog walking the corgi puppy next door hardly counts as a day job."

"Especially if the last time you did was in March." Pop pumped the breaks. A large truck was pulling out from one of the condo construction sites. "If you truly wanted to start your own business as a dog walker, we'd support you. But instead of, say, making flyers or building up a client base, you've been wasting away your summer, hanging around with that one weird friend of yours." He glanced over his shoulder. "Adrian, are you hearing me?"

"I hear you." Adrian pointedly looked away. Times like this, he resented his name. Lectures were so much more annoying now that they knew how to address him properly. "And for the record, Zoomer's not my *only* friend."

"Well, even if she was, that'd be okay." Dad flicked the radio dial, scanning through stations. He settled on one playing retro hits of the nineties. "Oh, I love this song!" He tapped along on the dash. "Anyway, I like Zoomer—she's fun! And this goth phase she's in lately, it reminds of me of when *we* were young."

"Don't remind me." Pop scratched his beard scruff. "I had that ridiculous mullet. And you, all into the rave scene." He half coughed, half laughed, "Hey, do you remember the first time I had you over for Shabbat? You showed up in cut-offs, a mesh top, and *so* much eyeliner—Mom nearly had a heart attack!"

"You still remember what I was wearing?" Dad's eyes twinkled.

Pop bobbed along to the music. "How could I forget?" They snaked past the construction site and began to pick up speed, rolling through a series of green lights. "When I woke up the next day, my bed-sheets were streaked green from that cheap hair dye you used."

Adrian gagged in the back seat. "Can we not talk about this? Who wants to hear about your nasty bed-sheets?"

"Now I know you're exaggerating." Dad swatted Pop on his knee. "I don't remember the stains being *that* bad."

"You wouldn't," Pop tsked. "I was the one who had to bleach them clean before my folks could notice my 'best friend' hadn't actually slept on the couch."

"Anyway!" Adrian loudly cleared his throat, desperate

to steer towards a new topic of conversation. "If you happen to care, Zoomer and I have been hanging out with someone new. So, you know, we're not the total losers you think we are."

"Did I at least buy the laundry detergent?" Dad tapped his chin. "I must have helped a little bit."

"You'd think so, wouldn't you?" Pop grinned. "But you were busy rinsing off the—"

"So, this new friend!" Adrian's voice cracked as he raised it even louder. "He lives... Um. Well, his name is Sorel. And we've been hanging out a lot. "

"What kind of a name is that?" Pop turned onto a side road and started to search for parking spots. "Some sort of cheese?" He snorted at his own joke.

"Be nice," Dad shushed him. "We're glad you're making new friends, Adrian." He clapped. "Oh, how about this? Let's do a family dinner! Then you can introduce us properly."

"Sure but, uh." Adrian bit his cheek. "That might be kinda tricky."

"Yeah, when do you think we can pull that off?" asked Pop. "Today's my only day off for the next three weeks." They rounded a corner, still no parking in sight.

"We'll make it work." Dad brushed off his concern. "Here, look, there's a spot!"

"Fire hydrant." Pop kept them moving. "And what does that even mean—you can't just 'make' things work because you want them to."

Dad wagged his finger. "Not with that Debbie Downer

attitude!"

"Here we go again. *I'm* the problem for being a realist."
Pop took them in another loop around the block.

"I never said that." Dad pointed across the road. "Oh,
what about between those trucks?"

"Way too tight." The car rattled as they came up to a
stop sign. The check-engine light was flashing again. "And
you didn't have to say it, you implied it. You always—"

"Here works." Adrian unbuckled his seat belt and
grabbed for the door. "I'll just hop out."

"Are you sure?" Dad leaned around his seat. "I was
thinking we'd walk around with you a bit, maybe grab a
little treat before heading home..."

"With what money?" Pop clicked on the hazard lights.
"We just ordered takeout last night. *Again.*"

"I'm fine, thanks." Tucking his stack of résumés under
one arm, Adrian kicked open the back door. "I'm gonna
meet up with Zoomer after this anyway. We'll bus home
together."

"If you're sure." Dad tugged at his own seat belt. "Just
stay safe, okay?" Adrian nodded thanks and hopped to the
curb.

"You're gonna do great, kiddo." Pop gave a thumbs up.
"Knock 'em dead!"

"And remember, we love—" Adrian slammed the door,
cutting off the last of Dad's words. He felt a little bad, but
the car soon grumbled away, down the road and out of
sight. With a sigh, Adrian turned in the opposite direction,
marching towards the main strip of shops and restaurants.

His first stop was a cat café but his allergies got the best of him; he sneezed about four times while just asking for the manager. Next he tried a high-end crystal shop, but the staff gave him so much side-eye, he felt the need to hurry off before they could accuse him of shoplifting. The remainder of his afternoon was much the same. There was no point to all this posturing, Adrian reasoned. None of these places were ever going to call him back. In the end, he dumped his entire stack of résumés into a recycling bin and made his way to the nearest library instead.

Among the air-conditioned stacks, Adrian flipped through familiar titles. He considered picking up a sci-fi book for Sorel—if he liked *Star Trek*, he'd probably love some Ursula Le Guin or Samuel Delaney. And if Sorel couldn't turn the pages himself, Adrian decided he would read it aloud to him. The very thought of it—sitting curled up on the graveyard grass, introducing Sorel to *Trouble on Triton*—kept Adrian's heart pounding all the way to sunset.

EIGHT

eady or not, here I come!" Zoomer hollered across the graveyard. She clutched a bent wire hanger, a makeshift dowsing rod. She held it with great concentration, waiting for one side to tilt and lead the way. Adrian spotted a 50% OFF sticker on the hook end; Zoomer stole all her hangers from the thrift store. He stifled a laugh as she suddenly took off, weaving her steps and jumping over headstones as she tried to follow the wire's directions.

Adrian kept a few paces behind. Zoomer had warned him not to get too close. She claimed his "energy field" could "throw off her reading." But how good could a divination tool be if a passing pedestrian could throw it out of whack?

"Aren't these things only good for, like, finding water?" Adrian's question was more of statement. He'd seen *Coraline*, after all.

"Such a mundane way of thinking." Zoomer took a few more winding steps. "They find what you need them to find. In this case, our ghost."

"I wouldn't say he's *our* ghost," Adrian pointed out.

Zoomer shook the wire like it had lost its GPS signal. She paused to readjust the placement of her plastic choker, its silver pentacle bouncing just above the notch of her neck. Around her eyes, she'd traced several layers of thick black liner. Adrian had to admit, whether or not she had the spell-casting down, she certainly looked the part of a burgeoning witch.

Once satisfied with the arrangement of her accessories, Zoomer raised the twisted wire once more and shut her eyes. With a small stumble, she was tugged along by the wire's lead. Adrian kept up after her, the pair of them moving in a spiral, falling deeper into the shadows of the cemetery. She started to go faster and Adrian jogged along, kicking up fresh mud as they hurried down the narrow path.

That's when Adrian caught sight of him. Hardly more than an outline of himself, Sorel crouched behind the sloping oak tree. He lifted a finger to his lips and Adrian fought back a smile. Zoomer's focus remained on the dowsing rod, which began to lean ever so slightly to the right.

"Are you sure you're going the right way?"

"Shh!" she hushed him. "It's working!" The rod began to lead her directly towards a granite monument in the centre of the graveyard. Adrian shook his head and turned back towards Sorel, but the ghost had vanished. Zoomer turned mid-step and smacked the hanger directly against the monument. "Ha." She pumped her fist. "I found you! Show yourself!"

Silence. Zoomer's rod stayed firm against the stone. In the distance, there was the drifting sound of honking horns. The faint rumble of a train. Adrian looked around at the empty graveyard. "Maybe we should look over by the—"

"Ah, you caught me!" Sorel materialized with a snap, perched on the top of the monument. "Nice guess."

"It wasn't a guess." Zoomer wore a satisfied grin and held her hanger high. "It was divination!"

"Sure, sure." Sorel winked at Adrian. "So, does this mean I have to 'seek' now?" he hovered down from his lofty seat. "That hardly seems fair. It's not like I have a living-person detector."

"That's not my fault." Zoomer stuck out her tongue. "Like it or not, it's your turn—and no peeking!" She flashed a wild grin at Adrian and took off into the shadows.

"Alright, alright." Sorel gave an exaggerated sigh. "If I've really got no choice." He turned towards the monument, face pressed into the crook of his arms. "Ten, nine, eight..."

Adrian ran in the opposite direction as Zoomer, searching for his own hiding spot. He was aiming for a broad gravestone, set a few paces from the front gate. It was just big enough to hide him well from most angles.

"Seven, six, five..."

The grass was muddy, still wet from a day of rolling thunderstorms. Adrian sank his knees into it all the same. Over the last couple of weeks, the summer's heat had turned humid and electric, ready to whip up a downpour at any moment. He loved this time of year, when the city's cacophonous nature was drowned out by thrumming rain, the sky lit with streaks of lightning followed by chest-rattling thunder-claps. Sewer grates overflowed and the headlights of passing cars rippled down the streets; dark grey streaks ran down the concrete towers, as if they were being recoloured by a massive, invisible paintbrush. Huddled up in a blanket, Adrian would turn off the lights in his bedroom and study the windows of neighbouring apartments. Strangers eating their dinner, tucking their children in to bed, and some, like him, quietly watching the city wash itself clean. After a storm had run its course, the air was left crisp and cool for a few hours. The perfect time for a midnight round of hide-and-seek.

"Four, three, two..."

Adrian spied Zoomer, hunkered down in her own hiding spot. She was pressed right against the ground, practically vibrating with excitement. The game itself had been Zoomer's idea, of course. She had been hanging at the graveyard more often lately, focussed on expanding her witchy skill set. Sorel had protested at first, claiming to be a novice on all things paranormal. But after a little encouragement from Adrian, he'd agreed to give these experiments a try.

In what had become a nearly nightly routine, the trio

would gather beneath the wavering branches of the oak tree and try out whatever new craft Zoomer had cooked up that week. They parsed pictures on tarot cards, tested out the credibility of homemade Ouija boards, lit candles of every colour, and cast various spells—none of which seemed to have even the slightest impact on Sorel himself. While Adrian was not especially interested in becoming a full-on psychic, he was always happy to watch and play along. He had begun to spend his days counting down the hours towards sunset. In the wee hours of the morning, when he made it back to bed, it became hard to sleep. He was left tired-eyed and buzzing.

"One! Ready or not, here I come!" Sorel's voice echoed across the graveyard like a stone skipped on placid waters. He spun around and vanished from sight. A prickle of excitement ran up the back of Adrian's neck. Who knew being hunted by a ghost could be so much fun?

Electricity slowly gathered through the humid air. Adrian scanned the cemetery, searching for any sign of movement. The trees' leaves murmured to one another. The lights of cruising cars passed long shadows across the graveyard. Adrian's breath was tight and he tugged at the binder under his shirt.

Something flitted past the corner of his eye. Adrian turned quickly but found nothing there. Was Sorel messing with them? Almost definitely. Or maybe their hiding spots were really that good.

Between the apartment towers and shabby storefronts was a network of alleys, including one that sat nearly opposite the cemetery's front gate. From that direction came a loud crash, followed by the yowl of a cat. Adrian was startled by the noise but forced himself to stay quiet, refusing to expose himself on account of a stray tabby.

Sweat began to creep under his arms. His heart raced. Maybe this wasn't such a good idea, Adrian thought to himself. This game was a tad scarier when he was hiding from someone with the option of invisibility.

"Ahh!" Zoomer shrieked and leaped up. In an instant, Sorel appeared behind her and gave chase. He was clawing at the air, making a show of it all, while Zoomer weaved between the cemetery stones. The weight lifted from Adrian's chest—this was all a game, he reminded himself. Just fun among friends.

Rounding a sharp turn, Zoomer turned to stick out her tongue. Sorel almost nabbed her but she twisted and doubled back, bobbing just out of his reach. Screeching with joy, she took a lap around a dark red maple tree—but her laughter was cut short. Her foot fell into a nearby well in the grass, where a grave marker had sunken into the earth. Adrian had almost tripped over that spot several times before. He watched as Zoomer suddenly pitched forward. Sorel tried to catch her but the two only managed to crash. They tumbled together, out of sight.

"Guys?" Adrian stood up from his hiding spot. When neither answered, he began to run. "Are you okay?!"

Just as Adrian grew close, Zoomer sat herself up. She was clutching her knee, black leggings ripped and slightly bloodied. "I think so?" Her voice was raspy, like she hadn't used it in ages. "She must've— Wait, who—" Zoomer pinched her eyes. "What's going on?"

"Did you hit your head on a stone or something?" Adrian crouched beside her and looked around. "Where's Sorel?"

"What do you mean?" Zoomer blinked up at him. "Where's Z— Augh!" She cried out and gripped her ears as if suddenly hit with a piercing sound. Zoomer began to yelp and went rigid, slamming into the muddy ground. Her whole body began to spasm. Adrian gasped and reached towards her but she smacked the air, warning him to keep away.

"No!" Zoomer balled up her fists, wailing on her own head. "Get out! Get out! Get OUT!" Back arched, kicking and screaming, she lurched and rolled around like she was trying to put out a fire. Adrian could only watch in horror as Zoomer began to pry something out of herself; it came through her mouth, slippery and translucent like a shadow made of oil slick. She gagged and doubled over but didn't stop. A fistful of hair rose from the back of her throat. She gripped tight, yanking Sorel out of her, head first. He tumbled to the ground and landed silently in the grass. Zoomer was on her knees, gasping for breath.

Adrian's stomach turned. He tasted acid on his tongue. "Shit."

"What the hell was that?" Sorel groaned and rubbed his head.

"I could ask you the same thing!" Zoomer wiped her tongue with both hands. "What the hell did you do to me?!" She reached towards Adrian, who helped her stumble up. "You taste nasty by the way—like, yuck!"

"What?" Sorel pinched his nose, his form wavering out of focus. "Wait, did I just—?"

"Possess me?" Zoomer brushed the dirt from her clothes. "Yeah, you did. Creep."

"I'm sure he didn't..." Adrian's words slipped away from him. That terrible image of Sorel falling out of her, it was burned into his mind. No matter how he tried, he couldn't push it away.

"I ... I don't know how that happened." Sorel rose to his feet. His voice was muted, as if coming through several layers of thick fabric. "I'm—I'm so sorry." He reached towards Zoomer but she took a large step back.

"Just stay the hell away from me!" she snarled, still short of breath. Adrian could feel her hands shaking as she gripped his arm. Her nails were cutting into his skin. "Come on." She pulled away. "Let's go."

Mind reeling, Adrian's body was on autopilot. He was still living in that split-second moment where the two ripped apart, in all its impossible, nauseating unreality. He let Zoomer lead him back towards the cemetery's gate.

Only when they nearly had crossed through the exit did Adrian return into himself. Glancing over his shoulder, he saw Sorel still hovering in place. He seemed stunned. Adrian's heart sank with every step they took apart.

Wait, he wanted to say. *Slow down, Zoomer. Can't we talk this out?* But he knew she wouldn't hear it. He could tell in the way she marched through the iron archway without a single word, how she stomped along the rain-soaked sidewalk all the way back home—Sorel was dead to her. In more ways than one. When Adrian finally made his way back to his own apartment, looking down from his bedroom window, the graveyard was as empty as it ever had been before.

NINE

The elevator whined with the passing of each floor. A thin strip of light rose, vanished, and rose again in the space where doors did not quite shut. At last, the car softly groaned as it descended into place. After giving it some thought, the doors creaked open. Adrian stepped out into the carpeted hall of the eighth floor.

The scent of cigarettes emanated from Granny Z's apartment. It sneaked under her doorway and traced along the hall. Adrian had never actually seen the old woman smoke indoors. He'd not even glimpsed an ashtray or lighter anywhere in the one-bedroom unit. Yet the smell remained, pungent as it was resolute. Once, Adrian had asked Zoomer about it. She laughed like he was joking. Maybe she had just gotten used to it by now.

"Come in, come in." Zoomer's grandmother shuffled

past in her fuzzy pink slippers and matching housecoat. "Be sure to lock the door."

Adrian dutifully flipped the deadbolt. He slipped on the chain lock for Granny's comfort, too. There wasn't much in her apartment that would be worth stealing, unless the thief was a collector of decade-old television sets or weird, porcelain angels.

Those small ceramic figurines were Granny Z's most prized possessions. She had them carefully arranged throughout the living room, perched on the crown moulding and stacked up along the windowsill. A tiny blonde girl with puppy-dog eyes and one broken wing sat at the corner of her fold-out tea table. Granny paused to give her a small kiss before lifting the electric kettle and pouring its contents into a large, stained mug. "You want some, love?" she offered. "Groceries came in yesterday. Got myself some Earl Grey."

"That's okay," said Adrian. "Pop's trying to get us all off caffeine. No coffee, no tea."

"Isn't that just criminal." The old woman sucked her teeth. She squeezed the tea bag against one side of her cup, then set it aside on a napkin for later use. Tapping in a spoonful of sugar, she swirled her spoon, then topped it all off with a splash of whiskey. "I might have something herbal in the cupboard, if you'd like to look."

"I'm good, thanks." Adrian eyed the apartment's only bedroom. A dim glow flickered along the bottom of its door. "Is Zoomer around?"

Granny nodded and shuffled back towards her seat.

There was a deep impression in the recliner where she settled back into place. "Word to the wise," she said, tapping her nose, "she's in a bit of a mood."

"Thanks for the heads up." Guilt wound in Adrian's stomach as he stepped down the hall. Behind him, Granny was already gently snoring.

His first knock got no answer. Adrian tapped the door again and Zoomer groaned from the other side. "Go away!"

After a few seconds' hesitation, Adrian slowly turned the handle and inched his way inside. Candlelight danced across the room. Small flames burned in cups and bowls scattered across the floor, along bookshelves, and up onto the wardrobe where they doubled in its long mirror. Zoomer was hunched over by the window with a set of tweezers. She poked at a melting candle and did not look up. "What do you want?"

He wanted to know if she was okay. Except, just asking if she was "okay" hardly felt like enough. Adrian peered over Zoomer's shoulders. There was a small triangle submerged part-way in candle wax. "What're you doing?"

"What's it look like I'm doing?" Zoomer hissed. A drip of wax slipped along the tweezers and burned her fingertips. She flinched and quickly blew on it.

"Getting into a new kink?" Adrian hoped he could get her to laugh. No luck.

"Did you want something?" Zoomer pried the wax off her skin and dug out more from under her fingernails. "Or did you just come to make fun of me?" She rose and motioned for Adrian to move aside. He obliged.

"Yes," said Adrian. "Or, I mean, no? I've just been ... thinking about you."

"Sure, sure." Zoomer kept her back to him as she studied her bedroom bookshelf. Its rows were packed tightly, uneven spines shoved together at odd angles. She ran her hands along various titles and pulled them down, seemingly at random. She would flip each book open, scan through a couple pages, then toss it into one of the piles on her twin-size bed. A few missed and landed on the floor. "As if you actually give a shit."

"Of course I do!" Adrian hopped aside to avoid getting clipped by a green book, the size of a pocket dictionary. "I know what happened must have been really scary. Even though I don't think Sorel really meant to—"

"Steal my body?" Zoomer threw another book without looking. This time, it was a small red paperback that landed at Adrian's feet. "Totally violate me? Try to control me?!"

"That's one way to think of it." Adrian stooped to pick up the book. He put it on top of a nearby stack. "But you're the one who was all curious about his ghost powers—so maybe we call it an impromptu, hands-on learning experience?"

"Possession is no joke, dude." Zoomer cracked the spine of a heavy black tome and pawed through its delicate pages, stopping occasionally to consider diagrams of complex symbols. "I think Sorel is a lot more dangerous than we realized. If that's even his real name." She came to the centrefold and shoved it into Adrian's chest. The text was so tight, he could hardly read it in the low light. "I spent all night looking stuff up online but then my data almost ran out, so I went to the library and got these to add to my collection."

"You've read *all* this?" Adrian scanned the books with stickered spines on the bottom of the piles. Many of them were riddled with Post-it notes and dog-eared pages, revealing the layers of her cryptic research. "That's legit impressive."

"It's a work in progress," said Zoomer with a flip of her hair. "I'm starting with bits that seem the most important." She took the heavy book back from him and replaced it with another, this one full of glossy pages. It displayed a drawing of a small girl casting a long, twisted shadow. "Listen. This one says that really bad spirits sometimes disguise themselves as little kids. It's a trick, to make people trust them."

"Except, Sorel's not a kid." Adrian pushed the book back into her hands. "He's our age. Or, like, he was."

"Except, how do we know that for sure?" Zoomer flipped through the next few pages of the heavy book, revealing wall after wall of dense script. "Think about it. What would stop something like that from *looking* like a teenager, if it thought that would win us over?"

"He's not a *thing*, or an *it*." Adrian took the book back and set it on her shelf. "I get that what happened, what he did, it must have been terrible. But that doesn't make him a monster."

"This isn't even about that." Zoomer was already into

another one of her library books. This one was full of black-and-white photos, blurry grey streaks at the ends of dark hallways and handprints on frosted glass. "I need you to hear me on this. Even if it's hard."

Adrian crossed his arms but kept his mouth shut. If she needed a listener, fine. He could do that.

"The thing is," Zoomer explained, "most ghosts can hardly even manifest a full-body apparition." She pointed to a page with a picture of a plain-looking, two-storey house. As Adrian's eyes began to adjust, he saw a pale face looking out from the attic. "That's part of why it's so hard to get a proper picture of one."

"So what?" Adrian asked.

"So *everything*!" Zoomer slapped shut the book, nearly catching his nose in the process. "Sorel's totally visible, like, any time he wants to be! And he can hear us—he talks back like it's no big deal."

"Now you're gonna blame him for being a good communicator?" Adrian's question was dripping with snark.

"Dude, we've seen him even move stuff!" Zoomer threw up her hands and began to pace. With each lap, a cascade of dust filtered into the candlelight. "Doesn't it weird you out?"

"I know, it's strange. *He's* strange." Adrian shuffled his feet. As much as he didn't want to believe what Zoomer was implying, he also couldn't shake the nausea that had settled into his stomach since that night. Adrian couldn't imagine what it felt like for her, to be so deeply invaded like that. Just watching the two of them rip apart had disturbed him so much, it still played in his mind on a loop. The panic on Zoomer's face—it had been like watching an animal caught in a trap. A trap that looked like a sweet-talking teenage boy, with eyes like a fresh-water pond and a voice that made Adrian's hair stand on end.

Yet there was another face frozen in his memory. Sorel's own expression had been that of utter shock. He seemed just as surprised as anyone else, and just as hurt when trying to sputter out an apology. Adrian's arms tensed as he recalled Zoomer's nails digging into him, the way she dragged him away before they could even try to talk. She might have been hurt in the moment, but Sorel was the one who got left behind.

Guilt sizzled on Adrian's tongue, daring him to speak the truth—Sorel wasn't some demon in disguise. And he certainly wasn't a threat. He was like them, lonely and in need of a good friend. All Adrian wanted was to go back to the graveyard, sit everyone down, and hash out all the sides to this story. Or better yet, rewind time to before everything had gone so wrong.

"Sometimes, yeah. I get kinda creeped by the whole sit-uation." Adrian shoved his hands into his pockets. "But of all people, you and I should know that you don't just ditch someone because they're different. You stick it out, try and understand."

"That's exactly what I'm trying to do." Zoomer sank down on the bed. "When ... when he possessed me, it was like I could see everything happening in the moment. But I couldn't control my own body." She shuddered and several of the books slipped towards her. "It was like getting squished down into this tiny little place. I didn't know if I would ever—if I *could* ever come back." A tear rolled down her cheek, a tiny mirror of the bedroom's candlelight.

"But you did." Adrian rested on the bed beside her. "You're here, right now, with me."

She took a long, slow breath. "I know." As she exhaled, Zoomer slumped into Adrian's shoulder. "I know." He nuzzled the top of her head and the two of them sat in silence for a long while.

Candle flames flickered and popped in hot wax. Wind rattled the windowpanes and the lights of neighbouring apartments began to fall dark. Most reasonable folks would be getting ready for bed by now, which meant Adrian was finally starting to feel like himself. Zoomer cuddled against him, so quiet he wondered if she might have fallen asleep. He brushed aside a tuft of her hair, as it was tickling his nose. "You don't really think what he did was on purpose," he whispered, "right?"

Zoomer yawned and rubbed her eyes. Her makeup was already well smeared. "Maybe not," she admitted. "But that doesn't change things. It might even make it worse." Stretching up, she offered Adrian an apologetic smile. "I know you want to trust him. I do too. But it's just too risky right now."

Jaw clenched, Adrian struggled to hold back the medley of counterarguments trying to worm their way out of his mouth: How can you talk about our friend like he's some kind of health hazard—a threat level we've got to assess? What do you mean it doesn't matter if he meant it? Doesn't that change everything? Have you even thought about how he must feel right now, wondering if we're ever coming back?

With a sniffle, Zoomer wiped her nose on the sleeve of her black T-shirt. Her face was still puffy from crying. Shame washed over Adrian, drowning all the words he knew he would never say. How could he try and convince her not to be upset? He'd seen the way she had wrestled for control of her own body—of course she was nervous at the thought of going back, returning to the place where it had happened. He was supposed to be her best friend. Yet here he was, thinking of ways to box up her fear for the sake of someone they'd really just met.

There was clattering at the window. Adrian sat up with a start. The pyramid-shaped candle had melted down to a smouldering wick and dropped something to the ground. "Finally." Zoomer hopped off the bed and grabbed her tweezers. "It's ready!" She snatched up her prize, a small square of wax-covered foil. She pried the wrapping apart, revealing a glittering crystal inside. "This is just what we need. Some proper protection." Adrian watched as she polished the stone using an old sock. After a few good scrubs, she motioned for him to hold out his palm.

It was still quite warm, and he had to pass it back and forth between his hands for a few moments until it cooled off. It was nearly transparent, save for a thick purple vein that ran through its centre. "And this is supposed to help how, exactly?" Adrian asked.

"It's quartz!" said Zoomer, as if this was the most obvious thing in the universe. "That line in the middle, that's amethyst. According to the box, anyway."

"The box?" Adrian dared to ask. Zoomer passed along a crumpled cardboard container, the cover of which read: PHANTOM CRYSTAL CANDLE—REVEAL YOUR PRIZE INSIDE!

"It came with my witch kit!" she told him, confidently.

Adrian snorted. Even at the worst times, Zoomer managed to find the silliest solutions. "You're sure this isn't just, like, some rock candy that they repackaged and marked up?"

"Obviously not!" Zoomer snatched back both the package and the stone itself. "Sugar would melt. Right?" She examined the crystal up close, eyeing it over, and then gave it a quick lick. A second later, she made a face and groaned in disgust. "Okay, that's definitely a rock. Why'd you make me do that?"

"Make you?!" Adrian laughed. "I was joking!"

"Sure, whatever." Zoomer smacked her tongue. "The point is, this thing is going to help stop our old pal Casper from trying to jump our bones. Literally."

Against his better judgement, Adrian's heartbeat started to race. "So, we might be able to go back after all? With this, uh, protection?"

"Maybe." Zoomer traced her fingers along the crystal, studying the strip of colour that ran through its core. "First I need to figure out this whole ritual-ward thing. That'll take some time, just to even figure out what books are right about what." Her gaze drifted towards Adrian, and she must have seen the pitiful look on his face. "Look, it's okay to be upset," she told him. "I know you like him."

"That's not— I don't." Adrian bit the inside of his cheek. "I mean, I don't *not* like him. I just—"

Zoomer put a finger to her lips. "Like I said. I get it. But if he's such a great guy, he'll understand if we keep our distance for a while."

"Right." The brief hope in Adrian fluttered out like a doused candle. "Sure."

"Also, we should have a safeword." Zoomer tapped the quartz against her chin. "Just in case he tries to body-snatch us in our sleep or something. Some way we know we are who we say we are."

Could Sorel really do that? Adrian wondered. He rested back on Zoomer's bed. "Now you're being paranoid."

"Excuse me, it's already almost happened!" Zoomer snapped. "And like, you don't even know how ghosts work."

"Whatever." Adrian shrugged. "So, what's this code gonna be? 'Beetlejuice'?"

"Too obvious." Zoomer paced across her room. "Hey, what was that short story we had to read for English last year? The one with Simon de Canter-whatever?"

"'The Canterville Ghost'?" Adrian scoffed. "You want *that* to be our safeword?"

"You're right. Too esoteric." Zoomer grabbed a large scrunchie and pulled her hair up. "It needs to be something that can come up easy in conversation."

Adrian studied the shadows dancing on her popcorn

ceiling. "What about something totally weird?" he wondered aloud. "Like, Granny Z's mac and cheese!"

"Oh my god, that's perfect!" Zoomer clapped.

"Perfect?!" Adrian sat up with a start. "I was kidding! What about the fact I'm lactose intolerant—and I thought you were going vegan?"

"Firstly, I was *pescatarian*." Zoomer wrapped a thread of hair around her finger. "Also, that was last month. Get with the program." She let her curl spring back into place. "Besides, the fact it doesn't make any sense is what's so brilliant! You'll be all like, 'Want some Granny Z's mac and cheese?' And I'll say, 'No, thank you, please!' Ha!"

"I guess that works," Adrian mumbled. He hadn't meant to come up with the solution so quickly—a passphrase meant there was a real threat to keep at bay. How did they go from being Sorel's friends to making safeguards against him?

As he glared at the flame of Zoomer's window-ledge candle, its wax began bubbling over. It was rapidly dripping onto the bedroom carpet. "Um," Adrian nodded, "is it supposed to be doing that?"

"What?" Zoomer gasped. "Um, definitely not!" She fell to her knees and started trying to catch the wax, cursing as it singed her fingertips. She glanced back at Adrian. "You gonna just watch me struggle?!"

"I was thinking about it." Adrian shook his head, slid off the bed, and blew out the flame. It flickered once and went dark. The scent of smoke and burnt carpet lingered long after.

TEN

The apartment always smelled like vinegar on Sundays. Pop insisted on making all their cleaning supplies from scratch. He swore up and down that his home-brew spritzer was just as reliable as store-bought disinfectants. Dad wasn't quite so swayed. Maybe because, somehow, it always became his job to spend a day hovering over a pot of boiling water and white vinegar. No matter how many drops of tea-tree oil or lavender he stirred in, the mixture always came out with the same acetous scent. It left Adrian craving French fries and sea-salt chips when it was his turn to clean the kitchen counters.

Finger on the trigger of the spray bottle, Adrian pushed a small blue cloth in figure eights. Each pass left thin streaks in its wake that slipped out of existence as quickly as they arrived. Illuminated by the rays of sunlight, they shared a brief dance across the countertop. Adrian's attention drifted towards the living-room window. While a midday sun cast the city in gold, the graveyard remained a series of long shadows. It held its secrets close, disclosing nothing to the outside observer. The cemetery trees were full, dense branches sheltering several graves from view, including the only one Adrian truly wished to see.

Though who could say if Sorel was there at all, anymore? Two weeks since their last visit, his patience must be running thin. Did he still pace, invisible inside those fence-post walls? Or had he given up entirely and gone wherever spirits go when they're finished with this mortal coil?

Adrian pressed a hand against the windowpane and closed his eyes. Zoomer's words of warning had been churning in his mind. The worst part was, she had a point. Even if Sorel hadn't meant to hurt her, the fact that he *could* was dangerous enough. They were completely without knowledge of his full power. Even Sorel himself had appeared surprised. The only thing that was certain was their own lack of protection. They had to keep their distance. It was the only logical option.

Except, Adrian speculated, didn't almost everyone have the capacity to do harm? That hardly seemed reason enough to cut them off, without so much as a proper goodbye. Zoomer promised it was just for a while, until she could find a way to shield them both. But how long was that going to take? Another couple weeks, at least. Probably more. Meanwhile, Sorel—if he was still beholden to the graveyard—was left to wonder when his so-called friends might deign to visit again. Despite Zoomer's words to the contrary, it didn't feel right ghosting the ghost.

The timer on the stove went off. Adrian snapped back to the present. A smudge in the shape of his palm remained on the glass. He gave it a squirt of cleaning solution and wiped away the mess. Stowing the rest of his supplies beneath the kitchen sink, Adrian slipped on a pair of oven mitts. The freezer-bag fries had cooked just right—crisp and bronze, steaming hot. He inhaled deeply with great satisfaction.

It took a few minutes for the fries to cool. Adrian inspected each one before arranging two equal portions. He set the handfuls in two plastic containers, where he'd already prepared two sandwiches, stuffed with the wilted remains of a takeout salad. It was an eclectic meal, but Adrian hoped it would do the trick. He clicked on the lid for each container and decorated them with hearts, drawn in dry-erase marker.

The door to his fathers' bedroom creaked open. Heavy footsteps meandered down the hall. Adrian tossed both sealed meals into the fridge and dashed to the couch. He shoved a few fries into his mouth on the way—they were still a bit too hot but he didn't dare make a sound. Just as Dad rounded the corner, Adrian pulled out his phone and pretended to scroll. They gave one another a passing nod.

"Smells good in here." Dad softly tapped his gut, stomach rumbling. "You making something?"

"Hm?" Adrian subtly swallowed down the last of his

stolen fries. He blinked at Dad, as if just properly noticing him. "No, uh, not really. But I think Pop left some food for us."

"He did?" Dad opened the fridge and spotted the two stacked containers. "When did he find the time to make this?"

"I dunno." Adrian ran his thumb along the phone screen, staring at nothing. "Maybe he got up early or something. Probably wanted to surprise you."

"Mhm." Dad eyed the dishes in the sink, the oven mitts on the counter. "Well, that was very thoughtful of him." He took one of the containers for himself and returned to his home office-slash-bedroom. As he went, Adrian fought back a grin.

Dad and Pop really did love each other. They had to, surely, given everything. Why else would they stick it out? Adrian only vaguely remembered the days when they seemed truly happy with one another. The older he got, the more those memories seemed like dreams. It's possible that version of his fathers had never really existed at all.

Everything in life was just too tight. That was their real problem. He and his dads were always bumping into each other in the apartment's narrow hallway, dancing circles any time two people needed the bathroom at once. When Pop got his latest job as an overnight custodian at the university, Adrian had thought maybe things might finally loosen up. His folks could have some space from each other. Dad would have time to clear his mind and finish that novel he'd been writing. Pop would make better money than he used to, which meant less stress for everyone.

Instead, somehow, things only seemed to get worse. Pop was surlier than ever, his patience wafer thin. Dad was perpetually hunched over his computer, yet Adrian had overheard him on the phone with his publisher the other day, asking for more time. The draft just wasn't ready. It seemed his fathers always managed to step on each other's toes—even when they weren't in the same room.

There was the rattle of keys in the door, the subtle click of the lock. "Oh, hey kiddo!" Pop smiled wearily as he stepped inside. "You're up early."

"It's a quarter after one." Adrian motioned towards the stove-top clock.

"Oh." His father blinked at the digital display. "So it is." He dropped his work bag and slumped down to untie his boots. Adrian pushed over on the couch, giving room for Pop to plop down beside him.

"You pull another double?" he asked. Pop answered with a tired nod. "Let me get you something to eat."

"I'm okay, thanks." Pop sank into the sofa cushions, eyes already closing. "Just need a little recharge before going back."

"You're working *again* tonight?" Adrian whined his way up, heading towards the fridge. "That can't be legal."

"Overtime is overtime." With a yawn, Pop fully tipped over. He sank his bald head into a throw pillow, on the cusp of snoring. Adrian just sighed.

When the snapping of the Tupperware lid didn't wake him, Adrian tried wafting the food right under Pop's nose. That did the trick—with a snort and a sniffle, he opened one eye. "Dad made it," said Adrian. "I think he knew you'd be hungry after work."

Digging an arm out from under himself, Pop cautiously took a bite. "Hm." He nibbled on one of the crispier fries. "Not too bad." As he sat up and started on the sandwich, footsteps returned to the hall. Dad must have forgotten something.

"See you later or whatever." Adrian grabbed a couple of his Pop's fries for himself and began to back away. "I'm gonna, uh, go do my homework." Right as he turned, he bumped up against a round, cushiony belly.

Dad smirked down at him. "Homework? In July?"

"Summer reading." Adrian sidestepped and continued his retreat. "It's a thing. Look it up." He scurried back to his own bedroom and only once the door was shut did he let himself fully breathe again. Pressing one ear to the wall, he held still and waited.

Bits of a muffled conversation. Adrian couldn't quite make out the words but their voices sounded sweet. Or, at least, not upset with each other. He grinned to himself—the plan had worked. Each father thought the other was making an effort. That had to count for something, didn't it? Adrian nibbled on the crumbs of their imagined dialogue.

It didn't take long for their tone to shift, however. Sing-song voices turned short, gruff, and jaded. Whispers, growing with intensity, like the gathering of sharp winds and heavy clouds. Adrian's chewing slowed and finally stopped. He swallowed, throat dry, wishing he'd thought to grab a glass of water before making his retreat. There was no way he'd be going back out there now. It'd be like walking into an oncoming thunderstorm without an umbrella.

A jackhammer's staccato played out below his bedroom window. A roadwork operation was in full swing, already having claimed more than half the street. Its overture was joined by the pulsing bass of the next-door neighbour's stereo—evidently, this was the perfect time to play some dubstep on repeat. A nearby dog chimed in with a touch of ceaseless barking, a piccolo mixed into the afternoon's orchestra. Amid all this clamour, Adrian could still follow every note of his fathers' argument. The subtle shifts, the rise and fall, the ultimate crescendo. The exact words were lost to him, but they didn't matter. He knew what they were saying. It was the same as it had ever been before.

Adrian crawled into bed. He pulled the covers over his head and, in that dark cocoon, let himself become enveloped by the warmth of his own heavy breathing. Pillows pressed against his ears, the beating of his own pulse drowned out all else.

He thought of Sorel. Not the ghost but the boy who once had lived. Who was he really—more so, who had he been? Did a spirit retain memories of its body's final moments, or what came after? Had Sorel been aware of himself as he was being buried six feet under? In utter stillness, Adrian imagined that moment. What it would mean to be so utterly alone, the walls closing in. Had Sorel heard the dirt hit the coffin, caught the muffled sobs of his mourning family? Such questions were frightening to consider, yet Adrian couldn't shake his curiosity. Sure, it sounded terrible, but at least death would have a finality to it. Maybe even comfort. The struggle to stay alive would be over. That alone was a tempting thought.

ELEVEN

Mud was caked onto the bottoms of his slippers. With each step, Adrian left a small indent in the dirt beneath his feet. Tall grass tickled his ankles when he stepped off the main path. An unusually cold wind swept through the graveyard. The solitary oak tree reached towards him, branches like the spindly fingers of grasping hands. The absence of its leaves gave him pause—had it not been summer just yesterday? Just as Adrian's mind began to grasp the question, another cold breeze snaked past and stole his train of thought.

He could not remember how he had made it to the cemetery. For some reason, that fact was untroubling. Adrian ran his fingers along the gritty stones, tracing the grooves of each name, the shape of mourning messages crafted by those left behind. Even when he tried to concentrate, he couldn't make out the words. The engravings bent and shifted into unfamiliar symbols. It hurt his head too much to try and parse them. Adrian turned away.

Sorel was sitting by his grave. He pinched a rose between his fingers, its petals slipping from his grasp as he tried to pry them free. Adrian tried to speak but no words came. He wanted to step closer, but when he lifted his foot, it couldn't find the ground again.

Adrian drifted upwards, as if gravity was a skill with which he'd become unpracticed. He passed right through the trees, their canopy of gnarled branches scratching at his arms and legs. He was falling skyward, up into the hazy orange night. If he could not stop his ascent, quickly, he would be lost to the sky forever.

With a silent cry, Adrian stretched his arm as far as it would reach. He clawed at the air, desperate for a handhold. At last, Sorel looked up, gasped, and leaped to help. But even as their fingers met, Sorel's solid hand slipped right through Adrian's grasp.

Adrian's stomach dropped. He fell faster, rising well above the graveyard. He passed along the apartment block and saw into Zoomer's window, the sill lined with candles. They all had burned to stumps. In the next room over, a man was standing behind Granny Z as she slept in her armchair. He was smoking a cigarette. Tumbling higher, Adrian passed his own unit, where silhouettes were arguing. There was no time to call for their help. Soon, all he saw were rooftops. The city opened up below, a patchwork of condo towers and sprawling neighbourhoods, L-shaped office buildings and scattered parks—all twinkling like a starry night.

An airplane passed just above his head. Adrian could hear the roar of its engine, feel its thrum pop his eardrums. He closed his eyes, a scream rising to his lips. No, not a scream. A name.

"Sorel!"

He woke with a start. Adrian blinked, staring into pure nothing. In the thick and stuffy darkness, all he could hear was the pounding of his heart. When that beat finally began to settle, it was replaced by the faltering melody of a poorly played trumpet. Adrian pushed aside the layers of blankets and pillows, rolled over, and reached for his phone. Though he hardly needed to check the time. The musician upstairs only ever practiced after midnight.

Adrian's clothes were stiff, his chest tight and sweaty. His mouth was dry and vaguely sour after sleeping with unbrushed teeth. He sat up and stared at the shadows of his bedroom for a full minute before getting out of bed. He double-checked his slippers but there were no signs of mud or grass stains.

It had all been so vivid. His first thought was to text Zoomer—she was usually up for some late-night dream interpretation. Mind still reeling, he couldn't seem to gather his thoughts into an intelligible message. After a couple failed drafts, his attention wandered towards the window instead.

If he told Zoomer about the dream, she'd probably just twist it into something sinister. It'd become an omen, a

THE HAUNTING OF ADRIAN YATES

dangerous portent. Yet another reason to stay away from the graveyard, away from Sorel. Adrian shut off his phone and tossed it back onto his bed. He grabbed a black T-shirt off the floor, some fresh underwear from his dresser, and a pair of mostly clean socks. After a once-over in the bedroom mirror, he cracked open his bedroom door and slipped into the hall.

It was an easy exit. Dad's snores drifted from his bedroom and Pop's shoes were gone from the rack by the door. Adrian's steps were completely silent. He knew each creaky spot along the floor. He hunkered by the doorway to lace his sneakers in the dark. The welcome mat promised to keep his secret, as did the deadbolt as it clicked open without a word. Adrian made sure to lock back up before running down the corridor.

TWELVE

The streets were wet. As Adrian had slept, the sky had grown dark, opened up, and zipped itself together again. The memory of a storm was contained within brimming potholes and tiny rivers cascading into sewer vents. Stepping off the curb, Adrian hurried across the street. Water had already sneaked under the broken seal of his sneaker and soaked into the heel of his sock.

The cemetery's fence glistened with reflections of the street lights. Raindrops fell along the curve of its arched entryway, dotting the shoulders of Adrian's wrinkled T-shirt. One landed on his face, a cold kiss against his cheek. The rosebush had grown taller in his absence, vines encircling the iron post.

The ground was soft, just like in his dream. A breeze cut through the humid air and tickled the back of his neck.

Adrian shivered and looked over his shoulder. "Sorel," he asked the darkness, "are you here?"

The only answer was the hum of traffic. Adrian set himself in a forward march towards the oak tree. At Sorel's grave, a handful of clovers had sprouted. Adrian frowned and knelt to pluck one, and at his back, a twig snapped. He spun in the direction of the sound. A small shadow scurried along the tree branches and a wiry red squirrel leaped downwards, ran towards the fence, and narrowly avoided a passing car while scurrying across the street. Just like that, Adrian was alone again.

Like the water seeping through his sock, a thought crept into Adrian's mind: Sorel might be gone entirely. He had no idea how ghosts were tethered to this world, if at all. What if they needed regular visits to sustain their after-livelihoods? Perhaps too much time had passed since their last contact. Adrian bit his lower lip, tongue flooded with the metallic taste of regret. Could it be that Zoomer's call to stay away from the cemetery had been the nail in Sorel's incorporeal coffin? Or maybe Sorel himself decided to leave, thinking they didn't want to have him around anymore.

Adrian slumped against the oak tree, landing among the mud and stray leaves scattered at its base. Picking up a nearby twig, he peeled back its wet bark, revealing pale wood beneath. He tried to snap it but the branch was too fresh. After a series of deliberate twists, Adrian was left with two broken halves linked by a vein of frayed pith. The shape looked a bit like Zoomer's homemade dowsing rod—it really wasn't so far off, when he thought about it. Adrian held the broken pieces in his fists and closed his eyes. "Sorel?" he asked again. "Are you here?"

There was a soft tug in his left hand. Adrian peeked and saw one half of the stick bouncing slightly. It nodded upwards and gingerly led him away. The weight in his hands shifted slightly, this time to the right. Adrian stepped along the grass, his muscle memory helping to avoid trampling on the graves. He was led in several circles, each one just slightly smaller than the last, until he arrived at his destination. With a thump, the dowsing rod had pulled him to the graveyard's singular monolith. Just like Zoomer's had done.

The stone's surface was marbled and damp. There was no sign of Sorel here, or anywhere else in the cemetery. Adrian shook the broken twig, trying to wake it. The night sky was growing heavy once more, the air thick and still. Adrian's time was running out. With a sigh, he tossed the stick aside and headed towards the gate. "What a waste of time," he berated himself. "What am I even doing here?"

"You know, I've asked myself that question many times," spoke a voice from behind. "Let me know if you figure out the answer." Adrian spun around and there was Sorel, propped against the monolith while examining his nail beds.

"You're alive!" Adrian gasped.

"Um." Sorel smirked. "Are you certain about that?"

"You know what I mean!" Adrian laughed and hurried back. "I was so stressed, I didn't know if you'd still be here." Arms open, he was about to offer an embrace but then stopped short. "Um." Awkwardly, he stuffed his hands into his pockets. "It's just really good to see you."

Sorel crossed his arms and eyed him over. "Mhm. Sure it is."

"Ah—I'm sorry," said Adrian, though he wasn't sure what he was apologizing for. Being too nervous to even give his friend a hug? Ditching said friend for two weeks, because his *other* bestie had told him to do so? "I wanted to come see you," he tried to explain, "but Zoomer was kinda tripped up after you guys, uh, had the incident."

"The possession?" Sorel tried to scowl but couldn't seem to hold it. He sighed and drifted downwards, the bottom of his shoes brushing up against the rain-soaked grass. "Yeah, well. It freaked me out too."

"It was an accident, wasn't it?" Adrian tiptoed closer. "You'd never intentionally try to take over anybody like that."

"How could you even ask me that?" Sorel sank even lower, the ground almost up to his knees.

"Well, *I* know that you wouldn't!" Adrian quickly doubled back. "But Zoomer, she feels like you're dangerous. She thinks we should stop coming here, at least for a while."

Dropping completely out of sight, Sorel reappeared a few paces away. Back turned, he was sniffling. Adrian had never considered whether ghosts could cry.

"It's okay!" he tried to reassure him. "It's all fine now. Or, it will be. I'm sure if you two just talk, you can explain everything!"

"Except, I can't." Sorel wiped his nose with the back of his shirtsleeve, leaving no stain. "I had no idea that was even possible. And I'm not sure I *could* stop it from happening again." He started to walk away, outline growing faint. "Maybe she's right. I am dangerous. You really should just leave me alone..."

"But—" Adrian grabbed after him but it was too late. Sorel stepped around the corner, like one might turn along a hallway, and promptly disappeared.

The graveyard was empty again. Litter danced along the fence. The long grass tilted in shallow waves. Adrian looked around for any sign of Sorel. Finding none, he returned to rest a hand against the cold, stone monument. "But, you can't just go," he whimpered. "I'd miss you."

"Well, same." Sorel reappeared, semi-solid and perched on a branch of the oak tree. Knees akimbo, he looked rather like a large bird. "Sorry for slipping out like that. I needed a second to collect myself."

"Oh." Hand to his chest, Adrian exhaled relief. "Okay. All good."

"This is all new to me, too, you know?" Using his thumbnail, Sorel picked at the gap between his front teeth. "I haven't been friends with living people in a bit. Not since—"

"You were alive?" Adrian ventured a guess.

"Ha! Pretty much." Sorel slid his way down and vanished. Mirthless laughter floated on the wind. When he rematerialized, he was leaning right over Adrian's shoulder. "Even then, it was pretty hit or miss."

"Shit!" Adrian jumped back. Spots flashed in his vision, like he'd been hit with a camera flash. All of Sorel's hopping around was giving him a headache. Rubbing his eyes, he asked, "Can you stay in one place for a minute?"

"I'll give it a try." Sorel's sideways smile glinted in the moonlight. "No promises."

Tamping down grass with his sneakers, Adrian sat in a dry-enough patch. Sorel drifted down to join him, still a foot off the ground. "Sounds like you've been lonely for a long while then," said Adrian.

"Worse." Yawning backwards, Sorel lay as if in an invisible lawn chair. "I've been *bored*. Being dead is so dull! I'd almost gotten used to it, until you came along."

Though Adrian knew it was selfish, he smiled. There was a special pleasure in being Sorel's main source of entertainment. He'd never been someone's whole world before. "Should I say I'm sorry?"

"Only if you mean it." Sorel shook his head, long hair spiralling behind him like campfire smoke. Adrian wondered how it might feel to run his hand through it. "When we're together," Sorel explained, "it reminds me of all the stuff I'm missing out on. When you go and I'm still stuck inside here, it's like I'm dying all over again."

"That's awful." Adrian grimaced. "Is there something I can do to help—maybe I can talk to Zoomer?"

"No," Sorel snapped. "She's right, you two should just stay away from here."

"But what about you?"

Drifting downwards, Sorel lay beside Adrian. The grass was undisturbed below his back. "I'll keep on keeping on." He waved at the grey sky, the tips of his fingers fraying again. They left traces like sand thrown to the wind. "You just move on and forget about me. Everybody else has."

"I could never." Adrian reached for what remained of Sorel's arm, hoping to keep him from vanishing completely. In an instant, he was hit with a cold snap. It was like grabbing a fistful of liquid nitrogen—Adrian gasped and pinched his eyes shut. He couldn't let go.

Every time he tried to pull his hand away, he sank deeper. His fingertips burned like they'd been hit with frostbite. The pain travelled rapidly up his arm and stabbed into his lungs. He'd lost his breath. Adrian's knees buckled and he was falling, swallowed by an endless ocean. He tried to scream only to gulp down freezing, salty water. His nose stung. His throat ran raw. All turned dark and numb. He was more than lost. He was gone.

◆◆◆

Rain pattered the back of Adrian's head. He felt his eyes open. He was bent over, face pressed against a wet gravestone. His lungs burned as they expanded for what felt like the first time in several minutes. After a few shaky breaths, his fingers dug against the mud and granite. His body pushed itself up, but he was a passenger in the experience.

"Adrian?" His name arrived, but in Sorel's cadence. "Oh no. Not again."

Thunder rumbled and shook the earth. The graveyard

was rich with the scent of wet moss and petrichor. What had started as a dribble turned into a deluge. Drops slipped from Adrian's wet hair and fell into his face; reflexively, he blinked and wiped it aside.

"I'm here." Just like that, Adrian's mouth was his own again. "It's okay."

Rivulets of rain snaked through cracks in the ground. It rippled over craggy headstones, welling in the curve of chiselled names and dates. Adrian spotted a dry patch beneath the oak tree. He gingerly stepped towards it. Just lifting each foot took a great deal of effort, like he was trying to move in a pair of oversized shoes.

"I'm so sorry about this," Sorel sputtered an apology. "I don't know why it keeps happening."

They arrived under the cover of sprawling branches. "It's fine, really," said Adrian as he crouched beside the trunk. His palms were slick, fingernails caked in mud. But they were still his own. "I'm here. I'm still here."

"Thanks for not freaking out." As Sorel let out a breath of relief, Adrian's chest lightened. "I'll, uh, try to go now."

Adrian felt Sorel try to move back out of him but there was an instant sting behind his eyes. It was a wrenching pain, sharp and quick. Both of them cried out. "Stop, wait—" Adrian grabbed the sides of his head as if it might be yanked off otherwise. "Just hold on!"

"I can do this!" Adrian could feel Sorel's panic rising in his own throat. "Just—just give me a second to figure it out!" Each of his attempted exits felt like a run against a locked door.

"I said *stop*." Adrian inhaled sharply and Sorel held completely still. Slowly letting out his breath, Adrian suggested, "Why don't you just stay for minute?"

Sorel scoffed. "You can't be serious."

Adrian blinked up at the dark sky. Clearing his mind, he moved away from what felt like the driver's seat of his body. "Take the wheel for a while. I don't mind."

Rain had begun to make its way down the oak tree's gnarled trunk. It trickled along the bark onto Adrian's back. His fingertips tingled with that same cold as before, except this time it came at a steady pace. Unpleasant, sure, but manageable. Instead of drowning, he was wading out into the water, willfully enveloped by a rising tide.

Sorel squeezed a fist, then the other. Stretching his legs into Adrian's, he rose and took a step. There was no need to speak, they both knew where they wanted to go.

The loose sole of his sneaker slapped against cemetery mud. When they approached the fence, Sorel tapped Adrian's knuckles along the cool iron posts. Each bar rang, a single plucked note. They arrived at the gate, joyful panic pounding in their shared chest. Together, Adrian and Sorel stepped through the archway and out into the street.

THIRTEEN

Fluorescent lights burned away all shadows outside the 7-Eleven's storefront. Sorel winced and sheltered Adrian's face. A tone sounded as they stepped through the glass doors. Sorel looked around for its source. The cashier hardly looked up from their seat behind the register. Adrian turned away and led Sorel into the nearest aisle.

Their clothes were drenched. Each step came with a soft squish and left a muddy footprint on the tile floor. Sorel inhaled deeply. He soaked in the blended scent of gas, sugar, and overcooked hot dogs. A bubbly tune murmured through the store's speaker system. Adrian grimaced; this pop song had been on every station all summer long. He could already anticipate its awful chorus, which would undoubtedly stick in his head for the rest of the night. Even as he went to cover his ears, Sorel took over and started nodding along to the music. He shimmied his shoulders and tapped down the aisle, brimming with delight at the simple pleasure of hearing something new.

Dancing down the candy aisle, Sorel marvelled at the selection before them. Through Adrian's eyes, it was all so colourful and vibrant! Reds so bright they tickled the back of his tongue, paired with rich blues that drew him in like an open sky. And the yellows! Brilliant and captivating, they sparkled brighter than any starlight. Sorel ran Adrian's fingers across the many surfaces and stopped to squeeze a bag of cherry-shaped sweets. He giggled at the sound of crinkling plastic.

Before Adrian could stop him, Sorel had pulled the bag from the shelf, and it opened with a pop. He shoved a handful of the candies into Adrian's mouth. The flavours hit Sorel like an ocean wave, and he almost stumbled back in shock—Adrian felt it, too, sugar sweeter than he'd ever tasted, and sour so tart it stunned his tongue. His lips went tight and he started to cough.

The clerk looked up, annoyed. "You gotta pay for that."

"Mhm!" Adrian managed to answer. With his right hand, he reached for his wallet, hoping against hope that he might have some cash. Meanwhile, Sorel upended the bag to pack in several more candies. He laughed aloud as each one exploded with flavour.

The roof of Adrian's mouth was on fire. His jaw felt like it might cramp. He dragged Sorel away from the candy aisle and moved towards the back of the store, swinging open the fridge to grab a bottle of water. He snapped open the cap and took a swig.

"Seriously?" said the cashier.

Fresh, cold, and crisp—Adrian had never been so refreshed. He had no idea how thirsty he was until he was awash in sweet relief. It was like an ice pack was pressed on his temples, relieving a headache he hadn't even known was there. Sorel helped him chug almost the whole bottle in just a few gulps. When it was done, they came up together, gasping for breath.

"Far out." Sorel moved to grab another drink but Adrian tugged them towards the checkout instead.

On the front counter, they dropped the open bag of sweet-sour candies, the near-empty bottled water, and a pack of gum that Sorel snagged from the nearest shelf. The store clerk scanned each item, lips a flat line. "You on something, buddy?" Adrian shook his head, no.

"It's called being high on life, buddy," Sorel announced, adding a slant to Adrian's usual smile. "Try it sometime!"

"Will do," the clerk replied while ringing up their total. "Now, that'll be nine bucks. Card or cash?"

"Nine *dollars*?" Sorel choked on the price. "Get real!"

"That's what stuff costs nowadays." Adrian dug into his pocket. "What decade are you from again?"

The clerk blinked at them. "Are you calling me old?"

"No—" Adrian sputtered. "I was just—never mind." He quickly counted out a handful of loonies and quarters, the leftovers of laundry day.

"It doesn't matter," said Sorel. "But hey, how much to add some of those to the mix?" He pointed towards a pack of cigarettes stuffed into the cashier's pocket.

"A pack of reds?" The clerk snorted and gestured to a locked cabinet. "Regs go for twelve fifty, but I'm gonna need to see some ID."

"Um, we're okay actually." Adrian tossed the remainder of his cash on the counter, snatching up their candy and bottled water. "Thanks, though—keep the change!"

"Just a minute..." The clerk pushed the coins around in a quick count. "Hey, this is only, like, five bucks!" But Adrian and Sorel were already dashing back out the sliding doors.

Outside, the rain was pouring down in sheets. It glittered in the headlights of passing cars. Adrian led Sorel around back of the convenience store and booked it down the closest alley. Once they'd put some distance between themselves and that angry clerk, the pair tucked themselves beneath a small awning. Huddled together on a side street, they gulped on humid air, shared heart pounding.

"What a rush!" Sorel pulled their stolen candy out from Adrian's pocket. "Do you always do stuff like that?"

"No!" Adrian squeaked. "What the hell were you thinking?"

"You're the one who took the stuff and ran." Sorel bit into another sour gummy.

"Only because you had opened it all already!" Adrian smacked, tacky sugar getting stuck between his teeth.

"You worry too much." Sorel waved off his concern. "It all worked out, didn't it?"

"Easy for you to say," Adrian snapped. "You're not the

one whose face they probably caught on camera!"

"Camera?" asked Sorel. "When did they get a photo of you?"

"Oh my god." Adrian's mind had already begun to race. "What if they come looking for me? How am I gonna explain this to my parents?!"

"You're not going to have to explain anything," Sorel assured him. "Even if they got a picture, we probably just look like a freaky blur or something."

Adrian tried to scowl but his face wouldn't quite cooperate. He settled on a slanted grimace. "How do you even know that? Were cameras even invented yet, back when you were alive?"

"I think so." Sorel thoughtfully tapped the water bottle on Adrian's chin. "Yeah. For sure." He swallowed down the last few sips of their drink. "But we know I mess with that kind of stuff, right—like with Zoomer's phone-thingy?" Sorel used Adrian's hand to give a calming pat on his shoulder. "Anyway, what's done is done. Try and loosen up a little."

Adrian glared out at the street. As much as he hated to admit it, Sorel made some decent points. Chewing on the too-sweet, too-sour candy, he watched as rainwater snaked along a nearby, overflowing eaves-trough. It rolled over the drainpipe, down into the open mouth of a nearby sewer vent. After a good while, his heartbeat slowed to a more normal pace.

"Tomorrow I'll go back with the rest of the money," Adrian decided.

"If that's what floats your boat." Sorel looked down, twiddling Adrian's thumbs. "Um, but listen. I am sorry for messing around. I'm just not used to all this living stuff—it's a lot to take in all at once."

"Well, bad news. It doesn't get any easier." Adrian chuckled. "But hey, next time, maybe run it by me first before you start grabbing at whatever is in front of you."

"Next time?" Sorel perked up, a lilt in his voice. "You want to do this again?"

A smile traced its way onto Adrian's lips. This time, he knew it was his own. "Yeah. I kinda do."

The pair set aside the wrappers of their pilfered goods. Sorel leaned back against a slick, brick wall and lifted Adrian's left hand. In turn, Adrian overlapped it with his right. Their fingers intertwined and a shiver passed between them. It was the closest they'd ever been to really touching.

Without speaking, the pair sat and watched the rainstorm fade. It became a drizzle and eventually just a heavy mist. Stepping from their hiding place, they made their way along back streets and alleyways. They approached the graveyard in the wee hours of the morning, when the glass towers of downtown sparkled like fresh dew. Looking out at them from beneath the cemetery gate, Adrian had never noticed how beautiful they were before.

FOURTEEN

Zoomer sat cross-legged on top of an industrial-size dryer, bouncing along with its tumble-cycle rhythm. She shuffled a deck of shimmering tarot cards. "Okay, concentrate on your question," she instructed.

"Hm." Adrian lay on an empty laundry bag that he'd spread across the cold tile floor like a beach towel. A washer rumbled beside him, its window a swirl of soapy water and twisting colours. "Wait, *I'm* supposed to have a question?"

"Obviously!" Several cards leaped to the floor as Zoomer attempted to shuffle the deck.

Adrian pushed himself up on his elbows and passed back the errant cards. "Can't you just pick one for me?"

"It's like you're not even listening." Zoomer let out an exasperated sigh as she set the deck back into a single stack. The machine on which she perched settled into a gentle hum. "You're the one who asked for my help, least you could do is return the favour."

"Right." Adrian sat himself up. "Thanks, by the way. For sharing your laundry money."

"I can't believe you spent yours on random stuff from Sev-Elev." Zoomer sucked her teeth, looking for a split-second just like her granny. "And you didn't even think to share it with me!"

"It was kind of just an impulse thing." Adrian picked at the corner of his sneaker. A stray bit of rubber was coming off its heel. "But yeah. Sorry."

"Hey, I'm just glad you're finally figuring out how to have fun." She snapped her fingers in tiny applause. "Invite me next time though, alright? Thinking of you going solo is just depressing."

Knees to his chest, Adrian leaned back against the washing machine. Its pulse shook through him and, in his gut, the memory of last night swirled. There were no words to describe how *un*-alone he'd been last night. What had felt like horror to Zoomer, Adrian had experienced as an absolute high—the freezing rush as Sorel's spirit entered his body, the intimate entwining of their sensory experience. Surely, there was some way to tell her how exciting it had been, how freeing it was to let someone else take control.

Their separation was the only truly disturbing part of their evening. Adrian and Sorel had debated for the better part of an hour, trying to sort out the most seamless way to come apart. Would it be better to attempt it all at once, like ripping off a bandage? Or they could do a little at a time, as one might take careful steps into a cold lake. Sorel began by flexing his fingers and arching his toes, prying away bit by bit. To Adrian, the sensation brought up memories of putting hot glue on his hands just to peel it off. He had tried to help by tugging in the opposite direction, but each small gain was rapidly sucked back. The gravity of his body proved hard for Sorel to escape.

What started as curious flickers towards the surface became increasingly desperate. Sorel clawed at Adrian's wrists, finally launching with such force he had landed across the graveyard. Both of their heads were spinning for a good while after, but they had done it—just as they had willfully merged, they could mutually separate. Adrian was certain that with practice, both would get easier. Even after they said goodnight, the taste of those half-stolen sour candies stayed in the back of his mouth until morning.

"Hey, you coming for this reading or what?" Zoomer glanced over and waved him up. Wordless, Adrian rose to join her on the dryer. She chewed her thumbnail while studying the three cards before her. Face-down, they vibrated slightly, dancing on the smooth surface of the dryer. "Alright, let's see what you got." Zoomer flipped over the centre card first, revealing an intricate water-colour portrait of a mermaid and a deep-sea diver. "Ooh, the two of cups! Somebody's getting lucky."

Adrian picked up the card and examined it closely. Each of the figures had a small vial: the merperson's had a label that read LEGS while the diver's read FINS. "What's it supposed to mean?"

"It's the *lovers* card!" Zoomer pursed her lips with glee. She took a small handbook from her bag and flipped through several pages. "'Each of the lovers is willing to sacrifice something for the other,'" she read aloud. "Super romantic."

"Assured mutual destruction," Adrian grimaced. "Yeah, real cute."

"Hush!" Zoomer prodded his knee. "Wait, hold on one sec. Was that card upside down?"

"For me or you?" asked Adrian.

"Never mind. It doesn't matter." She tucked a strand of hair behind one ear, licked her finger and flipped to the next page. Where she touched, she left a lipstick residue. "It's just, like, you might be unaware that you're getting codependent with somebody. So, watch out for that."

"I'm supposed to watch out for something I'm not aware of?" Adrian shook his head. He set the card back down in the middle and tapped the one to its left. "Alright. Hit me again."

"This isn't poker," said Zoomer. Even so, she flipped the card with the flourish of a high-stakes dealer. On this one, someone hung up by one leg, dangling from the branch of a knotted tree. The figure was oddly calm, hair flowing in the breeze. "Oh! Well, *that* is interesting."

"What? What is it?" Adrian grabbed for the card but Zoomer got to it first.

She flipped through the book again, smearing even more black lipstick on its pages. "Right, of course!" Zoomer smacked a page near the front of her book. "The Hanged One. I knew that."

Adrian snatched the card back, chewing the dry skin on his bottom lip as he examined the design. "What's this one supposed to be about?"

"It means somebody likes to be tied up," she winked, and Adrian almost choked on his own spit.

"Cards can tell that?" he asked in a whisper.

"I think they just did!" Zoomer cackled at Adrian's scowling face. "Oh, that was too easy." She wiped an eye and turned back to the book. "For real, though. It's like, when you're stuck in something that maybe you can't even see—so you're just supposed to, like, just let it happen. You know?"

"Yeah, like that's not vague at all." Adrian scoffed and tossed the card back in place. "None of this is making any sense so far."

"You have to see them *all* to get the story." Zoomer flicked her wrist, revealing the final card. This one was a simple image, only coloured with black, white, and red. A bleached ram's skull grew thorny vines from its empty sockets, blood-red blooms sprouting along its broken horns. "Oh." There was a momentary pause in Zoomer's animated delivery. "Okay then."

"Let me guess, does that one mean 'you're gonna die in seven days'?" chuckled Adrian. "Pop loves that movie. He's so into retro crap." Zoomer didn't answer. After a while, Adrian drummed his fingers on the dryer and started taking other guesses. "Oh! Or is it like an opposites thing?

Like, this is the best one in the deck and it means, like, 'you're going to win the lottery.' I bet I could talk Dad into buying me a scratch ticket."

"Mhm. Sure." Zoomer still didn't look up, busily scanning through her codex. "Okay yes. It's the Death card. But it's, uh, totally not as scary as it seems, I think."

"You're kinda making it scary right now." Adrian leaned over, trying to glimpse the book's description.

"Yeah, no, my bad." She shook her head. "It's just, like, about transformation and rebirth, or whatever."

"Oh." Amusement flickered up through Adrian, dispelling his concern. "So, it's basically a trans card."

That got Zoomer to look up. She flashed a mischievous smirk. "That's actually the secret to tarot. The main deck basically just takes on the whole rainbow acronym—it's actually kinda obvious."

"Way obvious," Adrian agreed, his shoulders slumping back. He gave the card a closer look, running his fingers over its design. It was actually kind of beautiful. "Okay, so, we got them all out now. Can you tell my future yet?"

The washing machine dinged as it finished its cycle. A trickle of slimy water dripped from its base. All the machines down here were busted, just in different ways. "I told you, it's not like that." Zoomer hopped down from her perch to go collect her stuff. "What matters is what *you* see in the cards."

"I thought you were the one who wanted to learn how to interpret?" Adrian scooted after her. "I'm just here as a practice dummy."

"Fine. Just give me a second to think." Zoomer popped open the washer door. "Love, hanging, and death..." She picked up one of her shirts and gave it a twist, beige water spilling across the floor. "Sorel?"

"What?" Adrian spun around. "Here—how?"

"Chill, bud." Zoomer tossed her sopping shirt into a large grey laundry basket. "I was just thinking out loud. It just seems like there's a connection in the cards that leads right to him."

"Right." Adrian rubbed his neck, finding it suddenly stiff. For a moment, he'd been certain she'd put it all together. "But, uh, what makes you think that?"

"It just makes sense." Piling up the rest of her still-soaked laundry, Zoomer thought aloud, "He's dead, for one thing. And you two had some definite lover vibes."

"We did?" Anxiety was creeping its way back up Adrian's throat.

"I can't blame you if you're still kind of fixated." Zoomer hoisted her laundry basket onto her hip. "Honestly, I still think about him too."

The rumbling of the dryer went quiet. Adrian studied the back of Zoomer's head, his mind swimming with questions. But he could put none of them into words, except one. "You do?"

"Well, yeah." Zoomer slapped the washer door shut and motioned for him to get off the one working dryer. "You don't exactly forget the dude who tried to body-snatch you."

"Right." Adrian helped gather Zoomer's tarot cards

before collecting his own clothes. "Of course not."

"We can talk about it, if you want." She snatched his laundry bag off the dirty floor and tossed it over. "We're safe now. He can't get to us out here." Adrian could only nod. The clothes in the dryer were still damp but he could hang them up back at the apartment, on door-handles and the backs of chairs. "It's okay if you're still upset," said Zoomer as she lifted her basket and tipped it into the dryer's waiting maw. A medley of colourful socks, shorts, T-shirts, and undies all tumbled in at once. "The whole thing was kinda traumatic. I mean, mostly for me. But you can have your feels, too."

"Mhm." If that's still how she really felt, how was he supposed to explain that he'd been counting down the hours until he could go back to the graveyard? He kept thinking, maybe if he found the right words, she'd understand. But that was starting to look less and less likely.

"The cards said it best, though." Zoomer slotted in quarters for the dryer. "Sometimes you gotta just cut out the toxic people and let them go live their own life. Or, uh, death, in this case." She set the buttons to their highest setting and started up the cycle again. "Just, let go and move on."

"True." Adrian hoisted his laundry bag over one shoulder. "But, um, you *are* still working on that protection thing—the crystal or whatever it was?"

"Oh, definitely. Totally on my to-do list." Zoomer glanced up, catching Adrian's skeptical glare. "I'm serious," she insisted. "Last night, I watched *The Craft*, *Practical Magic*, and the first three episodes of *Sabrina*. All for research purposes."

"Great. Real good to know," Adrian flatly replied. He began to shuffle towards the door. "Anyway, I should probably go put this stuff away."

"You're not gonna wait for me?" Zoomer pouted as she grabbed her cards and started shuffling again. "That's bullshit," she said with a hollow laugh. When Adrian still moved to leave, she called after him, "Well, what're you doing later?" He shrugged. "Okay because, I was thinking, we could go sneak into that crappy fair that's set up down by the old mall—the rides look totally deadly, like, no way they're safety checked. Fun, right?"

"Sure." Adrian rested one hand on the exit. "But, I don't know. Seems kind of noisy and stuff—probably would be too much for me, you know?"

"Oh, right." Zoomer tsked. "Yeah, that's okay."

"Plus, I promised Dad I'd help make dinner." Adrian tried to force a laugh. "Last time he almost burned down the whole complex and—"

"I said, I get it." Zoomer cut him off. Tension rang out afterwards, enveloping the laundry room in silence. The dryer stopped mid-cycle and she kicked it with the back of her heel. "Anyway, I've got stuff going on too. So, whatever, no big deal."

"Right." Adrian pushed back against the door, weakly waving goodbye. "I'll see you later or something."

"Or something." Turning her back to him, Zoomer dealt herself a new tarot reading. Adrian was gone before she flipped the first card.

FIFTEEN

The day's roaming thunderstorms had settled into a humid night. Small wells of rainwater remained between the cracks in the road, soaking the roots of strong-willed dandelions. Sorel walked in Adrian's shoes, not even noticing the splash as he stepped into a puddle. He remained fixated on the glowing square of light carried in his palm. "This thing is incredible!" he marvelled. When the screen went dark, he saw Adrian's face mirrored back.

"It's a pretty old phone," said Adrian. "But it works alright I guess."

"You *guess*?!" Sorel rattled the plastic cup that held their fast-melting iced cappuccino. "I remember when the first kid on my block got a colour television!"

"You realize that saying stuff like that makes you sound like a total grandpa." Adrian squirmed a little at the thought. Even though Sorel looked—and now *felt*—like he was seventeen, there were still moments where the gap between them became undeniable. "So, question. If you, you know, died way back when or whatever, how old does that actually make you?"

"I told you, time works different on the other side," said Sorel, chewing on the straw of their drink as he searched for the last few drops of flavour. Adrian winced at the sharp hit of pure syrup—he never should have let Sorel make their iced cap a triple-triple. His teeth hurt and his hands were getting jittery from the caffeine. But damn, he felt how it made Sorel so happy. When that rush rose up in him, it was hard to say no.

At least they had been able to agree on ordering oat milk, after Adrian had done the work to explain how one even milks an oat. It was a good thing, too, since the last thing he needed was a date night feeling all bloated and gassy. With Sorel riding along inside him, Adrian wouldn't even be able to cloak his farts.

When he had mentioned that he was going out with a friend, Dad had slipped Adrian just enough cash to cover a Tim's run. Of course, his father had no way of knowing that going out with Sorel was a two-for-one deal. The remaining change jingled comfortably in Adrian's shorts pocket. Caffeinated and sugar-high, the pair weaved along the city streets with no particular destination in mind.

"Can't you just tell me if I'm on a date with someone old enough to be, like, my great-great-uncle?" Adrian nudged Sorel towards a garbage can and tossed in their empty cup. "You know I'm a teenager, right?"

"So am I!" Sorel insisted. They passed an antique shop and he studied Adrian's reflection in its glassy storefront. "It feels that way to me, anyway. I guess it sort of depends."

"Depends on what?" asked Adrian.

"How you're counting," Sorel brushed off the shoulders of Adrian's wrinkled shirt. "To me, it feels like just a few months since they put my body in the ground."

"Well, there's no way that's true," Adrian pointed out. "I would have noticed a funeral."

"I don't know what to tell you," said Sorel. "You're just gonna have to trust me." They turned another corner and came onto a busier stretch. The street was dotted with late-night bar-goers, people vaping and hailing taxis. A few city busses sat bumper-to-bumper, waiting for a green light. "You know, this area kind of looks familiar. I think I used to live around here."

"Really?" Adrian looked around as if living-Sorel might step out a doorway or poke his head out a window. "Can we go see your old place?!"

Reflexively, Sorel slipped a finger behind Adrian's ear, tucking back his non-existent hair. "I don't know if I could find the exact spot," he had to admit. "It all looks so different now."

"That makes sense." Together, they ran a hand over the brick wall of an old hardware store. It had recently been sold off and was now under renovation to become an artisanal cannabis shop; a newly minted sign proclaimed THE JOINT DISPENSARY would only welcome customers aged eighteen or older. Across the road, a large neon sign announced the local optometrist's office had been replaced with a vegan pizzeria. "You said this used to be a quiet neighbourhood, right?"

"Did I say that?" Sorel scowled. "Now that I'm here, all I remember is the noise. Babies crying, dogs barking all the time, and cars—" A motorcycle roared past them, lane-splitting through traffic.

"Racing?" Adrian finished Sorel's thought. "Yeah, they still do that."

Rows of storefronts, bars, and restaurants were stacked together, nearly all of them hosting small apartments on top. One flickered, a sliver of action movie visible between the gap in its blinds. A neighbouring unit had its balcony door wide open, coaxing in the evening breeze through yellow blinds. A few steps further, several windows were completely covered in shiny tinfoil, and yet another was stuffed with leafy plants to block out prying eyes. Sorel examined each one, and Adrian could taste his growing curiosity, the bubbling desire to peek behind the scenes and find out what kind of life the world held now.

At a crosswalk stood two women, holding hands. One was in cut-off overalls, the other a denim vest with colourful pins. Adrian had to stop Sorel from openly gawking. The pair spoke lightly about a show they were set to see tonight, and as the walk sign illuminated, they shared a brief kiss.

"Some stuff sure has changed." Sorel stared after the couple as they boarded a nearby streetcar. "My mom would've called those two a pair of 'tin lizzies'!"

One of the women glanced up and Adrian quickly turned aside, covering his face. "I've never even heard of that one," he hissed. "But you can't just go shouting stuff at people!"

"Whoops, sorry!" Sorel snickered. "I'm still getting used to this whole out-in-the-open thing." He let Adrian take the lead as they hastened down the block. "Like, have we talked about the fact you've got two dads? When I was around, that kind of thing wasn't even in science fiction books—did they, like, grow you in a pod or something?"

"What?" Adrian laughed as he checked the time on his phone. "What year do think this is?" A couple texts from Zoomer were waiting for him.

"You tell me!" Sorel waved Adrian's phone in front of his face. "You've basically got a *Star Trek* communicator in your pocket that connects to radios in space! But you're saying *pod people* are unrealistic?"

"Fair point." Adrian swiped aside his latest messages. He'd get back to her, later. "Though, this really isn't anything fancy. It's practically a flip phone."

"A flip … phone?!" Sorel fiddled with the buttons on the side of Adrian's cell, only managing to make the screen go dark. He jostled it a few times, trying to wake it up again. "You've gotta realize, on my end, that sounds equally far out."

Adrian slid the phone into his back pocket. "You know, I heard the first folks to make these things actually got the idea from *Star Trek*. Funny how some things go full circle, eh?"

"More like, trippy as hell," Sorel laughed. They passed a nightclub with a packed patio where a queen with a teal wig smoked a thin cigarette. Adrian kept them moving, even as Sorel dragged his feet. "I swear, if I'd seen more people like *that*, maybe I'd still be alive."

"Yeah, well." Adrian walked with his hands in his pockets. "There's still plenty of folks coming after people like us. And there's all kinds of new insults now, even if most aren't bold enough to shout them in your face." Looking over his shoulder, he had them round a corner onto a more residential street. "Remind me to never introduce you to the concept of internet trolls."

"You have trolls in this time?" asked Sorel. "Never mind. I don't know if I can handle learning any more big reveals right about now." They passed by a lane-way house that was partially under construction. Down the road lay the shadows of climbing condos. "One thing I'll say for my time, the houses were spaced apart a bit better. I remember when I..." He trailed off, resting a hand against Adrian's chest. "When I lived with my mom and my sister. We shared a one bedroom. A walk-up." He exhaled, the taste of nostalgia on his breath. "It had terrible insulation. Always freezing in the winter."

"But great light come spring." Adrian's hand rose to touch his cheek, recalling the warmth of the sun as it poured through the dingy window. The scene knitted together in his mind like it had always been there, as real as any memory of his own. Dusty floors, curtains coated in cigarette smoke. The scent of wet dirt, fresh herbs in a windowsill. "Your sister liked being east-facing. Better for growing her basil and oregano." He blinked and the scene faded. Back in the present again, they were getting a dirty look from an old man smoking on his porch.

"How did you..." Sorel's question faded. They both already knew there was no answer. "I didn't even remember that, until you said it."

Hustling away from the old man's glare, Adrian whispered, "I know."

They darted through the long shadows, past a series of closed doors. As they approached another busy intersection, Adrian floated the question, "Did you want to walk around and see your old place? Maybe we could help you remember—"

"Hold that thought." Sorel peered towards the horizon. An array of lights flickered across low-hanging clouds. Colourful pinpricks that grew sharp before fading again in an endless, spiralling dance. "What is that?!"

They crested a hill and the light source fell into view: a large Ferris wheel, steadily rotating. Each spoke was a rainbow refracted through the evening mist. "Must be for that parking-lot fair," Adrian thought aloud. "Zoomer's been bugging me to check it out all week."

"Well, what are we waiting for?!" Sorel quickened their pace.

"Oh but—I don't know if that's a great idea." Adrian stumbled over a crack in the sidewalk.

"What's the problem?" Sorel righted Adrian back onto two feet. "Come on, it'll be fun!" With spritely ease, he weaved them through a web of alleyways and across a set of unused streetcar tracks. In a matter of minutes, they arrived at the edge of the fairgrounds and he marvelled up at the wheel, taking in its full height. "Wow," Sorel grinned to himself. "I forgot I knew that short cut."

Behind Sorel's excitement, Adrian's dread was quickly rising. Muscles tense, he slowed them to stiff and jarring steps. "This really isn't my kind of thing," he tried to explain. "I'd rather just go home."

Sorel pushed onwards, like he was wading into a high tide. "What *is* your thing, then? Moping around in graveyards?"

"Kind of, yeah." Adrian was rapidly losing ground. Sorel's motivation was overwhelming, and he was only growing stronger. Approaching the fairgrounds, a ticketbooth operator gave them a very curious look.

"Well, you can mope when you're dead." Sorel gave one last push towards the entry gate. "*I'm* gonna have some fun while I can. And so are you."

Sixteen

Oil-slick puddles rippled across the strip-mall parking lot, warping the fair's flashing lights. A handful of meagre pop-up rides ran their cars on an endless loop. The poorly patched speaker system eked out discordant carnival tunes on repeat. Games of chance and fast-food stands were huddled together beneath canvas tops, their dollar-store prizes and discount hot dogs still damp from a day of heavy rain. The reek of Porta Potties mingled with that of cotton candy. Sorel inhaled deeply through Adrian's nose. "Isn't it beautiful?"

"It sure is something," Adrian muttered. His left sneaker squelched with every reluctant step.

The ticket booth was staffed by a middle-aged woman, her greying hair tucked into a loose braid. Adrian motioned that he was on the phone, even though he clearly had no earbuds. She didn't seem to care that he was, essentially, talking to himself. She barely even looked up while getting their entry fee sorted. Passing back a few tear-away stubs, she informed him, "We're closing in an hour."

A pebble of guilt rolled in Adrian's gut. Zoomer would have eaten up this whole sad affair. He could almost hear her snarky observations, see the clever look she'd wear when sizing up the carnies. She'd probably know ways to cheat every game in this place, and they'd walk away with arms overflowing, taking home far too many cheap stuffed animals. Maybe he should call her, after all. It's possible she wouldn't be too upset that he was hanging with Sorel again—at very least, Adrian could try to bribe her with caramel corn or a spiralized sweet potato.

"Oh, let's get one of those!" Sorel made a beeline towards the corn-dog stand, ready to burn through Adrian's remaining pocket change. The meat was questionable but the breading was so sweet, it might as well have been coated in sugar. And it probably was. Since the fair was closing soon, the cart seller was giving them away for half price, so Adrian agreed to go back for seconds, and then thirds.

"These are actually pretty good," Adrian admitted as he chewed the bready crumbs off their shared popsicle stick.

"You're telling me!" Sorel grinned, picking out a splinter stuck between Adrian's teeth. He wiped his fingers on Adrian's shorts and moved to toss their used stick over his shoulder. Adrian managed to take control, guiding them to the park's overflowing trash bins instead. "Okay, hunger managed. What's next—maybe the spinny-cup ride?"

Towards the centre of the fairgrounds, a circular track of twisting cups spun at an alarming speed. "After three corn dogs in a row?" Adrian held his stomach. "No thanks."

"Right." Sorel gave his torso a thoughtful pat. "Been a while since I had a stomach to get sick with. I guess we can take some time to digest." He pivoted towards a series of gaming booths. Just as he was gearing up to toss a softball into the mouth of a cartoon clown, there was a piercing screech. Adrian had to clap his hands over both ears, almost doubling over.

A robotic voice was barely audible through the speakers' piercing feedback: "The park will be closing in forty-five minutes!"

Just like that, the grounds' small yet dedicated crowd began to buzz with new life. Selfie-snapping couples and parents chasing sugar-happy children all hurried to get in their last few rides. The endless Ringling music grew louder and more frantic. Adrian winced, ears still ringing. He tried to back away but slipped on the ball he'd dropped, tumbling into the sticky side of a vendor cart.

"Hey, watch it, kid!" barked a tall, hairy man in a carnival T-shirt.

"Sorry," Adrian whimpered. "Sorry." His temples pulsed with leftover caffeine, stomach twisting it together with undigested corn dogs. Something burned up the back of his throat, all the way into his ears. Operating on instinct, he shrank away from the crowd—except, the rest of him didn't follow. Instead, Adrian's consciousness alone slipped from his body's driver's seat.

The swirl of lights and sounds was muffled, like someone had pulled a blanket over his head. He was only somewhat aware of Sorel taking over, guiding them out of the bustling crowd. "Hey, are you okay?" Sorel's words echoed back to him down a long, empty tunnel. "Adrian—what's going on? Where did you go?"

Adrian tried to answer but his voice wasn't strong enough. All he could do was crouch within the cubby-hole he'd found inside himself. Something was pounding. It took a few moments to realize it was his own heart. He wondered, how many pumps did he have before it gave out entirely? The very thought made the beats quicken.

In that small, tight space, a memory clawed its way in. It started like so many did—with a sharp jolt, an elbow to the gut. Bent over the side of a trash can, vomit sizzled at the back of his teeth. A blur of curious faces looked on, hushed words of worry. A strong arm grabbed his shoulder and yanked him up. It was Pop. He clutched Adrian in one hand, a shiny white ticket stub in the other.

He had slipped through time. Adrian was just eight years old now, and his fathers were treating him to a day at Wonderland. Even the distant memory of all those people, all that noise, made him feel dizzy. Pop said something, gruff and short. The way he did when he hadn't slept enough. But then, Dad was there. A gentle touch on his back, telling Adrian it was okay if he didn't want to go inside the park. They could go home. Pop gave a gruff complaint about the cost of a day pass but Dad told him to back off. *Adrian.* In the memory, he used the right name. *Don't worry about anyone else. Turn inwards, focus on your breathing.*

From somewhere along the edge of his perception, Adrian found his lungs. A deep breath in, held, then released. And again. Someone was helping him, calming his heart rate. Sorel's voice drifted down that long, dark tunnel. "You still in there?" His hand filling Adrian's own, squeezing his palms. "Please, say something."

Slowly, Adrian inched his eyes open. At first, all was darkness. Then his vision began to adjust. He was inside a booth, cramped, a dark curtain drawn on one side. Below the velvet fold, passing shadows. The ripples of rainbow puddles.

"I'm okay." Another long breath in, a steady exhale. "Where are we?"

"Somewhere safe, and quiet," Sorel promised. Seconds later, a screen lit up before them and a loud chiptune started playing. A red button flashed and the machine demanded two dollars and fifty cents, in exchange for five photos. "Okay, well. One out of two isn't so bad."

"Not great either," Adrian laughed. It took all his effort just to stay upright in the photo booth's awkward, plastic seat. Upon returning to his body, he found it stiff and painful; his head swam, lungs burning like he'd been underwater.

Sorel still clasped Adrian's hands together. "You had me scared there for a second."

"Yeah," said Adrian. "Me too."

Outside, crackling music still played on loop. The warm, sticky scent of the fairgrounds mixed poorly with the musty air of the photo booth. They sat together in silence for a while before Sorel ventured to ask, "So, what was that?"

"*That* was why I don't come to these kinds of places." Adrian shook his head, trying to clear the webs that hung along the corners of his mind. "Sorry if I scared you."

Sorel pursed his lips. "I should be the one apologizing, I shouldn't have tried to push you to do everything, all at once."

Adrian shrugged. "I know you were just excited. I was too."

"Alright then, you ready to go home?" Sorel peeked around the photo-booth curtain. "I think I can get us to the front gate pretty quick..."

"What, so soon?" Adrian fished out the last of his change—two toonies and a couple quarters. "We haven't gotten our pictures yet." He pushed them into the machine while Sorel bounced his knees in excitement.

Utter glee pulsated throughout Sorel's being. It was downright infectious. "You really want to stay?"

"Come on," said Adrian. "Let's live a little." He smacked the big red button. The camera flashed and they were bathed in light.

Seventeen

Adrian squealed as the ball connected with the final pin. There was a short, melodic tone as the carnival game lit up to announce a winner. "You've got a great arm!"

"Aw shucks." Sorel grinned and pointed towards his chosen prize. "I might've had a little practice, back in the day."

"Uh, sure, kid." The booth operator plucked a stuffed animal from the wall—a small, black cat—and tossed it to Sorel's waiting hands. "Last one of the day. Congrats."

Clutching his prize, Sorel led them from the booth. A pack of tweens hurried to the last few open rides and he easily sidestepped the crowd, simultaneously avoiding a large wad of gum that lay underfoot. As for Adrian, he was quite happy to let Sorel take over their navigation. It allowed him to focus on the adorable stuffy in their hands.

"It's so cute!" He smiled down at his own reflection in the toy's plastic eyes. "What're you gonna name them?"

Sorel mulled over the question as he tucked into a nearby queue. "How about, Sorel Junior? SJ for short?"

"Oh man," Adrian stifled a laugh. "You're not one of those people who want to name their kid after themselves, are you?"

The line moved up a step. A tall, blonde couple glanced back, giving them an odd look. Adrian turned aside, pretending to be interested in the mall parking lot. "I don't know, I might've been." Sorel shrugged. "Guess I won't get to find out now."

"Oh. Yeah." Adrian gently petted the cat's fuzzy head. "Sorry. I kinda forgot."

"Yeah," Sorel smirked. "I do too, sometimes."

Beyond the line of food carts and rickety theme-park rides sat a flat, darkened structure—what used to be the Galleria. It had not been an especially notable strip mall but it was a staple of the neighbourhood. That is, until developers had sunk their teeth into the property late last spring. Now newspapers covered its long windows and a heavy padlock sat on the front door. In a year, their billboards promised, the whole place would be gutted completely, flipped into yet another stack of condos that would blot out what was left of the view.

Though the grocery store had always been hopelessly understocked, the post office chronically understaffed, and the dollar store blatantly overpriced, Adrian felt a pang of loss seeing the old place in such a sorry state. When word of the Galleria's terminal condition had become common knowledge, some local artists scraped together enough grant funding to run an exhibit in its hollowed-out corpse. The showcase was a temporary gallery, a statement on the living tomb of stagnant capital—so all its posters had said. Zoomer had begged Adrian to go and see the show for themselves, but he put it off until it was too late to get tickets. Now, all that remained of the artistic installation was a neon sign affixed to the mall's empty façade: Love Me Till I'm Me Again.

As they inched forward in line, Sorel studied the halo-lit words. "What's that supposed to mean?"

"Your guess is as good as mine." Adrian shook his head. "Hey, so, was this place around when you were alive?"

"I'm not sure." Sorel sucked his teeth. Adrian could sense the strain it was to look backwards; stepping into the past felt like pushing through a swamp, muddy and thick. "I think—no. Yes. They were just gearing up to the grand opening. Before that, it was an old auto factory." The picture pieced together, for Adrian too. "I had an uncle who worked there and he'd come over for Sunday dinners..."

"Smelling like the bottom of a grease pan." Adrian gagged on the taste of the memory.

"Yes, exactly!" Sorel snapped his fingers.

Adrian glanced towards the couple in front of them. They seemed well distracted, trying to take nighttime selfies with various filters. Once certain they were free of eavesdroppers, he wondered aloud, "Sorel, do you think there's something about us doing this, um, thing that we do, that helps you remember stuff from when you were alive?"

"I think so, yeah," Sorel nodded. "Before, it was like I'd been drifting out at sea. Then suddenly, you were there. Like, an anchor or something. Or, maybe a lifeboat?"

"If you're at sea, you probably want the second one," Adrian laughed. Quiet settled over them, punctuated by the occasional fanfare playing at a nearby ring-toss tent.

"So," Sorel asked, "did the mall turn out to be any good?"

"Not really." They took another step forward, almost at the front of the line now. "But there were a couple decent kiosks." Adrian spoke under his breath as the operator took his ticket. "And a pet shop where they used to let me hold the kittens sometimes."

"That sounds awesome!" Sorel grinned, and a bubbling sensation brimmed in Adrian too. It was like he'd just downed a whole can of pop. He relished the feeling, getting drunk on Sorel's pure and easy joy.

With a wave of approval from the Ferris wheel technician, Sorel and Adrian shuffled to the middle of a cold, hanging seat. Its metal bar came down with a hard slap and clicked shut. Their feet swung lightly, barely touching the ground. The stuffed cat was tucked between Adrian's knees. Once they began to lift, Sorel spoke again.

"You know how I said that it's only been a few months since they put my body in the ground?" he asked, and Adrian nodded. "I want you to know, I wasn't messing with you. That's really how it feels to me."

"But how long has it been—?" Adrian's question hic-cupped briefly when a sudden stop jolted their seat. He gripped the safety bar, out of instinct. "For real. You can tell me."

"Based on the year you said it is..." Sorel drummed his fingers, running some quick math. "I'd guess, five decades? Give or take."

The number smacked Adrian even harder than their sudden stop. Sorel was fifty years his senior? Except—he wasn't really. Now that they'd spent some time together, he could tell when Sorel was stretching the truth. Even so, he had to ask. "Are you sure?"

"As much as I can be." Sorel looked down at the new riders, loading in below. "Some parts are still blurry. But I know I wasn't even eighteen when it happened." He shook his head and Adrian shivered, the memory of curly hair grazing his shoulders. "And I know my mom and sister took it pretty hard."

"It must have been tough, to lose you so young." Adrian coaxed one of his hands to leave the safety bar and pressed it to his chest. He cradled their shared heartbeat. "Sorry. I guess that's sort of obvious."

The crowd across the fairgrounds had thinned. Only a few, dedicated attendees still milled about the multicolour pop-tents. "It wasn't to me," Sorel admitted. "Not back then."

Adrian pressed back against the sticky plastic seat. "Were you able to talk to them at least?" he asked. "The way you do with me?"

"Didn't know how," said Sorel. "I didn't have much time to practice either, since any time they weren't around, I just sort of ... wasn't."

"Wasn't?" Adrian echoed, unable to cloak his curiosity.

"I'm not sure how else to put it." Sorel absent-mindedly picked at a frayed patch on the knee of Adrian's jeans. "I'd blink and days would have passed—weeks, months, whatever." The more he fiddled with it, the faster the stitching became undone. "I had lots of visitors at first. When they were there, I'd exist again. Fifteen minutes here, an hour there. Sometimes, I'd show up while they were still coming down the street! I could hear them talking to me sometimes, saying prayers." Sorel wrapped a thread around Adrian's finger and pulled it taut. "Even when they weren't at my graveside, if they were thinking hard enough about me—there I'd be. Once or twice, I managed to show up in their dreams. But all that stopped after Mom died and my sister moved away." He gave another firm tug until the strand finally snapped. "Figures."

The tip of Adrian's finger was going purple from lack of circulation. Gently, he retook control and unwound the knotted thread. "Maeve. That was your sister's name, wasn't it?"

"I think so, yeah," Sorel murmured. "I don't know how I forgot that."

"So, then what did you do?" Adrian shook his hand, blood rushing back into his finger. He dropped the loose thread off the side of their chair and let it blow into the wind.

"There wasn't much *to* do." Sorel swayed Adrian's legs, bouncing on the footrest. "I remember other funerals, other souls. But when you first turn over, it takes a lot of effort just to even stay in one piece. Even with visitors, a lot of folks just sort of fade away."

"But not you," Adrian pointed out.

"No, not me. And no, I don't know why. Some of us aren't so good at passing over." Sorel scoffed, "I always was a late bloomer."

The wheel started to turn again. Their seat wavered in the night air and Adrian was hit with a fresh wave of nausea. He shut his eyes, waiting for it to pass. When he wasn't looking, he could almost imagine they weren't high in the sky but instead on a boat somewhere—rocked lightly by gentle waves. The illusion *almost* worked to quell his sickness. "Did you get to see your mother, again—after she passed?" he asked, partly just to keep his mind off of gagging.

"No dice," said Sorel. "She was buried somewhere else. Probably in the churchyard, near my Gramps."

The wheel swung a bit too fast. The water in Adrian's daydream was getting choppy; he clenched his teeth, growing seasick. "Why aren't you there, too? Seems wrong to separate you like that."

"Too big a sinner, I guess." Sorel managed to coax a laugh from Adrian's sickly throat. "Even in death, I'm the odd one out."

Their chair lurched to a halt. Adrian's gut sloshed and made him wince. Acid crept into the back of his mouth.

They must have been high up by now, and he knew Sorel desperately wanted to take a peek. But he also knew Sorel wouldn't force him to do so. Not until he was ready.

Sorel turned to face the wind. It tousled Adrian's short-cropped hair. "After my family moved on, I thought I would too. Instead, I got more sensitive. Someone just glancing at my grave would summon me up. With practice, I learned how to stick around a little longer every time, even with no one to keep me company." His laughter was rich with a bitter aftertaste. "Sounds kinda pathetic when I say it like that."

"Not to me." Adrian slid his palms along the safety bar and overlapped them.

"Well, thanks." The swaying of their chair had settled. With a deep breath, Adrian permitted a peek at the view.

They were at the top of the wheel. The city's lights danced bright as a galaxy of stars. Among the downtown skyscrapers, the tallest spire was decorated in waves of soft blue and pastel pink. Traffic flowed along the gridded streets, red and yellow. Dark trees marked rows of residential homes, porch lights glowing gold against the night. They all blurred together, the overlap of many interwoven stories.

"It's beautiful." Adrian was surprised at how much he really meant it.

"Isn't it?" Sorel ran a thumb along the back of Adrian's hand. "It's funny, I was in such a rush to leave the world, until I did. Then, all I wanted to do was see what might have happened if I'd stayed. Not that I had much of a view after they knocked down all the houses around the cemetery and turned them into big ugly blocks."

"Oh." Adrian glanced in the direction of his own apartment building. "Sorry about that."

"Don't be. There's nothing to be sorry for." Delicately, Sorel stroked along Adrian's wrist. Goose pimples rose across his tender skin. "When you're dead, things just come and go like that. It's sort of like you're sitting on a moving train. Everything just flies by before you even get a chance to really see it. You're always just looking at your memories of what was there a second ago."

Adrian looked out towards the lakeshore. Just beyond the city's sparkling view, dark clouds hung heavy with the promise of more rain. "Weirdly, I think I know exactly what you mean. It's usually a pretty lonely feeling."

"Well, now it doesn't have to be," Sorel whispered. "We've got each other."

The Ferris wheel jolted again and started its descent. The city's dance spiralled out of view. On their way back down to earth, it felt as if they had all the time in the world.

EIGHTEEN

Adrian gasped for air. Cheeks sore, his lungs were on fire. He couldn't remember the last time he'd laughed this hard. "And then, when the kid said—"

"Yeah, yeah, he said—" Sorel tripped over his words, rushing to beat Adrian to the punchline, "'I see dead people!'"

"And I was all like, 'What, like it's hard?'" The bed creaked as Adrian rocked across the mattress, Sorel clutching his chest. Their shared giggling fit built up and broke like waves, washing over them for several minutes. Every time one would calm, the other would pick up again, until at last they mutually drifted back down to earth.

With a contented sigh, Adrian stared up at the popcorn ceiling of his bedroom. "I still can't believe we goofed so hard on a scary movie. We could make a podcast just roasting that kind of stuff!"

"I've no idea what kind of pod you can cast," Sorel said, still tittering. "But *I* still can't believe you can watch a whole movie on that thing you call a phone!" With Adrian's hand, he grabbed a stray pillow and tucked it under his head. Feet resting against the wall, he wondered aloud, "So, what do we wanna do now?"

Before Adrian could answer, a door slammed in the hall. Heavy footfalls made their way towards the living room. "Sorry," Adrian muttered, "I thought Pop was working tonight."

His fathers were at odds even more than usual lately. Yet any time Adrian tried to ask what was wrong, it was as if all the air had been sucked from the room. Within his presence, their disagreements dissolved into sidelong glances and barely hidden scowls. Did they think he was that obtuse that he wouldn't notice their tension? Or, he wondered on less-than-optimistic occasions, are they so wrapped up in hating each other that they can't even pretend to care anymore?

"It's fine." Sorel tapped his fingers along Adrian's chin. "That reminds me, when exactly are you planning to introduce me to your folks?"

"Oh! Um." Adrian's heart leaped and he sat up straight. "I didn't realize you'd want to do that."

"Relax!" Sorel tapped Adrian on the nose. "I'm just kidding."

"Right. Sure." Adrian reflexively ran his fingers through his hair, a habit he'd picked up from Sorel. "I knew that."

The argument next door rose a few octaves, then all at once went quiet. The palpable silence was perhaps even worse. In absence of their bickering, tension permeated the whole apartment. Adrian was left to imagine the worst— maybe one of them had finally walked out.

Hands shaking, Adrian started to shrink into himself again. Sorel stepped in, giving just enough of a squeeze that Adrian could stay in the present. Together, they shared a deep breath in and let it out slowly. "How about you walk me home?"

"I'd like that." Adrian shuffled off the bed. His head was still dizzy, like he'd been underwater for too long. But it didn't take too much concentration to slip away. It was easy to get on his shoes without a word from his parents—Adrian wasn't sure they even noticed him coming and going anymore. Dad was fussing in the kitchen, rapidly stirring a bubbling pot on the stove. The smell of burnt rice wafted through the apartment. Meanwhile, Pop sat slouched over on the couch, his glowering face lit up by a laptop screen as he scrolled through pages of a spreadsheet full of bold red numbers.

Adrian mumbled that he was off for a walk and swung open the front door. He was immediately faced with a fist hanging in the air. Zoomer was standing on the other side poised to knock. "Oh." She blinked in surprise. "Hi."

A knot clenched in Adrian's gut. He could already feel Sorel's churning irritation at seeing Zoomer again. They'd never really debriefed the whole friend breakdown, but now didn't seem like the right time.

Shoving himself fully into the driver's seat, Adrian cobbled together a friendly grin and stepped into the hall. "Hey bud. It's been a minute."

"Yeah, no kidding." Zoomer leaned back on her heels with casual disinterest, as if she'd just so happened to appear at Adrian's doorstep. "Your phone busted or something?"

"I don't think so." Adrian's hand instinctively went to his pocket. The weight of his phone rested against his leg.

"Then why haven't you texted me back?" Zoomer peered over Adrian's shoulder into the open door of his apartment. "It's been, like, a week since we hung out."

"Who's at the door, kiddo?" Dad asked from the kitchen.

"It's just Zoomer," Adrian called back.

"Oh, perfect!" Hopping over, Dad wore a slightly singed apron and matching oven mitts. "Are you joining us for dinner?" he asked with a toothy smile. "There's plenty to go around."

"Actually, I forgot." Adrian stepped aside to grip the door's round handle, ready to close it as soon as he got the chance. "Me and Zoomer have plans tonight."

"We do?" asked Zoomer. Adrian shot her a silent glare.

"But what about dinner?" Dad pouted. "We were just about to sit down as a family."

Before Adrian could stop him, Sorel held a hand to his grumbling stomach. "You know what, I *could* eat!"

"But, uh—I'll just have to wait." Adrian quickly slipped back into control. "Keep a plate warm for me, alright?"

Dad looked as if he might protest a little more, but Pop interjected from the couch. "That's fine with us, kiddo. Just don't be back too late. And bring your phone!"

"Yep. Got it. Good." The words popped out of Adrian's mouth like pinballs. "Later!" He dodged around any remaining questions, giving the door an extra hard tug. Next, he took off down the hallway in a straight shot towards the elevator.

"Dude, hey." Zoomer followed closely after. "What's the rush?"

"Um." Sorel came up with a quick line and passed it off to Adrian, "Dad burned dinner again. You really don't wanna taste it."

"Damn." Zoomer tsked. "Yeah, we're better off going hungry then." She leaned on the wall as Adrian repeatedly stabbed at the elevator's down button. "Anyway, it's a new moon tonight and I was thinking, what if we head down to that spot the mower always misses—you know, near the maintenance door? We could gather some herbs, do a little witchy ritual."

"Mhm. Sure." At last, the tiny arrow pointing downwards turned a dim yellow. "But I need to do a, uh, thing. First. Can I meet you after, maybe?"

Zoomer crossed her arms and stuck up her nose at him. "Okay, that's it. As my best friend, you *have* to tell me what's going on."

"What?" Adrian wheezed, trying to quell Sorel's voice as it pressed up his throat. "What makes you think something's wrong?"

"I know you're mad at me." Zoomer glowered at her cracked nail polish. It glinted in the hallway's flickering lights. "If you're still feeling messed up about the whole Sorel situation, you can tell me."

"Of course I am—" Sorel started to answer but Adrian cut him off.

"Am *not*. I am not." Looking up, Adrian watched the slow climb of numbers above the elevator door. "I don't want to get into it. I really have to go."

"Go where?" Zoomer kicked her heavy black platforms on the fraying hall carpet. "Man, I'm not happy about it either. Sometimes I kinda even miss the guy, but—"

"Then why are you being such a little shit about it?!" Adrian slapped a hand over his mouth. Lips hidden, Sorel sneaked in a satisfied grin.

"*Excuse* me?" Zoomer reeled back. "What did you just say?"

"Sorry, sorry, sorry," Adrian grabbed the wheel back from Sorel and tried to right their shared ship. "It's just, like, um. If you're upset, and I'm upset, why don't we just go talk to me—" He gritted his teeth. "I mean, with me. To him. Go with me to talk to him."

Falling quiet, Zoomer stared deep into Adrian's eyes. It seemed all but certain that she could see both the people looking back. "You've been back there, haven't you?"

"Who, me?" Adrian clenched his sweaty fists, willing the numbers on the elevator to rise faster. "What makes you think that?"

"Oh my god." Zoomer's voice began to quiver. "You're

going to see him right now, aren't you?!" Her words echoed up and down the hall.

"Shh!" Adrian glanced back towards his apartment. Thankfully, the door stayed shut. "So what if I am?" he hissed. "It's not that big a deal."

"Not a big deal?" Zoomer wrinkled her nose. "I told you, he's seriously dangerous!"

"Well, maybe you don't know him as well as you thought." Sorel wound Adrian's jaw back into his own control. He turned away from Zoomer.

"Wha— You—" she stammered, gobsmacked. "Well, fine. But maybe *you* can't see what's right in front of you, because you're crushing on a goddamn dead guy!"

The elevator's bell rang. Its doors creaked open and Adrian stepped inside. "Whatever," he replied, for once speaking in unison with Sorel.

"But, you promised." Zoomer's frown twitched at its corners. She glared after him. "You promised to stay away until I could protect us."

"How long was I supposed to wait?" Adrian smacked the button for the first floor. "A week, a month?" After several tries, the button lit up with recognition of his request. "Tell me, Zoomie, how long does it take for you to get your crap together and actually follow through with something on your to-do list?"

A ripple of pain ran across Zoomer's face. A second later, she shut down into a scowling wall. "Screw you." She turned and marched away. "I'm out of here."

The elevator doors began to shut but Adrian caught

them with his foot. "Wait!" he called after Zoomer.

She paused at the far end of the hall. "What?"

Adrian opened his mouth to apologize but instead heard himself say, "You think *he's* the dangerous one, but just look at yourself." Sorel glared through Adrian's eyes, wrath brimming in his throat. "You're obsessed with me, and I know it's because I'm your only real friend." Adrian clenched his teeth, trying to hold back the words. But Sorel was too determined. "You're possessive and controlling, totally insecure. You can't allow us to be happy, so you make up all these reasons to keep me to yourself." To top it off, Sorel tossed in a touch of slang that Adrian had taught him—a final twist of the knife. "You're toxic."

Shoulders shaking, Zoomer turned and pushed through into the stairs. Fluorescent light spilled out from the open door, casting her in a silhouette. "Whatever," she growled. "I hope you get your damn soul stolen by your creepy-ass ghost boyfriend." The door slammed shut with such force, it shook the cracks in the hallway's thin plaster.

NINETEEN

With a sputtering jolt, Adrian and Sorel began their slow descent. With every floor, Adrian's heart sank deeper into his gut. He was only faintly aware of when the elevator stopped and the doors whined themselves open, then the distant smack of his sneakers through the lobby followed by the kiss of fresh night air. Sorel led them through the familiar stream of headlights and flashing crosswalks, distant sirens, and barking dogs. All blended into the endless haze of another sleepless city night.

◆◆◆

The grass was cool on his cheek. Adrian made his way back into consciousness. He didn't have to open his eyes to know exactly where he was. No matter how thick the summer heat, the ground of the graveyard was always cold. His body felt oddly empty. The outline of Sorel sat beside him on the grass, prodding at the clover bed beside his gravestone.

"Sorry." Adrian pushed himself up, his palms slick in the mud. "Guess I kinda zoned out. Looks like you got us back okay."

Brows furrowed, Sorel pinched a clover between his fingers. The stem bent a little at his touch but would not break. Sorel came away scowling at his empty hands, saying nothing.

The silence between them made Adrian's stomach flutter with nerves. "Do you think we should talk about what just happened?" he asked. "I know you're mad at Zoomer but that went kinda far. We should probably at least try to apologize." On his third try, Sorel managed to pluck the clover from its roots. Adrian nodded in approval, and noted, "You're getting better at that."

Sorel spun the flower like a pinwheel between his fingers. "Do you know I wanted to be a cat?"

"What?" Adrian scoffed. "Is that supposed to be some kind of metaphor?"

"Nope. Just the truth." Sorel held the flower to his nose, then frowned. "When I died, I wanted to come back as a little black cat—the kind that nobody owns but everyone knows. I'd spend all day chasing squirrels out of gardens, sleeping in trees. People would leave me cream on their doorsteps."

"I'm pretty sure dairy is actually bad for cats," Adrian

pointed out.

The clover slipped from Sorel's grasp and fluttered to the ground. This time, it refused to be picked again. "Sounds about right," muttered Sorel. He ran a hand over the patch of clovers on his grave but they would not stir. "Point is, that's what I figured would happen. A do-over, reincarnation, whatever you want to call it." Leaning on his elbows, he shook out his ginger curls. "Or maybe it would all just end, that sounded okay too." He groaned, passing through his own gravestone as he rolled to one side. "Of all the stuff I thought could happen, I never expected I'd get stuck!"

"You weren't counting on the whole heaven thing?" Adrian tilted closer, hand on his chin.

"Ha!" Sorel laughed, contemptuously. It echoed across the graveyard, making Adrian's skin prickle and run cold. "Stuck in an immortal afterlife where I'm forever visiting with all my most religious relatives? Yuck." He sneered at the starless sky. "Besides, I wouldn't have been welcome there anyway."

Adrian wrapped his arms around himself. "Well, maybe that makes two of us."

Sorel's sharp eyes flitted towards him. "Yeah, maybe."

"Sorel, I—" Adrian reached out a sympathetic hand, barely brushing against Sorel's pantleg. In an instant, visions swirled behind his eyes: Waking with dirt in his mouth, calling for help without making any sound; clawing towards the surface with invisible grit beneath his fingernails; breaking through only to find the world changed.

Everyone he'd ever loved was gone, and worse, those that remained had forgotten him. All that was left was the vacuous call of inexistence.

Adrian felt the weight of muscles unable to ache, the maddening monotony forged while pacing in an iron cell. The material world was a battle forged through continual effort, earned by treasuring the tiny dramas of scurrying ants and spiders weaving their webs. He suddenly and intimately knew what it meant to struggle with his own morbid curiosity, to wonder what scraps remained buried six feet under his own nameplate.

The visceral nature of Sorel's afterlife washed over Adrian like a wave of salt water. It stung in his nose and made him sputter. "Sorel?" he reeled back, returning to his own senses as he gasped for breath. "That's. You—?"

"Shit." When Adrian opened his eyes, Sorel was doubled over and rubbing his temples. "You've gotta warn me before you do that."

"I didn't mean to." A question sat on Adrian's lips as his senses slowly returned. "What I saw just now, was that your death?"

He nodded. "Kinda, yeah."

"But you were—it was..." There were no words Adrian knew that could describe it. "Terrible." The phrase seemed so tiny, flippant in comparison to all he'd felt. If that's what Sorel had been going through for five decades, it was little wonder he needed company.

"Pretty much." Sorel wore his sidelong smile. "Guess I ended up in hell after all. And my punishment is, I get to watch everybody else keep on living while I stay forever doomed to scare away anyone who even tries to get close to me."

"I'm not scared of you." Shuffling back, Adrian rested himself against the oak tree. He patted the ground, inviting Sorel to join him.

With a sigh, Sorel accepted his offer. He drifted over and slouched against the knotted bark, shoulders fading through it. "Thanks, I guess."

Above them, dense leaves rustled softly. "I'm sorry about Zoomer," said Adrian. "She just doesn't know you like I do."

"Do you really know me, though?" asked Sorel.

Adrian stopped to think. "I want to," he decided.

Sorel didn't answer for a good long while. When he did, his words were faint, easily mistaken for a gentle breeze. "I just didn't know it would be like this. All I wanted was a break."

"I get it." Adrian fiddled with the frayed end of his shoelace. "I've thought about it too. Needing a break." The threads began to unweave between his fingers but Adrian kept on picking. "Being alive is exhausting. I'm, what, just supposed to keep going along—finish high school, sit on the wait-list for top surgery, work a bunch of crappy jobs? Maybe I get married and spend the rest of my time arguing and suffering until I get all wrinkly and gross?" He flicked his broken laces and kicked at the muddy ground. "If *that's* what life is, then no thanks. I never asked to be born into this world where everything is expensive and broken and sucks."

"But at least you get to live it." Sorel flicked his wrist skyward. The oak's full branches were visible through his open hand. "You get to feel it, taste it, see it. You can go wherever you want, *do* whatever you want!"

"You've seen my life, right?" sneered Adrian. How had Zoomer put it once? "Every day is the same shit. Sometimes it just stinks different."

Sorel wrinkled his nose. "Poetic."

"Well, how about this?" Adrian pressed against the bark. "You never got to come out, right? Well, I did. But people already knew—they can always tell, I just gave them a word for it." He winced. The back of his binder was riding up, pinching his skin. "And now I'm, like, all visible and shit. Everybody sees me and that's supposed to be good, but nobody *actually* notices how crappy I'm feeling. And it's, like, all the time?" He turned away, picking at a knot in the tree. "I don't even know why I feel this way. It's supposed to be all better now, me being me or whatever. But it's like I'm trying to build a house next to a black hole—I'm always one step away from falling in." A chunk of bark came off in his hand. Adrian just stared at it. "I wouldn't exactly call that living."

"What would you call it, then?" asked Sorel.

Adrian peeked back at him, mulling over the question. "How about not dying. Presently."

Sorel grinned. "That's got a ring to it."

"It does, doesn't it?" Adrian smiled.

Side by side, they lay back to watch a dark blanket

of clouds drift by, illuminated by the city's endless light. "Hey," Sorel spoke up. "Do you have your phone on you?"

"Always." Adrian fished into his pocket. "Why?"

"Could you look something up for me?" Sorel propped himself up on an elbow. "I've had this song stuck in my head for ages. I don't know if you would have heard it but it was on the radio all the time when I was a kid. My mom used to borrow our neighbour's 8-track player so she could play it on repeat."

Adrian's fingers were already tracing across the screen's glowing keyboard. "What's the name?"

Sorel spelled it out, peering over his shoulder. "That's it!" He pointed with excitement. "Wow—there are so many versions."

"Some stuff just stays popular." Adrian tapped on the top result. The first few notes trickled out his speaker and he set down his phone in a small divot on the oak tree, letting music fill the graveyard.

Sorel bobbed his head and began to hum along; by the chorus, he was singing, *Take my hand, take my whole life too...* Peeking one eye open, he grinned at Adrian watching and offered his hand. "Shall we?"

Rising in one fluid motion, they began to sway together. They had practiced the art of interlacing well enough, by now. They'd learned how to slow the process. A familiar static built between them, an intimate emergence moving at their own pace. Sorel's fingertips traced Adrian's wrist, down the bend of his arm. Adrian's face pressed into the curve of Sorel's neck, lips grazing across his chin. With every fleeting glance, rivulets of electricity sparked between them. It was like trying to dance with a frozen river or a crackling storm.

The phone speaker fizzled out like an old record. The playlist moved on to another rendition of the same song. Neither Adrian nor Sorel cared to change it. They were lost in one another now. Adrian sighed into Sorel's mouth, his warm breath passing through and misting into the night air.

There could be no more waiting. Together, their two selfhoods became entangled. Flowing in and out, they occupied the same space and time with ease. Neither could be sure whose touch was whose. It no longer mattered.

Adrian had always held a portion of dread in his heart. A fear, bordering on a fixation. He could anticipate, with perfect clarity, all the ways his first intimate encounter would inevitably go wrong. Sometimes it was just a tablespoon of doubt, adding a bitter flavour to every flirty text or first date. The closer he would get to realizing his fantasies, the greater his anxiety would become, until he was brimming with a pure panic that threatened to spill out in all directions. The risks of revealing his body to another always left him seasick. Adrian suspected many people in his position might feel the same way. Even with someone who "got it"—who even maybe lived it—there was always an awkward waltz to be had, soft toes waiting to be crushed.

Except, not this time. Not with Sorel. When his touch slipped along Adrian's back, cradling the bend of his waist,

Adrian could trust his hands as if they were his own. Better, even. As he released all control, Adrian started floating. He was watching his own body as Sorel took over. And it was so beautiful.

The lines between them built and vanished like sand along a rising tide. Adrian let himself ride each cresting wave. Sorel's breath tight in his chest, Adrian flexed and twisted with delight. All his old worries seemed so small. Everything would be taken care of from now on. Adrian let himself unravel. He passed into nothing, a no-place that was everything, sustained by the knowledge that Sorel would always lead him back to shore.

TWENTY

ad rubbed the takeout chopsticks against each other, sanding down their tiny splinters. Pop methodically doled out dark brown rice noodles on three identical paper plates. Satisfied, he passed around each serving before settling into his usual spot on the living-room couch. Adrian sat cross-legged on a pillow beside the coffee table, trying to remember the last time they had all sat down for a meal. The television rested oddly silent, its dark face a mirror of their queer Rockwellian tableau.

"Would you pass the chili sauce, dear?" Dad asked in a perfectly saccharine tone.

Pop handed over a few of the small packets that had come with their meal. "Here you are, darling."

Adrian glowered but neither father acknowledged his scrutiny.

There was a buzz in his pocket. Adrian hardly had to guess who was texting. There were three new messages from Zoomer, plus an unplayed voicenote. A preview of her latest text made him pause.

Granny Z: we should talk …

A boulder of regret sat in the base of his throat, leaving no room for appetite. What was he doing, leaving her on read? Zoomer was supposed to be his best friend. He ran a finger across his lock screen, bracing himself to finally read what she had to say. He at least owed her that much.

"No phones at the table, Adrian," said Pop. "You know that."

Adrian looked to his dad to intervene—or at least be on his phone too, acting as a bad example. But Dad was eating quietly, glancing up only to add, "Listen to your father, Adrian. Please and thank you."

Adrian shoved his phone beneath his floor cushion and made a silent promise. *I'll text back later. For real this time.*

After several minutes of listening to his fathers' fastidious chewing, Adrian could hardly stand it anymore. "Alright, let's get this over with. You're getting a divorce, right?"

Dad almost choked on a mouthful of tofu. He smacked his chest. "Why would you say that?"

Adrian crossed his arms, uninterested in playing games. "You think I don't see what's going on? You've been at it for weeks and now, all of a sudden, you start acting way too sweet?" He waved at the array of takeout boxes from the Thai restaurant down the street. "And then you're just ordering my favourite food, for no reason? You're obviously gearing up to give me bad news."

Pop grunted in a manner that told Adrian he was mildly impressed. "Well, you always were a smart one. I'll give you that."

Dad cleared his throat. "I hate to break it to you, bud, but we're actually not getting a divorce." He rested a hand on Pop's knee. "We do have something to talk about, though. As a family."

"So, it's a separation, then. Time apart." Adrian munched on a forkful of broccoli. "Whatever you want to call it. It's for the best."

"Did you want to tell him?" asked Pop.

Dad nodded and washed down his last bite.

If they weren't getting a divorce, what could be such bad news? *Maybe one of them is dying.* As soon as the thought arrived, panic set in. Adrian's mind raced. He could see it all now—months of testing and meds. The sting of hospital disinfectant and fluorescent lights. Gripping tight to weakening hands. A goddamn funeral.

He couldn't do it. Even given his recent encounters with an occupant of the afterlife, Adrian wasn't ready for one of them to go ahead and join that side. And if it really was happening, he didn't want to know. Except, he had to. Voice wavering, he dared to ask, "Are you—?"

"We're going on vacation!" Dad placed an arm around Pop, grinning like he was posing for a picture.

Dead silence. Adrian blinked at both his parents, waiting for the punchline to this perplexing joke. "But, we never go anywhere."

"That's not true," Pop protested, earning himself a stern look from Dad. "Fine. Then all the more reason to spend some time together as a family."

"We're taking a road trip, out to the East Coast!" The corners of Dad's smile slightly twitched. A flake of green onion was caught between his teeth. "We'll stop by some campgrounds, really make a journey of it. And at the end, you'll get to see Nana and Gramps—isn't that great?!"

"*You're* excited to see Nana and Gramps?" Adrian asked.

"Well, sure." Dad bit the inside of his cheek, making him look a little like a stunned fish. "I may not be their biggest fan, but—"

"Understatement of the year." Pop snorted. Adrian giggled too.

Dad ignored the sideline commentary. "*But,* they've generously offered to put us up for a couple months. So, we're taking the offer!"

"A couple *months*?!" Adrian reeled back like he'd had the wind knocked out of him. "Seriously, what is going on. Are we running from the law or something?"

"Nothing is 'going on,'" Pop firmly insisted. "Nothing you need to worry about, anyway."

"That's right." Dad bobbed in agreement. "We've been wanting to take a trip like this for a while but never found the time. But now, your pop's schedule has opened up, so—" Pop quickly hushed his partner but Adrian had already caught on.

"Opened up, how?" Adrian braced himself against the edge of the coffee table. He searched his fathers' faces for the truth. "Just tell me. I can take it."

Dad weighed his words carefully. "Pop has received some, let's say, unexpected time off."

"You got fired?" Adrian gasped.

"They're calling it a layoff." Pop scowled at a stain on the living-room carpet. "Corporate thinks the day crew can handle the night shift, so long as they work late and come in early. Goddamn greedy sons of—"

"We're trying to see this as a *blessing*." A vein on Dad's forehead ran so thick, it looked like an elastic band ready to snap. "As you apparently noticed, things have been tense at home lately. This will be a good chance to spend some time together, to reconnect."

"Oh yeah, that's a great idea." Adrian pushed back his dinner plate. "Nothing like shoving yourself into a car for god knows how long and driving out to the middle of nowhere while your relationship is on the rocks. Really smart choice."

"We get it, you're not a fan of the idea." Pop began to raise his voice. "There's no need for the attitude. This is happening, and you might as well come around to it."

The tension in the room grew thicker. Dad opened his mouth, likely to try to smooth out the situation, but just ended up closing it again. Adrian stared down at his socks, one with a hole in its toe and the other fraying at the heel.

"When do we leave?"

"Next Monday," said Pop.

"Monday?" Adrian voice cracked. "Are you joking?!"

"I know it's soon." Dad softly put a hand on Adrian's shoulder. "The thing is, we found someone looking for a place asap. And we could really use the extra income, like, yesterday."

"Like, a sublet?" Adrian shoved his dad's hand off, trying to hold back the shudder in his throat. "Is this a vacation, or a move?"

His fathers looked to one another for the answer. "We need some time to think, look over our options," said Dad.

"I hear the rentals are much cheaper out east," Pop added.

Adrian's nose pinched with anger, tears blurring his vision. "So, I'm just supposed to drop everything and hit the road with you in less than a week?"

"Try not to worry too much about the logistics." Dad began to tidy the table. "We're hoping this is just a short breather. We'll do home school for the fall semester, and hopefully you can be back in your regular classes by winter."

"Home school?" A cold sweat formed across Adrian's neck. "But, I can't—what about—" All the words he couldn't say ran though his mind at once. *What about Sorel? What if something happens to him—or to me?* "What am I supposed to tell Zoomer?"

"Oh, bud." Dad gave a sympathetic look on his way towards the kitchen, leftovers in hand. "I'm sure she'll understand."

"Do you even know these randos who are supposed to

rent out the place?" Adrian waved frantically at their small apartment home. "Why don't you go, and I stay here. I can water the plants, watch over everything."

"We're not about to just let you stay here alone with strangers from the internet," Pop tsked. "The plants will probably do better off without us anyway." He laughed at his own joke and Dad chuckled along with him.

The pounding of Adrian's heartbeat rose to fill his ears. Everything inside him was screaming, *How can they laugh at a time like this?!*

"Adrian, we know this is a lot to process." Dad spoke gently.

"Yeah, no shit!" Adrian kicked the coffee table, knocking over his own water glass. "This is great. Just great."

"Adrian!" Pop snapped up. "Feet *off* the table."

"Whatever." Adrian rose and stomped towards the door. "I'm out of here."

Pop called after him but he couldn't care to listen. Even if he'd wanted to, the pounding in his head drowned out the conversation. Adrian was shoving on his sneakers as heavy footsteps approached from behind.

"I said, I'm going out!" he whirled around, ready to scream right into Pop's angry face. Except it wasn't Pop.

In stunned silence, Dad clutched a small takeout container. Adrian's name was spelled across the top in cursive script with a small heart over the *i*. "I was just going to ask if you were finished with your pad thai."

Though Adrian's mouth hung open, words wouldn't come. He simply shook his head and turned to leave. He was careful to not slam the door, at least. In the dim-lit hall, regret burned his near-empty stomach. Behind him, he caught the hushed tones of a hasty argument. Adrian didn't have to stay and listen. He knew what they were talking about. If his parents weren't going to divorce before, they might now.

TWENTY-ONE

very step down the stairwell was like falling off a cliff. His foot would hang in the air for what felt like far too long, until the ground rushed up to meet him. Each time, he was shocked by the firm slap of concrete, how it smacked into the loose rubber of his shoe. The clap of its impact volleyed along the bare walls, a percussive soundtrack for his long descent.

Adrian squinted under the harsh fluorescent lights. They flickered his shadow off and on. His sweaty palms gripped the railing as he spun around another bend. Normally, he could make this trek with his eyes closed; he had walked each flight so many times before. He knew the streaks on the walls, the crumbling edges of the steps. These should have been as familiar to him as his own hands—more so, maybe. Yet, as he rounded the next corner, his mind went one way and his feet another.

Stumbling down several steps at once, Adrian caught himself on the landing below. He fought to regain his breath, cheek pressed against the cool metal of a heavy door. Its number was emblazoned in chipped, yellow paint. Even if it had been blank, he would have known exactly where he stood.

There was a tug, an impulse to grip that cold handle and swing it open. He would race down the hall to Granny Z's apartment, falling into the embrace of all those tiny angels caked in second-hand smoke. He would spill everything into his best friend's lap, watching her grow furious on his behalf. Granny would fiddle with her kettle while not-so-subtly eavesdropping. They'd tell him he could stay there as long as he wanted. He was always welcome. He would have a place to eat and sleep and breathe, without the constant background noise of his fathers' muffled arguments.

Adrian shrank back from the door, as if he'd touched a hot stove. In his gut, he knew that Zoomer's home was not his to visit anymore. Not after all he'd said. Even if it had been Sorel's words in his mouth, they had rung too true. He could have fought harder to stop them. Better yet, he could have told Zoomer the truth about who was in that conversation with them. Instead, he'd let Sorel light the match. The bridge between them was now burned into charred pulp.

Nowhere else to go, Adrian continued downwards. Another flight, and another. He passed the exit to the ground floor. The outside world held no sanctuary for him now, only the promise of glaring lights and pedestrians with no sense of personal space. Even the graveyard was no longer his secret hideaway. He wasn't ready to go and break the news to Sorel. There would be no hiding it from him, and his impending departure to the East Coast was hard enough to bear on his own. All Adrian could do was focus on the steps in front of him. He went past the first level of underground parking, then the second. At last he came to the end of the well.

The final level of the apartment staircase led to nowhere. A small enclave with no exit, littered in empty bottles and cigarette butts. It was a planning error made manifest, so the story went. Adrian had heard that the original building design had been more grandiose; there were rumours of penthouse suites and a long bridge to connect with a sister complex across the street. The architects had sketched out three levels of a parking lot below. But before the full vision could be realized, the lead developer had suddenly resigned.

The details of the scandal were told differently each time. Some people around the complex said he'd fled the country, after his company had been caught mixing in sand to beef up the concrete. Others argued it was an issue with the weathering of the structure, a fatal flaw that ticked away behind the scenes. In time, they said, the roof and walls were set to rot through. It could be that the guy had just taken on more projects than he could handle, perhaps gotten loans from less-than-scrupulous investors. *Or maybe his parents got divorced,* spoke a sour voice in the back of Adrian's mind.

Eventually, a new company swooped in and bought the building for a song. The top few floors were lopped off from the schematics, as was the illusory skybridge. The third basement level was filled in, and some said this was an attempt to strengthen uneven foundations. All Adrian knew was that the final level of the stairway had somehow survived, transformed into a dark cavern with no exit. It was the perfect place to run to when you had nowhere else to hide.

Sitting on the steps to nowhere, Adrian caught his breath. His head was dizzy with adrenaline and sweat dripped into his eyes, blurring his vision. He instinctively moved to his pocket and found it was empty—he had left his phone upstairs. There was no going back for it now, of course. Besides, who was there to call?

A long, slow sigh slipped through Adrian's lips. He leaned back, looking up at the infinite twists of the stairs above. A memory trickled back to him.

Someone was on the phone, saying their "daughter" wasn't "socializing well" at school. Dad was concerned. He said they should seek expert help. Pop arguing over the cost, looking into what was covered by provincial insurance. An unanswerable question between them, one that still cut across Adrian's heart: *what is wrong with her?*

The words hung in the apartment for days. It was like a bad smell, rotten eggs forgotten in the back of the fridge. Dad and Pop just took turns blaming one another, perplexed by the struggles of their strangeling child. One afternoon, sick of the growing stench at home, Adrian announced he was going to meet up with some friends. Before his fathers could ask for follow-up, he had already slipped into the hall. That was the first time he had sought refuge down here, a not-girl hiding in a not-basement.

In the darkness of this no-place, he could sit in peace for a few hours. Adrian would bring library books or a sketch-pad, make up games for himself. He'd count the number of steps from the fourteenth floor to the basement, see how high he could jump and tap the wall. He might attempt to levitate pencils or move pennies with his mind; such silly ideas were a quick bust, but what mattered was that they passed the time. Once home, he regaled his fathers with stories of adventures with new-found playmates. A gentle round of fibbing that put all their minds at ease.

When feeling especially brave, little Adrian would dare himself down to the cavern below. A game of chicken for one, urged on by imagined monsters. How many steps downwards could he take before scrambling back from the dark? His mind would whisper into existence the shape of grasping hands, just out of sight. Before the last stair, Adrian would inevitably scare himself. He'd scurry backwards with a scream of horrified delight, race all the way back up to the apartment and leap into bed, giggling to himself. Then, he'd leave the light on all night—just to be safe.

Back at the old steps, Adrian's heart still remembered the thrill. The racing breath of a child still learning to play, the promise of a ghostly spectre ready to snatch his foot as soon as it passed into the shadows. Kind of ironic, he thought to himself.

A whimper rose from the darkness. Adrian sat up, fully alert. His rational mind said it could have been the building shifting. Maybe those issues with structural integrity weren't just talk. This whole place could collapse at any moment, and he would just be sitting there. Nowhere to hide.

An image flashed through his mind: the complex in a smouldering heap. Adrian had a pang of glee as he imagined his fathers, gripping one another with grief. Their son's body, too far down to even be pulled from the rubble. At least then they'd feel guilty, he told himself. Maybe they'd even bond over his passing, his young death a blessing in disguise. A weight lifted, a chance for them to start over.

Again, a hiss from the shadows. Adrian snapped back to attention. There was no denying it now. Something was down there. Heart racing, he gingerly crouched forward. He began inching down each step, like that game he used to play. Except this time, there would be no squealing and running away.

A raspy cough, a gasp. A ... hiccup? Adrian paused. He'd never heard of a monster who could hiccup. Though maybe he shouldn't generalize.

Crossing the last step of the stairway, Adrian was completely swallowed by the dark. There was nothing but pure silence. Adrian's head pounded. He peered around, eyesight slowly adjusting. There was something in here with him. He was sure of it now. What at first had appeared as shadow slowly morphed into something solid.

It was squatting in the corner. A figure, curled against the wall, coughing in sharp, juddering movements. Head slowly turning, its bloodshot eyes glared directly at Adrian.

"What the hell are you doing here?"

Adrian's voice cracked. "Zoomer?!"

TWENTY-TWO

Knees to her chest, Zoomer scowled at Adrian. "Who the hell else would I be?" She huddled in the darkest corner of the cavern below the stairs, cheeks streaked with eyeliner. "Get your own crying spot!"

Adrian crouched to his knees. "Make me."

"Seriously?" She shoved herself deeper, burying her face against the cold concrete. "Just leave me alone. Go hang out with your ghost boyfriend or whatever."

"He's not my boyfriend." Slumping down, Adrian shot out his foot to kick away a dusty beer can. It rolled in Zoomer's direction. "I don't know, maybe he is. Why does it matter so much to you, anyway?"

"Why does it matter?" She copied him with a nasal tone and smacked the can back in Adrian's direction. It missed by a long shot, ricocheted, and landed in a cobweb.

"I don't know, maybe because I was trying to protect your ass? But no, you just *had* to go back there, because you're so hungry for some of that ghost dick—or whatever the hell he's packing."

"This is why I didn't want to tell you." Adrian stuck up his nose at her. "No matter what he said, what he did, you'd never trust him."

"Yeah, well," she huffed, wiping a string of snot across her sleeve. "He did break my phone. And try to body-snatch me."

"You know that stuff was by accident," said Adrian. "But whatever. You just don't understand."

"What's there to understand?" Zoomer glared. "You're my best friend and you ditched me for—for some guy! Dead or alive, that just sucks."

There was a terrible silence in the cavern of the stair-well. Adrian tried to swallow but found his throat dry. "Even after all this," he asked, "I'm still your best friend?"

"Obviously." She sniffled. "Dumbass."

Adrian cracked a smile. "You're my dumbass best friend, too."

"Good." Zoomer tried to dab her cheeks but only managed to streak eyeliner further. "You know, all that stuff you said before, in the hall. It hurt but I knew you were just upset. What really sucked more was knowing you lied—and right to my face!" She tucked further into herself, voice muffled. "We're supposed to tell each other everything. At least, I thought we were."

"I know." Adrian slipped closer. "I was just scared that

you'd get upset, so I tried to hide it."

"Great plan." Zoomer rested a cheek against her knee and laughed weakly. "Because I'm definitely not upset now."

"I'm sorry." Adrian carefully reached towards her. "I should have said something sooner. And all that awful stuff about you being toxic—I didn't mean any of it."

Zoomer tugged at a lock of her hair and watched it spring back into place. Adrian's open hand waited for her, and tentatively, she grasped it in her own. Suddenly, she yanked him into a full embrace. "I literally missed you so much," she cried. "You have no idea how much it sucks here without you—you're legit my only friend!"

Adrian felt himself shaking, and at first, he thought it was Zoomer trembling in his arms. But the feeling cascaded upwards until he, too, dissolved to tears. "I missed you too," he admitted. "Everything at home sucks so much. All I wanted to do was go to your place and tell you everything."

Tears forming wet patches on each other's shoulders, Adrian and Zoomer held one another there, in the darkness of that place that was never supposed to be. They cried heaving, terrible sobs, the kind that only come when people are so far past their breaking point that it is impossible to do anything other than weep and weep. When at last they could catch their breath, they lay among the dust and garbage, hands clasped. Adrian told Zoomer the truth about everything: the first time he sneaked off to see Sorel in the graveyard, their shared run to—and from—the 7-Eleven, the

Ferris wheel, their midnight make-outs.

For the longest time in all their friendship, Zoomer stayed quiet. She listened carefully, hair splayed behind her across the grimy floor. "Wow," she spoke at last. "I never knew you could keep a secret so well." Rolling onto her stomach, she studied Adrian in the darkness. "So, how do I even know you're really *you* right now? Tell me something only the real Adrian would know."

"After all that messy crying, you really don't think I'm me?" Adrian's voice was hoarse, throat dry. Zoomer shrugged. "Fine. Ask me anything only I would know!"

"Ooh, I love this game." Wriggling with delight at her temporary power, Zoomer weighed her options. "Okay, here's a good one. Who was your first kiss?"

"You're really going there?" Adrian groaned. "I'll never know how you convinced me to play spin the bottle after we had eaten, like, three loaves of your gran's garlic bread."

"And a whole can of your dad's sauerkraut!" Zoomer faux-retched at the memory. "The world's stinkiest smooch—plus your cheese-farts afterwards, yuck!"

"Those weren't my fault!" Adrian insisted. "I hadn't cut out dairy yet."

"Worst. Sleepover. Ever." She snorted. "Alright, fine. It's you."

"The one and only," said Adrian. "But look, you don't have to worry so much. Sorel really isn't a bad guy, he just gets caught up in his feelings sometimes."

"Yeah, maybe." Fingers tracing shapes on the dirt floor, Zoomer drew a pentacle. She decorated it with elemental designs. "What really freaks me out, though, is I knew something was up when I saw you. But I couldn't figure it out. I had no idea Sorel could even leave the graveyard like that."

"Only when he's riding with me." Adrian leaned over and traced a smiley face in the middle of her design. Zoomer swatted his hand away.

"So, be real," she said, flashing her most wicked grin, "what's it like to ride ghost D, though?"

"Zoomer," Adrian squealed, "it doesn't even work like that!"

"What, like I'm supposed to believe you're the top?" Zoomer snorted and went back to her doodles. "But, um. How does it work then?"

Why hadn't he thought to bring some water? Adrian's tongue was getting so dry, dust gathering in the back of his mouth. He struggled to find the words to tell her. "It's like, I can see and feel and hear everything, when I want to. Or, I can sink away and just be, like, still." Eyes closed, he tried to find that place inside himself. It was so easy to just curl up into it, whenever Sorel took control. "When I'm there, sometimes I'll get a glimpse of something from his life, too. A taste, or a smell. It's almost like a kind of time travel." His head was getting buzzy, like he'd been holding his breath. Adrian shivered. "Sometimes, I get kinda high from it. It's just so freeing, letting someone else take charge, totally releasing all control. There's times I don't know if I even want to come back. But he always pulls me through."

"Woah." Even in the shadows, Zoomer was clearly

blushing. "Hot. Very kinky."

"It is not!" Adrian's cheeks ran hot. "I'm just— I'm not explaining it right."

"Hey, not trying to yuck your yum, dude." Zoomer raised her arms in surrender. "No kink-shaming here." She started to laugh and Adrian couldn't help but giggle with her, their shared joy reverberating all the way back up the apartment's long stairwell.

TWENTY-THREE

Adrian must have stepped in gum. Down the block and around the corner, every other footstep came up sticky. Mentally, he recited a self-made script. He'd practiced it plenty of times by now, editing and paring down all the words he wished he didn't have to say.

Zoomer had tried to talk him out of it, a dozen times already. She told him it wouldn't matter. According to Sorel, he didn't experience the passage of time in the same way as living people. She assured Adrian that a few months apart would hardly be a blip on his afterlife calendar. If anyone needed some hand-holding, it was Zoomer herself. They'd just barely reconciled and now his fathers were going to drag him off to the middle of nowhere, Nova Scotia. How was that fair? There must be another way to convince them, to let him stay.

They had debated introducing Sorel to his parents. Once they knew he had a boyfriend, maybe they would understand his need to stick around. Adrian gave the idea serious consideration, but it just didn't seem all that practical. Dad might buy it, but Pop? He'd never been the spiritual type. It seemed much more likely that they'd question Adrian's sanity before even agreeing to a cemetery visit.

What's wrong with her? That question still burned fresh in his mind. He couldn't risk it. And even if they could prove Sorel's existence, what if his fathers reacted like Zoomer? The presence of a nearby ghost, one with a particular penchant for their son, could make them run even faster. They might even stay away for good.

No. This was the better way to do it. Honest communication was the keystone to a good relationship—that's what all the social media therapists were always saying.

The graveyard's arched entrance loomed into view. Adrian stopped short at its precipice. He watched the yellow grass extend before him, rippling like ocean waves in choppy wind. With one last deep breath, he stepped over the edge.

"Sorel?" called Adrian. "It's me."

The city's orange ever-light cast the yard in twilight shadows. The sun had set hours back. The moment Adrian called his name, Sorel appeared, perched on a wayward gravestone. He waved, smiling wide, "Hey babe! I'm ready for our movie date."

"Crap," Adrian hissed.

Sorel spun into the air with excitement. "It's been

forever since I saw anything in a theatre! Do they still sell popcorn—can we get it with extra butter?!"

"I'm sorry, I totally forgot," Adrian winced, kicking at the dirt. "I don't even think any movie theatres are open this late."

"Oh." Sorel stopped his skyward dance and dipped back down to earth. "That's okay. We can just go for a walk, or maybe go back to your place?"

Adrian turned away, unable to hold Sorel's gaze as he told him, "Actually, we need to talk."

"No," Sorel said, quite simply.

"No?" Adrian repeated. "You don't even know what I have to say."

Sliding backwards, Sorel crossed his arms over his chest. "I may have been dead for a while now, but I know what that line means. And I'm saying no, we're not breaking up. Not tonight."

"It's not like that." Adrian stepped after him.

"Isn't it, though?" Sorel scowled. "Don't tell me—you met someone else, somebody with a pulse, and realized it's time to drop this dead weight?"

"Of course not!" Adrian let out a nervous laugh. "There's never been anyone but you."

"Then Zoomer got to you, didn't she?" Sorel paced like a caged animal. His outline turned translucent as he walked through a beam of moonlight. "You think I'm some kind of monster. She's making you cut ties."

Adrian shook his head. "Actually, I told her about us and she's sort of come around. At least, enough to not be mad anymore."

"So that's it!" Sorel flicked his wrist. "Being haunted isn't so thrilling anymore, now that we're not a secret to your friend!"

"Can you not be like this? If you'd just listen," Adrian's words were getting all bunched up, forming a lump in the back of his throat, "I'm trying to tell you something important."

"There's no need." Sorel's edges began fizzling. "You're ending things. The 'why' doesn't matter." He started to fade out of sight.

"Please, wait!" Adrian cried after him, "It's not my choice, it's my folks—they're making me!"

As if rounding a revolving door, Sorel stepped back into view. Brows furrowed, he asked, "What's that supposed to mean?"

"Pop lost his job." The words still didn't quite seem real. "We have to go live with my grandparents for a while, out on the East Coast."

"How long is a while?" Sorel asked, sharply.

"A couple months, at least." Adrian's voice was flat, as if spoken by someone else. He could still hardly believe all this was happening. "I know it sucks. I want to stay but..."

"Then, stay," said Sorel. "Just tell them you won't go." It was so simple when he put it like that, so matter-of-fact, Adrian was tempted to agree.

"I don't know." Adrian kicked at a pebble in the grass. "I don't think they'd get it."

Sorel hovered side to side, weighing his options. "Fine,"

he decided. Twisting mid-air, he appeared at Adrian's side. "Then I'll come with you."

"That's not a great idea either." Adrian took a step back. "We've never even done a full overnight."

Sorel waved off his concern. "Sure, but what could go wrong?"

"How about anything, and everything?" Adrian paced circles in the grass. "What if we get separated somehow? What would even happen if we split while you weren't in the graveyard?" Nightmarish visions flooded his mind, Sorel slipping out of his grasp, being torn in two. "You could die—or disappear forever!"

"Already did the first one," Sorel pointed out. "I'm not too worried about the second."

"But *I* am!" Adrian's voice wavered. "I could never forgive myself if something happened to you, because of me." He clutched his heart. "Not to mention, even if we could somehow make it all work, there's the fact that we'd be stuck in a car with *both* my fathers! If Zoomer could tell something was up, they could figure it out too."

"I doubt it. You and I both know, they're so caught up hating each other, they hardly even notice you." Adrian's lips parted as the weight of those words hit his gut. "What," Sorel shrugged. "That's the truth, isn't it?"

Fists balled, Adrian took a deep breath. "I am sorry that you're so upset," he spoke slowly, careful to clearly enunciate each syllable. "But this will be worse for me than it is for you. Just a blink, and I'll be back."

"Except, what if you aren't?" Adrian looked up,

expecting that wry smile to be waiting for him. But Sorel seemed genuinely upset. "What if they never let you come back?"

"You don't have to worry about that," Adrian promised. "I've got school to finish. I'll come see you every day, after class." Even as he said it, Dad's promises of home schooling echoed in the back of Adrian's mind. Then there was Pop's speculations on the cost of rental places out east. They really could be gearing up to stay, permanently.

"What if you get busy?" Sorel's visage briefly wavered. "Or make new friends—what if you forget about me?"

"That won't happen," said Adrian, trying to convince himself, too. "I know this is scary, but I promise."

"How can you promise that?!" Sorel shot into the air. "You don't know—you don't know anything!" Looming over Adrian, his words shook the air with rumbling echoes. His eyes drained of their colour, becoming a whirling storm. "No. This is not happening. I'm not getting left alone again."

The wind picked up. Adrian sank his heels into the ground, keeping steady. "Sorel, you don't have to freak out. Everything is going to be okay."

"It's not okay! *I'm* not okay!" Sorel raised his voice, then shook his head. He blinked and was suddenly himself again. He fell to the ground like a stone and lay still. "Adrian," he whimpered, "I need your help. I think something's really wrong with me."

"What do you mean?" Adrian stooped to Sorel's side. "What's going on?"

"I didn't want to worry you." Sorel lay crumpled on the ground. "We've just been having so much fun. I didn't want to ruin it."

"How could you ever ruin this?" asked Adrian, knees sinking into the mud.

"By telling you the truth." Sorel clutched his arms around himself. "Adrian, I've been lingering. Before you get here, after you go. It's like I'm stuck, even worse than usual."

"Maybe it's because I'm thinking of you so much?" Adrian suggested with the hint of a smile.

"I don't think that's it." Sorel began to shudder, teeth chattering as if he was suddenly cold. His breath was visible, a translucent cloud that dissipated at his lips. "Sometimes it lasts for hours, or days. And it's terrible being stuck here for so long, nothing to do or even read, no one to talk to." He blinked, tears vanishing before they hit the ground. "I'm just so, so lonely."

Resisting the urge to rest a hand on Sorel's back, Adrian offered words of comfort instead: "It's alright. I'm here now. There's got to be something we can do—Zoomer might know some kind of spell?"

"No. I don't want her." Sorel began to violently shake, head juddering. He snapped towards Adrian, eyes wide and frantic. "I don't want anyone but you!"

"What?" Adrian fell backwards, palms slipping in the wet grass.

A sickening grin crept across Sorel's face. "Let's run away together," he hissed. "Go somewhere new, start all over."

"What're you talking about?" Adrian stumbled to his feet. "You're not making sense."

"Just think about all the fun we'd have!" Sorel scraped along the ground, his sing-song voice like a whistle on the wind. "So many new adventures!"

"Even if I wanted to go with you, I can't just drop everything." Adrian looked over his shoulder. The gate seemed to stretch away from him, the graveyard lengthening before his eyes. "I'm not even done high school. I don't have money or a driver's license, or anything!"

"But we'd have each other!" Sorel's grasping hands were picking up speed. "Isn't that enough? Isn't that everything?!" An awful sound burst out of him. It was like a knife scraping against ceramic, or a rusty nail down a chalkboard. It took a moment for Adrian to realize—Sorel was laughing.

Adrian ran for the exit. Sorel raced after him and blinked out of sight. That terrible cackling echoed off the gravestones, pounding in Adrian's ears. When he turned, Sorel was ahead, blocking the path. Those pale green eyes had drained again, holding nothing but a restless storm.

"You're so selfish," Sorel spat.

Adrian was choking on his own hurried breath. "Why would you—"

"If you knew what I was going through, you'd never ask me to do this." Sorel's words rumbled like encroaching thunder. "To wait around and be forgotten, again."

From somewhere in the depths of Adrian's mind, he recalled an article that Zoomer had forwarded. It was months ago, during a short stint when she was set on becoming a psychologist. "Ten Easy Ways to Set Healthy Boundaries." Having already stated a clear "no," expressed his own feelings, and listened without judgement, Adrian jumped to step four: taking personal space.

"Maybe we need a break from this conversation." He spoke softly as he sidestepped Sorel. "I'll go tell my parents that we can't leave just yet. Then I can come right back here, so we can keep talking."

"You have no idea what it's like." Sorel hardly seemed to hear him. "Sitting around, alone. Not able to touch anything, or smell, or even breathe." He shimmered, the shape of him starting to blur. "And then someone comes along. They show you how to feel again. And you just never want things to go back to how they were before."

"I am leaving now." Adrian searched Sorel's face for any hint of the person he thought he knew. "You need to let me go." Twisting his step, Adrian faked a move to the right and then lunged towards the gate. Sorel spun after him, a second too late.

"No!" Sorel cried out. His voice was suddenly small and meek again. "Please, I didn't mean to..."

This time, Adrian did not turn back. There was no more time for excuses or reasoning. The archway was a breath away. He tumbled towards his escape.

Suddenly, a loud rip—something breaking. The sole of his sneaker had finally given way. It flung from the base of his shoe, sending him on a direct trajectory into the road. Headlights swerved. Someone honked. Adrian's arms flew over his face, braced for impact. From the corner of his eye, he saw Sorel leap after him with an arm outstretched.

A freezing hand grasped Adrian's ankle, just before it cleared the gate. A shot of cold ran up to his chest and burst forth, followed by a terrible numbness. The world twisted in all directions. He fell, and fell, and fell, further than he ever thought possible. A sinking weight dragged him ever deeper until he could not tell up from down.

With a smack, Adrian landed on wet earth. Eyes bleary, he witnessed a golden halo. He stared at the vision in awe. The blurred edges of its circle came into focus. He was looking up at a street light.

Tires squealed in the distance. A driver shouted something while speeding off into the night.

A silhouette leaned into view. Someone was standing over him, speaking quickly. Adrian recognized something about the voice, though he couldn't make out the words. There was a ringing in his ears. Slowly, he parsed a face—his own.

"I'm sorry," he was saying. "I'm sorry, I'm sorry, I'm sorry."

Adrian reached towards the warped reflection of himself. His hands were translucent as they passed through the hazy light. Before he could grasp at the familiar stranger, there was a sudden pinch at his fingertips like he'd stuck them into an electric socket. Adrian shrank back, nursing the pain. A ripple extended from the point where he had made contact, revealing an invisible barrier. It stretched across the graveyard's gate. Adrian's other self was safely crouched on the sidewalk outside it.

When Adrian tried to speak, it came out faint. Wind snaking through a cracked window. He could manage only a single word. "Sorel?"

"I'm really, really sorry," said the ghost wearing Adrian's skin.

Sorel clambered to his feet, one sneaker short. Lips twisted with guilt, he turned towards the street. The road was now empty, deadly quiet. Taking one shaking step, then another, he broke out into a sprint. He ran as fast as his new body could take him.

Adrian was too weak to give chase. Part of him knew he should be worried, upset, but the feelings wouldn't stick. All that he was, or had been, began to run. The dripping yolk of a broken egg. Darkness crept in. The void was calling, sweetly.

The spirit that had been Adrian sank into nothing and revelled in its embrace. The last sensation he experienced was a distinct sense of tipping backwards. It brought back vague memories of trying to sleep while drunk. Except, he wasn't nauseous, or dizzy, or worried about a hangover. He wasn't anything at all.

TWENTY-FOUR

Sorel was counting doorways. He paced along the carpeted hallway, quite certain that this was Adrian's floor. He hovered briefly by each entrance, listening for movement. There was the occasional chatter of late-night television, a couple of loud snorers, the vague sounds of someone practicing an instrument and not very well, either.

He was fully freaking out. Breath shallow, every inhale and exhale took extraordinary effort. Even little movements in this body were an awkward, clumsy dance, a constant juggling of blinking and sniffling, squishy flesh and sloshing organs. It was exhausting! Being alive had never seemed so daunting when he had been with Adrian.

Adrian. A bitter guilt burned in Sorel's throat as he thought the name—or was that heartburn? Adrian had mentioned having a sour stomach.

Slowing down, Sorel gripped his chest. There was still fresh dirt under his nails. What was he doing, spinning his wheels like this? Burning time. He'd just run off with his boyfriend's body! What exactly was the next step in his plan—bust into Adrian's apartment, scrounge up some supplies, then hit the road in a pilfered skin sack?

No way. Sorel turned on his heel and set himself straight. Well, as straight as he could be given how tricky it was to walk on Adrian's uneven legs. He'd never noticed before but the two were definitely different lengths. Adrian must have automatically corrected for it during their dates. Regaining his balance, Sorel marched towards the elevator. He had to go back to the graveyard before it was too late.

He cared about Adrian. Even in the midst of all this confusion, that point stayed true. Sorel was more certain than ever, now that he could feel the shiver of a rising pulse, the goose pimples down his neck. Sweet, patient Adrian. There he was, staring back at him from the warped silver of the elevator doors. Doe-eyed with a look of perpetual surprise, an apple chin and lips like two halves of a heart, elegantly kissable.

Sorel's hand wavered over the call button. Adrian's hand, he corrected himself. He just happened to not be using it at this particular moment. They'd soon be reunited, of course. Because Sorel would give the body back. Because he loved Adrian. Because returning was the right thing to do.

Except, would he be there? asked a whisper in the back

of his mind. It reminded him that Adrian might not be in the cemetery. He might not be anywhere at all, anymore. Sorel had seen some spirits come and go within a matter of minutes. *Not to mention*—the voice grew a little louder—*how could he be sure that it would work?* He had never taken a vessel like this before. What if the trade-back didn't take? Then he and Adrian would both be out of a body. That seemed like a net loss.

It had been so long since Sorel had fingernails to bite, he'd almost forgotten the nervous habit. The voice inside warned that, though things looked bad, they could always get worse. He envisioned horrified pedestrians as they discovered Adrian's corpse in the morning, face-down in the dirt. What would his fathers say, or Zoomer for that matter? It seemed hardly fair to risk so much grief. Maybe Sorel should keep the body, if only until he could be certain how to safely restore its proper occupant.

No, he wasn't going to talk himself out of this. Sorel pushed the call button several times until he heard the elevator's cables stir. He was going back down there, pronto. He'd track down Adrian somehow and talk through this whole situation. They'd make a plan, as a team. Who knows, Adrian might even be happier as a spirit—there was a good chance he'd let Sorel keep his life after all. That could happen, right?

"There you are!" The approach of heavy bootsteps jostled Sorel's train of thought. From down the hall, a broad man approached him with purpose. He had eyebrows for days and a salt-and-pepper beard. Sorel jumped and managed to smack an elbow against the wall—fresh pain ricocheted up to his shoulder and he winced, unused to being so solid all the time. "Where have you been?!" the man demanded.

"Me?" Adrian's voice was always so stringy and nervous. "I—"

"Do you have any idea what time it is?" The man tensed his jaw. "And where the hell is your other shoe?"

Sorel looked down. Adrian's left sneaker was missing, his sock caked in mud. "I ... lost it." That was close enough to the truth.

"How do you—?" They were interrupted by a hacking cough next door, the shuffling of footsteps. With a grunt, the man took Sorel by the shoulder and guided him away. "Your dad has been tearing his hair out, worried sick about you. I was calling your cell for hours, only to find it buried under a couch cushion!"

"Oh!" Sorel held back a gasp. The pieces were coming together. His past encounters with Adrian's fathers had taken the form of brief glimpses, seen through Adrian's hurried eyes. "Pops?" He racked his mind for what Adrian might say. "I'm sorry?"

"I don't want an apology." Pop fumbled with a handful of keys. "I want you to take responsibility for your choices. What if you had gotten hurt, or been kidnapped!"

"But I didn't." Sorel wriggled against Pop's weighty grip. How did corporeal beings struggle like this all the time, so easily overpowered by brutal force? "And truth is, I've gotta get back out there. There's some stuff that still needs taking care of."

"I'm sure." Pop rattled his key but the apartment's deadbolt wouldn't budge. "Unfortunately for you and your 'stuff,' you are fully grounded for the rest of the weekend." He shoved his shoulder against the door, trying to force it open. "Where is your dad—the damn lock's stuck again."

"It'll only take a second, I swear!" Sorel ducked away. "And it's really, really important."

Pop caught him by the wrist. "I'm sure it *really, really* feels that way. But you are not going anywhere until your bags are packed and your attitude is in check." The lock finally clicked open and Pop crashed his way into the apartment, dragging Sorel with him. Stumbling on his unfamiliar feet, Sorel landed onto the floor with a hard smack.

"Adrian!" Instantly, Pop knelt at his side. The door fell shut behind them, taking with it any light. "Are you alright? I didn't mean to—"

Cheek pressed onto a square of peeling wood-grain vinyl, Sorel's world spun. He was dizzy, not from the fall but from everything leading up to it. The air had all rushed out of Adrian's lungs and he couldn't seem to get it back.

"I'm okay," he wheezed. "Just tripped."

"Are you sure?" Pop patted down Adrian from shoulders to knees. "Nothing broken?" Sorel nodded and Pop slumped over with relief. "I thought I..." he shuddered, unable to even finish the thought.

"I'm okay," Sorel said again. He meant it, this time. Apparently this body had a way of finding its breath again, even when he did not. Pop was still sniffling, wiping his eyes while Sorel propped himself up. Something was stuffed in Adrian's pocket—a grey handkerchief, worn smooth, almost threadbare. It smelled faintly of dirt and vinegar.

He extended it to Pop without a word, who took it and nodded thanks. "I didn't know you still used Pop-Pop's old hankies."

"I guess so. Does that bother you?" The answer didn't really matter. But the longer Pop kept talking, the more time there was to plan an escape.

Pop ran his thumb along the faded paisley pattern, the remnants of monogrammed initials in the corner. "This was one of his favourites, did you know that?" Sorel started to nod but Pop muttered, "No, of course not. You were so young when he passed."

"Right," Sorel murmured, eyeing the door. How long would it take to leap for the handle? If he could manage to get Adrian's legs working right, how far might he get down the hall?

No, running off wasn't going to work. The last thing he needed was Pop giving chase, following him to the cemetery and finding out the true scope of the situation. Now, if Sorel could soothe him into submission, that would be a step in the right direction.

Moonlight slipped through a gap in the curtains. Silent tears glimmered down Pop's rough face. "My father was a complicated man. That's how my mom used to put it." He spoke softly, dabbing his cheeks. Once finished, he carefully folded the handkerchief into a neat square. "Do you know, he never said he loved me?"

Sorel stared at Pop, completely at a loss. What would Adrian do? Sitting up, he lightly tapped one of the big man's broad shoulders. "That must have been hard."

"Goddammit, Adrian." Pop blew his nose. "You're such a great kid. After everything that's gone wrong the last couple years, I just—" His voice caught and he took a moment to clear his throat. "I just hope you know that your dad and I, we love each other. And we're really, truly trying." Stuffing the hankie into his breast pocket, Pop took Sorel by the hand and stared intently into his eyes. "Most of all, we love you. I never, ever want you to question that."

It had been so long since anyone had said that to Sorel. He looked down at the dry skin on Pop's hands, the cracks along his knuckles. Those were marks earned through a life of late nights and thin meals. Pieces of a story that Sorel recognized. His mother had hands like that.

Behind Pop's tired eyes, he saw her—rising before sunrise, holding her shoes so as not to wake the landlord who lived downstairs. An orange left on the counter for breakfast. How many hours had he spent waiting by the window, watching for her return? By the end of the day, her voice was always scratchy like an old record; she ate dinner in silence, having used up her words on the spoiled children of rich families across town. Sorel could almost feel her blistered touch, hear the uneven click of her two-sizes-too-small heels. Her perfume, a single luxury that she treasured, worn only on Sundays. The scent of her was present now, clear as it had been when he was so young and small that she could pick him up, rest him on her hip, and kiss his sorry head.

In that moment, this was no longer some stranger in a dark apartment, telling stories. This was his parent, the one person trying to keep their family afloat during an endless rising tide. Sorel opened his arms and Pop whimpered, returning the embrace.

"We only want what's best for you. You know that, don't you?"

"I know." Sorel buried his face in that shuddering chest, hugging the mother he could never hold again. "I know."

The sky was a narrow line of periwinkle. A siren sounded in the distance and a dog started barking in a neighbouring unit. After what felt like ages, Pop and Sorel pulled apart.

Pop snorted and wiped his nose onto the handkerchief. "These things really are vectors for disease, you know."

"Yeah, probably," Sorel shrugged. "So, what do we do now?"

"For starters, we should both try and get some rest." Pop groaned his way up to one knee, bracing his back. "Been a long night."

"I'm not that tired," said Sorel. Though in truth, he could feel the ache behind Adrian's eyes. When was the last time he'd gotten a good night's rest? "And I still have my stuff to do."

"Can't you just humour me for once?" asked Pop, rubbing sleep from his eyes. "Go lay still with your eyes closed for ten minutes and then decide if this *stuff* of yours really can't wait."

It was hard to argue with that. Sorel couldn't rightly give Adrian's body back all sore and tired, after all. "Fine. I'll try."

"Atta boy." Pop clapped his knee. "Now, come on. Give your old man a hand." He grasped Sorel by the arm and attempted to stand, but Sorel himself was not yet accustomed to his new centre of gravity. They quickly tumbled over and crashed back onto the floor. "Holy crap, Adrian," Pop sputtered, "what the hell was that?"

"Shit—sorry, man!" Sorel burst out laughing, turning onto his back. "I think we gotta just live here now."

"Ha!" Pop chuckled hoarsely. "Alright, *man*. I guess we do."

TWENTY-FIVE

drian was not dead. That was one thing of which he could be certain. A dead person wouldn't have such a splitting headache.

For some time, he had been undone. The loose threads that had held together his consciousness had frayed into the abyss. His being was no longer a product of sensation and reaction, of memories and feelings, but instead a fine mist, a web of imperceptible particles that just so happened to once have been a boy. All the pieces of him had been transformed into the parachute seeds of a late-summer dandelion, blown apart by gentle winds. It was utter bliss.

Until the pounding started.

A terrible crashing reverberated through his unspun consciousness. It gnashed at him, piercing flesh that was not there. Adrian writhed in protest as he was knotted back together in a series of twisting jerks. His head, now firmly reattached to his shoulders, pulsed in agony. He balled up his fists, curled his toes, and reclaimed his voice with a wordless scream.

Adrian blinked. He'd forgotten that was an option. Vision coming into focus, a pair of beady eyes stared back at him. Tufts of speckled red fur. Tiny claws clutched an acorn; chittering teeth grated on the nut's soft green surface. The source of that terrible noise—a common red squirrel.

The ringing in Adrian's ears began to fade and dulled to a body-wide ache. He parted his lips, inhaled, and was hit with a violent urge to cough. The squirrel froze and twitched its tail. A second later, it shoved its snack into one cheek and scampered between the fence-posts, leaving Adrian to his hacking fit.

His chest finally stopped spasming and Adrian curled onto his side. He was motionless, out of breath. The graveyard's yellow grass brushed along his cheeks yet he could not feel it. The earth rumbled, the hum of lazy mid-morning traffic. Across the road, the quick steps of pedestrians clicked past. A couple joggers circled the iron fence but did not step through its gate. He waited patiently to fall back into blissful emptiness.

Around noon, the sky broke open. Adrian watched the droplets pass through him; the ground was not cold, the water not wet. All was empty and grey.

"You going to just lay there all day?" Adrian heard the question clear enough but he made no move to answer. It was likely a passing conversation, someone driving while chatting on the phone. Or maybe his own internal dialogue was attempting to break free and exist outside himself. He could hardly blame it for trying.

"Now don't be like that." The voice spoke again. Adrian had not anticipated his internal voice to have a Southern twang. "Come on now, let's get you up." Something brushed against his shoulder and Adrian stirred for the first time in hours—could it have been days? His sense of time had been rattled as much as the rest of him. The force gripped his upper arm and dragged Adrian to his feet, which now hovered a few centimetres above the ground.

The voice was in fact not his own but instead belonged to a wide mouth coated in shiny purple lipstick. Adrian's saviour had tall, coifed hair the colour of a nebula. The updo perfectly framed their round, friendly face. Dangling earrings sparkled like stardust and tinkled lightly when Marty tilted their head.

Marty. How did Adrian know that name? He couldn't source it, the thought was just there in his subconscious. Giving him a quick once-over, Marty sucked their teeth in tacit approval. "Looks like you're still in decent shape, all things considered. What's your name?"

After the fit from earlier, Adrian was hesitant to open his mouth again. His throat was raw. Words came slow. "You don't already know?"

"Well, aren't you a quick one." Marty tugged the hem of their tight black sweater. Shimmering gems decorated their shoulders and ran down their sleeves. "To tell the truth, my susser's not what it used to be. Not to mention, there's something to be said for old-fashioned courtesy."

"I'm, um." It took a few moments for the abstract shapes in his mind to form themselves into a solid answer. "I'm Adrian Yates."

"Very good." Marty grabbed Adrian's wrist and tugged him along like a stray balloon. "Yoo-hoo! Folks, we've got a fresh one!"

"Wait, aren't you gonna—" Adrian stopped short as the graveyard began to shift.

One moment, it was empty as always: a series of glistening, mossy stones laid along muddy pathways. The next moment, everything tilted to the left. The world spilled sideways, twisted and loudly popped. Two strangers appeared beside one of the cottonwood trees, one standing tall and the other seated in shadow. Except, they hadn't just materialized like Sorel might have done. Rather, Adrian's mind rapidly knitted together another version of events in which the pair had always been there. Though he no longer had a stomach with which to feel sick, the meeting of such disjointed realities was distinctly nauseating.

"Marty, you pick up another stray?" The seated figure spoke gruffly, arms crossed. Adrian sensed another name approaching his awareness, but it skittered back through the rustling grass before he could catch it.

"What was I supposed to do?" Hand on their waist, Marty stuck out their hip. "Poor thing had two feet in the fade!"

"And you pulled him out of it?" A woman stepped

forward—no, Adrian thought, that was too mundane a description of her movement. She flowed, like goldenrod swaying in a summer breeze. High cheekbones and luminous eyes, the colour of warm amber. She was layered with lustrous fabric that billowed around her like a cloud and brought out the richness of her skin. Despite her intimidating stature, there was a grounded nature to her voice that made Adrian instantly feel at peace. "Marty, we have spoken about this."

"But I had a *feeling* about this one!" Marty made a mid-air pirouette. "There's just something familiar-like about him—not to mention, he was practically begging for my help, weren't you Aiden?"

They smacked Adrian on the back, shoving him a step forward. "Oh," he mumbled. "It's Adrian, actually." He went to shuffle his shoes but found one was missing; his sock looked wet but his toes weren't cold.

"Tomato, tom-*ah*-to," said Marty, twirling their wrist. Whenever they moved, glitter followed through the air.

The ethereal woman narrowed her eyes at Marty before kneeling to greet Adrian, hand outstretched. "It is a pleasure. You may call me—"

"Niya." Adrian spoke her name as it occurred to him, "Niya Amani." He savoured the taste of it, like blackcurrant jam. "Sorry," he caught himself. "I don't know why that keeps happening."

"No offence is taken." Niya smiled, gently. "Sensing heartnames is a natural talent. Though I have rarely seen a new spirit acquire it with such haste."

"Told ya he was special." Marty winked out of sight for a split second and reappeared on pointe, balanced on a slender tree branch. It wavered only slightly below their weight. "Raj, you coming out or what?"

"Don't tell the kid my—ugh." A rough grunt came from the shadows. "Fine. Whatever." Black, fingerless gloves gripped the rims of a sticker-covered wheelchair and gave a firm shove. The final member of the trio inched into view, wearing a heavy scowl, a plaid button-up, and a denim vest. "Yes, I'm Rajam. And no, you're *not* getting my surname."

"Try not to take the 'tude personally, Hayden." Marty covered their mouth to not-so-subtly whisper, "Ze's just an old stick-in-the-mud."

"Ze...?" Adrian asked and something glimmered in the corner of his eye. It was a button, fastened on the pocket of Raj's vest. A green background with black text: ZE/ZIR. Like everything else, the grammatical fact rewrote itself into the fabric of reality. Adrian sensed it as easily as he could hear Marty's bubbly laughter or feel the weight of Niya's calculating gaze.

"Of course, I need no introduction, but that's hardly stopped me before!" Arms raised, Marty kicked into a sideways splits. "I am the one, the only, *the* Martina DeLousia Lamour!" They leaped up like a high diver and fell into a mid-air death-drop. After a few seconds holding their final pose, Marty peeked one eye open and hissed, "That's your cue. For the applause?"

"Oh!" Adrian quickly clapped his hands. Except, they

hardly made an audible response. He tried snapping his fingers instead but it was the same, like they were submerged in water. "Um, I'm not sure ... what's going on?"

"Interesting." Niya touched her lips. "I see you are still developing the capacity for auditory projection."

Adrian blinked in confusion and looked to Marty. "Was I supposed to understand that?" he asked.

"Gimme a second, I gotta figure out how to explain this." Marty stood to dust themself off, though their sweater had collected no dirt. "Try to *think* of the sound as you make it. You can't just expect your hands to do it on their own anymore."

"Hm." Flexing his fingers, Adrian tried again. After a couple of attempts, he managed to make a noise—but his clap was still slightly out of sync, arriving a second too late.

"Better." Niya steepled her long fingers against her chin. "You have potential, I will grant you that."

"Thanks?" Adrian smiled, meekly. "And, uh, smooth moves Marty. I don't think I've ever seen anyone dance like that."

"Well thank you, kindly." Marty pulled out a small compact to check their bouffant. "That flip's just a little something I picked up at a TDOR after-party a while back."

"I've never heard of that day having an after-party," said Adrian, glancing around the graveyard in search of his missing sneaker.

"Not among the living, of course." Marty's mirror vanished as it snapped shut.

Adrian pinched the brim of his nose. His eyes were

starting to hurt, like he'd been staring at a screen for too long. "So, okay. Rewind for a second. Are you all for real dead?"

"As disco," said Raj, knocking on the arm of zir chair. "Yourself included."

"Now that is unnecessary." Niya straightened a wrinkle from her dress. "Disco could come back in fashion."

"How about doornails then?" said Marty. "Dodos, dinosaurs? Take your pick, we're all the same in the end."

"Especially you, Marty." Raj wheezed as ze laughed.

"Hush." Niya quieted her companions. "Let us not confuse the poor boy."

"How can you be especially—?" A throbbing force struck Adrian and he clutched both sides of his head, crying out. "What's happening?!"

In an instant, Niya was beside him. Her hands pressed on his temples, cool as a fresh-water stream. She was syphoning the pain. "Take it slow," she guided him. "Your new condition will need some time to process." After a few moments, he could stand on his own again. "Try not to worry about the details for now. Just know, we are all spirits. Expressions of consciousness, travelling along this plane."

"So, you're ghosts," said Adrian. Still dizzy, he rubbed the fireworks behind his eyes until they began to fade. "Ghosts that use neopronouns and go to the Trans Day of Remembrance?"

"Try and work on your listening, Damian." Marty tapped their ear. "I only do the *after-parties*. The main event is a tad depressing for my taste."

"And watch who you're calling 'neo.'" Raj adjusted the glove strap around zir wrist. "My shit's been around for three decades, at least."

"Right. Okay." As Adrian turned, he spied his sneaker. It was broken in half, lying near the cemetery gate. How had it gotten there? The more he reached towards that memory the quicker it slipped away. "You're just so different than any other ghost I've met." He had *felt* Marty's smack on his back, heard the tap of Raj's knuckles. And then there was whatever Niya had just done. "You're all so ... lively?"

With a flick, Marty had a dainty, handheld fan. "Flattery will get you everywhere, darling," they winked.

"Comes with experience, kid." Raj popped a wheelie and spun a tight circle. "More time you're on our side, more practice you'll get."

"You have met others, like ourselves?" asked Niya. The subtle dip in the gentle tone of her voice told Adrian she was genuinely surprised. He wanted to explain, but the broken pieces of his sneaker kept distracting him. They shone like firelight, coaxing him closer. He drifted like a moth towards the moon. Niya followed at an arm's length. On some level Adrian knew, if she didn't stay close, he would lose himself again.

The shoe was fully bisected. The sole had ripped clean off and was lying in the muck. On its other half, the jagged edges of torn fabric glistened like a fresh wound. The tongue lolled open, revealing a scribble of Sharpie marker. What did it say? If only he could get close enough to read it.

Marty snapped their fan. "Now, Cayden—"

"*Adrian*," he said again.

"—there's no need to be afraid." Marty vanished from one end of the graveyard and appeared at the other, standing over Adrian's broken footwear. "You're in dead-good company now."

"No, you don't understand." Adrian knelt beside the fragments in the grass. "It says *Adrian*." Of course it did. Some of the fog around his memories had parted. He had written his name in there, back when he was—not here? Unlike this. Pre-dead.

"Don't go getting all sentimental on us now." Raj rolled over. "The body's just a vessel and all that. You were doing so good up til now!"

"No." Adrian reached for the shoe but his fingers passed right through it. "I'm not dead."

Marty held their fan over their mouth, failing to hide their lavender smirk. "If I had a dime for every time I heard that one."

"Be nice," Niya shushed. "Look how tender this one is. He needs our support to grapple with such an early demise."

"Yeah, well, we don't have time for all that." Turning sharply, Raj came to a hard stop. "We're already supposed to be at the AIDS memorial by now."

Adrian's vision was blurring again. Trailing shadows encroached on all sides. He opened his mouth to speak but his voice had fled from him once more.

"Raj has got a point." Marty rolled up their shimmering sleeve to reveal a watch made of pure light. It was hard for

Adrian to even look directly at it. There were no discernible numbers, no minute or second hands. "I'd feel a mite guilty leaving him here like this, though."

"We can swing back through and pick him up later." Raj waved over zir shoulder, already heading towards the graveyard's arch. "Maybe that other kid who hangs around here will find him."

Other kid? That's right. Adrian remembered now, someone else had been here. If only he could rope together the fragmented pieces of his memories. There was something important he was forgetting.

"You make a fair point," Niya sighed and began to withdraw. "Adrian, we will return as soon as we are able, I promise you. Try to hold together until then."

"Yeah, just try to chill." Raj hollered, "Get your afterlife on!"

"But..." Adrian had managed to speak but it was too thin, less a word than the creak of an old gate. That sinking feeling was coming back. He wasn't ready to disappear again. He had to be heard. "Something is wrong."

"I know," Marty crouched beside him one last time. "It's scary. But you're gonna be alright." They rose to join their friends. "Catch you in a while, baby crocodile!"

"No!" Adrian scrambled to his feet. "You can't go, I won't let you!" The last of his strength whipped together and rose beyond himself. He was on the wind, scampering between the cracks in headstones. He grasped at the space Marty had occupied seconds ago. They were gone, but the echo of their sweater hadn't faded just yet. He grabbed a fistful and yanked, hard.

"Hey!" Marty popped back into view. "Now, cut that out!" They spun away but Adrian held fast. Translucent sequins ricocheted in all directions. "I said stop!"

In an instant, Niya was between them. With just a brush of her fingers, Adrian's strength melted again. "Release," she whispered and he was unable to resist, any more than an ice cube could help melting in the hot sun. "Your life is over, now. Let go and be at peace."

"But, my body." Adrian dropped to his knees, falling into the dirt. "It's..."

"Buried and gone." Raj reappeared with a grimace. "Deal with it. We all had to."

"It's not, though. I swear." The earth turned liquid, sucking Adrian up to his waist. He desperately tried to explain, "You don't get it, I'm not in the ground!"

"Cremated, then." Marty shrugged, counting off options on their glimmering fingers. "Composted, dissolved, maybe mummified?"

"Perhaps donated to science," suggested Niya. "Turned into a tree?"

"Or at the bottom of the ocean, getting eaten up by crabs and sharks!" Raj rubbed zir hands with excitement as the others just stared. "What?" ze snapped. "It could happen!"

"None of that!" Elbows braced against the earth, Adrian was numb from his chest down. "My body is *alive*, it's still out there!"

The trio exchanged a series of bewildered looks. "Then

how come you're not in it?" asked Raj.

"Please do not tell me this is another one of those near-death experiences," Niya murmured to Marty. "This is why I don't do the hospital roundups anymore." Marty shrugged and mouthed an apology.

Adrian buoyed himself against an unseen current; he was now sunken up to his shoulders. "It's my boyfriend—well, I don't know if he's my boyfriend, exactly. We haven't really had a talk about labels or anything."

Raj spun zir fingers in a circle. "Get to the point, kid. We don't got all day."

What *was* the point he was making? Adrian was losing track of things again. His last embodied moments were all folded in on top of one another. Trying to parse each one in order was like uncrumpling a paper airplane to reverse-engineer how it had been made.

"We were arguing." That much he remembered. "He was upset about ... something. About me, leaving." That's right. Adrian had been going somewhere. "I tried to go, and he grabbed me. I blacked out. When I woke up, I saw *me*. My body, running away."

Marty clicked their tongue. "Well butter my biscuit, I *did* recognize you! You're that fleshy little flirt that Sorel's been after!"

Tilting her head, Niya hummed in agreement. "Ah, yes. I see it now. Apologies, it is so hard to recognize spirits before they are free of their skin."

Plucking a toothpick from behind zir ear, Raj chewed on it thoughtfully. "I don't get all the fuss about *living* dates, anyway. There're plenty of singles over on this side of the veil."

"Wait, you know—?" Before Adrian could ask his question, he lost his hold on the ground and started to slip again. Try as he might, his hands just fazed right through every rock and twig. Frantically, he reached upwards for help. "What is this? What's happening to me?!"

"You're fading, again. Like a newbie." Raj dug out a fleck of nothing from between zir teeth.

"Try and stay focussed." Niya crouched, the hem of her skirt just barely out of Adrian's reach. If only he could stretch a little more. "Pull yourself up by thinking about what makes you want to stay."

Panic riled in Adrian's throat, strangling his words. "But—but what if I can't?"

"You'll break into a billion tiny pieces, end up scattered across the cosmos, fading into oblivion." Raj was laughing again. Or, was that a cough? It was getting hard to tell. The trio's voices were getting distant, or was it Adrian who was drifting away?

"Will you shush?" Marty snipped. "You're gonna scare the poor thing!"

But ze was right. Adrian could feel it. He wasn't just sinking into the ground, he was dissipating. There was almost nothing left of him. Even the memory of breath had been stolen from his lungs; he couldn't cry, couldn't scream. His chin went under, then his ears. His mouth filled with rocks and mud. The nothingness was calling. But he did not want to go.

TWENTY-SIX

The blinds fell with a snap. Sorel yanked the dangling cords, twisting the slats. Again, they collapsed in on themselves. Had the mechanics of these things changed since he'd been alive? They didn't used to be so difficult, that was for sure. Giving one last tug, he finally got them to fly upwards. Daybreak crashed through the window. With Adrian's tired eyes, Sorel blinked into the sunlight.

Aside from a few easy-breezy clouds, the sky was endless and bluer than he'd ever dared to remember. Rows of sparkling towers, brick apartments, slanted houses, abandoned lots, and packed parking lots, all smashed together like the layers of a broken cake. Lines of cars snaked around the grid of streets, bicyclists swerving through breaks in traffic. The city spilled out in all directions and ran up against the shoreline of a broad lake. Had the water always sparkled like that? Sorel could almost feel it, lapping on his skin as he waded up to his chest. His sister calling for him from the sand.

He took a long, slow breath. They still had a few days before the trip. He'd make time to go to the beach before they left, for old time's sake.

A single ink-blot stood out against the morning's radiance. A faded patch of grass, sheltered by overlapping trees. From his window, the graveyard seemed so small, even quaint. Yet the sight of it numbed his toes. It was a menace, a speechless threat against the glory of his new life. Its only saving grace was its emptiness. There was no sign Adrian had been there at all.

"Knock-knock!" The bedroom door pushed open, making Sorel jump. The blinds fell, painting pinstripes across the bedroom and over the smiling face of Adrian's dad. Apron around his neck, he proudly clutched a platter of dark brown muffins. "Anybody hungry?"

Sorel's stomach rumbled. "Sure," he said, snagging one of the larger muffins off the plate. "Why not?"

"It's just a box mix from the corner store," Dad shrugged, sheepishly. "They only had oat bran left. I know it's not your favourite."

"Are you kidding?" Sorel had already polished off the muffin top and was picking crumbs off his shirt. "These are stellar!"

"Stellar?" Dad smirked and set the plate onto Adrian's dresser. "Okey-doke, then. I guess I'll reveal my ulterior motive."

Sorel looked up mid-bite. Was it over already? Were they going to interrogate him, demand where their real son had gone? Dad ducked from the doorway and, a second later, reappeared with a hiking backpack. "I thought you could use this for the trip."

"I'm using *that*?" Shovelling in the rest of his muffin, Sorel smacked his hands. "You for real?"

"I know it doesn't look like much." Dad plopped the bag onto Adrian's bed and started rifling through it. "But your pop and I used it on our honeymoon. You can fit lots more in here than you might think, if you pack right." He pulled out a few stray socks and loose receipts. "It'll need some cleaning, I guess."

"No, I meant, you'd really let me use this?" Sorel came up behind him and started tugging at the many zippers, exploring its varied pockets. "Far out!"

"I gotta say, I'm loving this new attitude, kiddo." Dad helped shake out the backpack. "When Pop mentioned it at first, I thought he was being sarcastic." He sorted through the last of the bag's trash and forgotten nostalgia.

Once Sorel was set to pack, Dad stood with one hand on the door-handle. "Adrian, bud, I'm sorry we're putting you through this." He scratched at a day's worth of stubble on his chin. "Even if you're feeling better about it lately, I know it's not an easy situation. I'm not exactly stoked about having subletters rooting around in our stuff while we're away, but the cost of renting a whole moving van just isn't in our budget right now."

"Hey, take it easy." Sorel ducked past him and into the

bathroom, coming back with a handful of toiletries to pack. Mango strawberry shampoo? Damn, the future was so rich with little luxuries! "I think you're making the right call. This is gonna be fun!"

"That's the spirit!" Dad tousled Sorel's hair as he passed. "Now, who are you and what have you done with my son?" Shampoo bottle in one hand and comb in the other, Sorel froze like a deer in headlights. But Dad just laughed and walked backwards towards the kitchen.

"Oh, wait," Sorel said, grabbing the plate of muffins, "you forgot these!"

"They're all for you," Dad shouted. "Pop and I had our fill!"

"All mine?" Sorel gawked at the veritable feast in his hands. "You're the best dads ever!" What a thrill it was to even say those words. To have not just one parent, but multiple—to be their most cherished child. What was Adrian thinking, getting so upset with them all the time? He had no clue how good he had it.

After sorting through exactly which clothes would serve him best on a long trip, Sorel recalled a lesson from his mother. He rolled up each item before he stowed it, maximizing space in his new-to-him backpack. Occasionally, he tugged at the elasticized undershirt holding down his chest. It was so uncomfortable. How Adrian had ever gotten used to wearing such an item, Sorel had no idea. When getting dressed that morning, he had briefly considered not putting it on at all. But after less than an hour without it, he was irked with a persistent scratching, an itch in the back of his mind that something was deeply wrong.

His body remembered the pressure of the fabric, the squeeze of the vest; it was waiting, impatiently, to be obliged. Eventually, Sorel gave in. Besides, he decided, it might seem odd to everyone else if Adrian suddenly dropped the practice. While sorting out sets of matching socks—something Adrian was sorely lacking—Sorel considered how many people might have used an undershirt like this one, in his own time. That is, if it even existed back then. They must have had their own methods, he mused.

Moving on to the dresser, the top drawer's knob popped off in Sorel's hand. After a couple tries, he managed to pry it open and the smile fell from his face. Among the wrinkled layers of Adrian's T-shirts and tank tops, a handful of keepsakes were nestled into place: a friendship bracelet with beads that spelled out Zoomer's name, a couple of postcards, a small collection of worn rocks and seashells. The stuff of life, unremarkable to anyone but the owner and those who cared for him. But in the centre of this hidden altar was a pair of pink ticket stubs and two photo strips. Adrian was seemingly alone in the booth, face frozen in a series of silly looks and candid glances. A golden hue hung around him like a halo, down his arms to where his hands were clasped.

Their hands. Sorel could hear the carnival music, smell the sickly mix of cheap sugar and vomit. He lifted one of the photo strips, fingertips prickling numb.

"Hey, bud," said Dad, as the door swung open again.

Sorel quickly shoved the drawer shut. "Hey, knocking

would be nice!" he snapped and turned to find it wasn't just Dad standing there.

"Don't blame me, your dad's the one with bad manners." Black lipstick and curly hair spinning with loose ends, Zoomer snatched a muffin off the plate on Adrian's dresser. "I *always* knock first." She hopped on to the bed, already dropping crumbs.

"I'm *so* sure." Sorel rolled his eyes.

"I'll give you two some privacy." Dad winked and pulled the door two-thirds shut.

Zoomer shoved the backpack off the bed to make more room for herself. "Yuck. I bet he totally still thinks we're dating."

"Whatever." Sorel scooped the bag off the floor and carefully set it upright against the dresser. "Did you need something?"

"Obviously!" Zoomer rolled onto her back, hair hanging off the end of the bed. "I've been waiting forever! I get that you're busy, but come on, gimme those hot deets." Sorel blankly stared at her. She waved a hand in front of his face. "What's the sitch with your ghostly boy-toy?!"

"My what?"

"I know, I know, you're not into labels or whatever." She stuffed in more muffin and chewed with her mouth open. "Seriously, though. How'd Sorel take the news that you're hitting the road?"

"Oh, that." Stepping to the closet, Sorel began to root through more of Adrian's wardrobe. "It was fine. No worries."

"That's it?" Zoomer whined. "Come on! First, you don't text me back for two whole days, then you just tell me it was 'fine'?"

Sorel did feel a little bad about that. He'd been trying to figure out this newfangled phone but it kept demanding some cryptic password. Whenever he tried too many times, it locked him out! "Well, there's not much else to say." He struggled over a pile of dropped hangers, digging into the back of the closet. "And I've got other things going on right now."

"Who are you trying to—wait a minute." She sat up with a jolt. "Oh my god. Oh my god, you totally hooked up, didn't you?!"

"What?!" Sorel nearly lost his footing. "Why would you even say that?"

"Oh, that seals it," she snickered. "I bet you had some serious goodbye sex, or whatever you wanna call it."

Hands, tender and warm. The softness of Adrian's stomach, the clench of his thighs. Images of their night together underneath the oak tree played out behind Sorel's eyes. How smooth it was to flow into one another, the rush of taking full control. His spirit filling up the body—then shoving Adrian out. Dirty hands. The gasping cry he made, lying on the ground and fading. The smack of one sneaker running down the road.

"No," Sorel said flatly. He stepped out from the closet and dropped a few items on the ground beside the bed. "It was nothing like that."

"Yeah right, don't even try to deny it." Zoomer raised

her voice and pounded a fist against the wall. "I bet he was all like, 'Oh Adrian, take me now!'"

"Would you be quiet?!" Sorel grabbed her wrist. "I said it wasn't like that."

"Jesus, fine!" Zoomer yanked herself from his grip. "I was just teasing." She scowled and rubbed at her arm. "That kinda hurt, you asshole."

Adrian's mouth reflexively mumbled an apology. For his part, Sorel tried to mean it. He was still sorting out just how much strength was too much or too little with fleshy people.

"Wait. I think I get it now." Zoomer narrowed her eyes. Sorel avoided her piercing gaze, focussed on keeping his poker face in check. "He dumped you, didn't he? That's gotta be it."

"Why would you—?"

"That little shit!" Cracking her knuckles, Zoomer rolled a scrunchie off her wrist and put her hair up. "If that freaky phantom broke your heart, I am gonna be down there so fast—you *know* I've been practicing my witchcraft. I've got some things that could make him wish he could die all over again!"

"There's no need for that!" Sorel stepped in front of her, hands up. "There was no dumping, I swear!"

"Oh." Zoomer looked at him sideways and she deflated back onto the bed. "Should've known, you're both too chicken for that. I bet you agreed to 'go on a break' or some crap like that."

"Actually, yes. In a manner of speaking." While trying

to roll up one of the sweaters, Sorel's hands started to go cold. He flexed them, trying to remember if there was a trick for making the blood flow in the right direction. "Truth is, I didn't go. Just couldn't bring myself to do it."

"That's it?" she scoffed and folded her arms. "The big reveal is you listened to my advice."

"Yep. It's for the best anyway." Sorel tucked a hand behind his ear, pushing back hair that wasn't there. He looked towards the window. "It's time to focus on the future."

TWENTY-SEVEN

Adrian awoke to a tap on his nose. It sent a jolt through his body, an electric current along frayed wires. He gasped, gripping his chest, rattled with the panic of a nightmare that felt far too real. Trying to calm his breathing, he waited for his senses to return.

He would wake to the beige walls of his bedroom, the stucco ceiling and yesterday's laundry piled on the floor. The upstairs neighbour would have put away his instruments and soon, the sun would peek through the blinds. Pop would stumble in, shedding his boots at the door. Maybe Dad would get up to fry a little breakfast. The pair would bicker over something innocuous, like whether turkey bacon was more cost-effective than tempeh. Later today, Adrian decided, he would go knock on Zoomer's door. They could share a cup of tea with Granny Z and then catch a bus downtown. With a tentative smile, he lay still in the day's budding potential.

A second tap snapped his eyes open. "There you are!" Marty smacked their hands, releasing a round of sparks. "Finer than frog's hair split four ways."

"Nicely done, Marty." Niya gave a round of tepid applause. "I was uncertain if he could be recovered twice."

"Let's not get ahead of ourselves," muttered Raj. "He could fall back in just as easy."

Though no clouds blocked the sun, the sky remained a dull and lifeless grey. The sight drained away any hope that the last few days had been a vivid yet terrible dream. Sitting up, Adrian found the trio resting around him in the grass. "How long was I out?" he asked.

Raj scratched the scruff of zir chin. "Living time, or real time?"

"Try to remain still," said Niya, the layers of her shimmering gown spread out around her like a picnic blanket. "You are still quite raw."

His tongue was gritty. Adrian grimaced, the essence of grass and dirt stuck between his teeth. He gulped a shallow breath and clutched his legs, finding them solid—to his own touch at least. Blades of grass still passed right through him; he was far from whole. His skin was still partially translucent, its colour and depth slow to return. "What the hell's wrong with me?"

"Nothing, per se." Niya's voice came gently, drawing out each word long enough that Adrian had time to catch up to it. "Pulled from your vessel as you were, it is a wonder that you have sustained at all."

"Think of yourself like a jello salad," Marty suggested. "You haven't had enough time to set." Their flashy sweater lay across their lap. It had several loose threads and gemstones missing, ripped in Adrian's frenzied pursuit. Conjuring a needle and thread, they began to mend the damage.

"Should we place bets? I give the kid twelve hours, max." Raj was still gnawing on zir toothpick.

"Hey," Adrian snapped, louder than he'd been expecting. It was hard to modulate his volume without a tangible set of vocal cords. "Can you not?"

"Don't get your ectoplasm in a twist," ze grinned. "You can get in on the action too. I'll give decent odds."

As Adrian opened his mouth to reply, a grating noise disrupted his train of thought. A pulsing hum, like someone had clicked on a fluorescent light or he'd wandered too close to a hydro tower. He searched for the source and found it behind him. The arch. Cold and brittle, even just to look at; its streaks of rust glimmered like open wounds, bleeding red across his vision. He shuffled away, the sound subsiding only slightly.

Past the iron fence, the world remained a hazy monotone. In contrast, the cemetery had never seemed so vibrant. The gravestones were no longer placid grey but rich with marbling undertones. Their elongated shadows painted the grass with strokes of dusky blue, curling moss shining verdant green. Among the scattered weeds, each dandelion was its own brilliant sun. A small crop of mushrooms, sheltered by a broken monument, wore soft caps of lavender and misty white.

Effortlessly threading their needle, Marty glanced up as if sensing Adrian's awe. "I topped you off with a little something extra, when I brought you back," they explained. "Just a temporary boost to keep you steady. It's hard to hold a conversation with someone who keeps fading."

Fading. That's what they kept calling it. Adrian shuddered. "Is that really what happens when you die, you just fall apart?"

Raj chewed over the question. "Can't say, really. Never had the opportunity myself."

"Here's the basics, hon." Marty passed their sewing needle through a gemstone like it was anything but solid rock. "When most folks pass on, they do just that—pass into whatever lies beyond. Some of us ... don't." With one last tug, they knotted the thread and cut it with their teeth. "Homos often seem to be the stick-aroundy types."

"Trans and enbies, too," said Raj with a flick.

"I was counting all of us together." Marty held up the sweater. The holes were patched and it sparkled even brighter than before. They smiled at their own handiwork. "Like I was saying, queers tend to linger. It's just a thing."

A sharp twinge ran up Adrian's underarms. Even in spectral form, his binder managed to pinch. "So, that's what happened to all of you," he spoke the obvious, trying to turn focus from his discomfort. "Then are you like Sorel, buried here?"

"Oh, honey, no!" Marty clutched their sweater to their

chest, gasping with horror. "I wouldn't be caught dead in this dumpy little spot—no offence, of course."

Niya's lips twitched slightly. "We are spirits who have accepted our own death and as such, we are not bound to a singular place," she explained. Long sleeves billowing, she gestured to the surrounding grounds. "However, we can be summoned. Sorel has been calling to us, though he may not know it."

"Bless his heart." Arms up, Marty threw their sweater back over their head. "Poor boy just hasn't been ready." They reappeared, hair still perfectly intact, smoothed out any remaining wrinkles, and patted their round belly. "Like I said, some spirits stay and some go. But a few, like your not-so-sweet sweetie, they get stuck doing a bit of both."

"He's spectrally constipated." Raj crunched zir toothpick, snapping it in half. Ze dug out a replacement from the breast pocket of zir vest. Adrian chuckled. All this was so absurd.

"That is one way to put it." Niya frowned at Raj, who clearly gave her no mind. "And for those experiencing this—*ahem*—liminal blockage, holding on to the living world only worsens their struggle." She tutted. "It is a very sad state of affairs, most often an issue with those who died unexpectedly or with unfinished business."

"I've met a few who can't even recognize they're dead," Marty said with a sour expression, like they'd just bit into a lemon. "Real toughies, those."

"Sorel knew." Adrian glanced back at the gate. Its warding power still emanated in an ominous hum. He cringed, unable to even look at it for too long. "And he definitely didn't want to stick around here any longer."

Niya nodded sympathetically. "Maybe not consciously. However, many young spirits find it difficult to move with intention. It takes time to leave the place where living people expect to find them."

"Not to mention, iron's a bitch." Raj jutted zir chin at the fence. "A pain in the ass to pass through, even for us."

"But he—I—" Adrian stammered, increasingly exasperated. This was all too much at once. "Why didn't he tell me?"

"Oh, don't take it personal." Reclining on one side, Marty drew a line through the air. They produced a thin strip of pure light and held it like an emery board, using it to tidy up their nails. "Part of the problem is, us and Sorel never managed to make a proper introduction. Been swingin' by this spot for a couple decades now but he hasn't picked up on us."

"It can be difficult for spirits to hear each other," explained Niya. "You might say, we are not always on the same frequency." She demonstrated by running her hands past one another.

"It's especially tough when the ghost in question keeps trying to force his way back on the living folks' signal." Twirling zir toothpick, Raj tossed it expertly into the grass. It landed near Adrian's knee and vanished on impact. "We thought Sorel had made some progress, but then he had a setback."

"Oh." Adrian's shoulders slumped under the gravity of

Raj's words. "So, this is my fault."

"Well, only a wee bit." Marty tucked their nail file down the neck of their shirt. "Hardly at all."

"We certainly do not hold anything against you." Niya spoke carefully.

Raj scoffed. "Speak for yourself."

The trio fell into quiet conversation, but Adrian hardly paid attention. A film reel had started up behind his eyes; it clicked softly, spinning through the last couple of months. Nights spent gallivanting around town, Sorel riding alongside, inside him. The carnal thrill of sharing his body, of releasing control. His burning curiosity about Sorel's past and the selfish glee with which he'd tromped through those memories. Adrian had wanted to know him, and to be known, on so many levels. He had chased that longing, all the while picking away at Sorel's progress. He could have passed on by now, or at least learned that there were others like himself. Adrian had thought himself the victim, but he was the parasite. He'd been draining Sorel of his chance at an afterlife. "I should have known," he whispered to the unbent grass. "It was too good to be true."

"...Which is why it's not so smart for spirits to spend lots of time around the living." Marty was in the middle of some grand explanation, not that Adrian had been listening. "When we remember what it was like to feel alive, we start to crave it. And if we start experimenting with possession, we can end up in a real pickle."

"Fucks us right up." Raj rested an elbow on the arm of zir chair, wistfully gazing skyward. "Can hardly blame either of you though, body-swapping's such a rush—sweet high, hell of a burnout."

"All this time." Adrian rose to his feet. "Sorel thought something was wrong with him, that he was broken. He was just waiting to be found." Without thinking, he let his legs lead him away.

Niya called after him, "Adrian, you cannot blame yourself for this." She spoke in hushed tones with her companions: "I thought we had more time with Sorel. I had not considered he would go so far."

"Looks like we have a runner," Raj grimly agreed.

Adrian slowly approached the oak tree. Its branches had never looked so full. A mosaic of green, from minty lime to opulent emerald. "It might have been an accident," he murmured.

"Then why isn't he back here now?" Raj rolled after him. Ze outpaced Adrian with ease and came about with a quick turn. "Face it, kid. You got booted out of your own behind, and not in the fun way."

Even if it wasn't on purpose, does that really matter? Adrian's lips trembled as Zoomer's warning played in his mind. She had been right. She was always right.

"Now don't go losing hope." Marty was there in an instant, hand on Adrian's shoulder. "We're here now. And all of us were once like Sorel, more or less."

"That is why we travel together now," said Niya as she descended beside them. "We help find other lost souls and guide them along the way."

"So, you're like"—Adrian puzzled over the best way to

put it—"gay guardian angels?"

"Hell yeah we are!" Raj pumped zir fist.

Marty smirked, their purple lipstick glimmering like a line of amethyst. "I don't mind the sound of that."

The corners of Niya's long mouth upturned slightly. "Now," she said, "given the circumstances, we may need to intervene with Sorel earlier than planned. Adrian, can you tell us more about what you experienced before he overtook you, any further hint at his motivation?"

Adrian furrowed his brows, grasping at the haze of their last interaction. It was still tough to suss out anything of substance. "I just know he was scared. He mentioned lingering. Being here even when no one was visiting."

"Well, I'll be!" Marty made a mid-air twirl. "You owe me ten bucks, Raj!"

Raj scoffed, "I'll get it to you in the next life."

Nodding, Niya explained, "Manifesting without assistance is a very good sign. Sorel must have been growing secure in himself, approaching readiness to break from liminality."

"In fact," Raj speculated, "if he'd been here instead of you, we probably could have picked him up and out of this little pit stop."

That thought, more than any other, turned Adrian's non-existent stomach. Despite all his meddling, Sorel had still been progressing into grown-up ghosthood. If Adrian had just left well enough alone, he'd still be in his body and Sorel would be ready to leave the graveyard, to go travel the spirit world. "Man, I really messed things up, didn't I?"

The trio looked to one another, apparently not in a rush to answer. "Darling, here's the truth," said Marty. "If being dead has taught me anything, you can't change the past. You can only take ownership of your own choices. And Sorel's got a doozy of a decision to own up to."

"What matters is that you are here with us, now," Niya agreed. "We will make a plan for what comes next, together."

"Yeah, don't sweat it, kid. We got your back." Raj grinned and flexed zir knuckles. "You're not alone anymore."

TWENTY-EIGHT

The future, what future?" Zoomer snorted. "Your impending road trip with those two soon-to-be divorcés?" She landed back on Adrian's bed, its springs whining. "Let's make a bet, how many days—no, wait, how many *hours*—before they lose it and turn the car around?!"

"Shh!" Sorel eyed the thin wall that separated Adrian's bedroom from the rest of the apartment. "Shut that down already."

Feet against the wall, Zoomer stared at him. "What's that supposed to mean?"

"It means, don't jinx it." Sorel returned to the closet and started sorting through more of Adrian's mess. "I just figure, they seem pretty set on the idea. No need to go in with a pissy attitude." He held up two hoodies, one with a busted zipper and the other with holes cut into the sleeves.

"What do you think, black or green?"

"Bleh. Neither." Zoomer made a retching face. "I can't believe you're seriously packing right now instead of going out there to negotiate. It's not too late to try and convince them to let you stay with me and Granny."

"Actually, I think my 'rents might be right." Sorel tossed aside the black hoodie and tucked the green one into his backpack. "They just want what's best for me. With everything that's happened this summer, we could all use a break." He caught Zoomer staring at him, her mouth agape. "Plus, uh, think of all the road stops! I can send you pictures from Canada's biggest cheese wheel—I hear they even let you take a piece with you."

"Wow. So cool." While she lay upside down, Zoomer's frown turned into a disconcerted smile. "Except that you're lactose intolerant."

"Right." Sorel clenched his teeth. How could he have forgotten that? "But I can still enjoy some quality cheese tourism, when I get the chance."

Before Zoomer could say another word, the muted tones of disagreement drifted from the living room. Heavy footsteps, punctuated by the thud of a slammed door. She flashed a knowing look. "You're seriously gonna tell me, you're not freaked about being trapped in a car with *that*?"

"They're just stressed." Sorel shrugged, deciding to leave behind Adrian's raincoat. It couldn't be that rainy out east. "Times are tough, they're trying their best." He pulled out a pair of brown boots at the back of the closet, maybe a size too small. They'd work well enough until he could replace his sneakers. "What we need is a fresh start. Maybe I'll even talk to them about staying for longer—I could look into universities over there." Sorel never imagined himself the bookish type but maybe he'd grow up to be one, now that he had the chance to do so.

There was a sudden smack against the back of Sorel's head. It wasn't hard but it was enough to make him double over, stumbling into the sharp edge of an open drawer. He looked down at what had hit him—a crumpled pillow lay at his feet. "What the hell?!" he snarled back at Zoomer. "What's wrong with you?!"

"What's wrong with *me*?" Zoomer clenched a second pillow in her fists. "Are you for real right now—you're casually planning on ditching me, and I'm supposed to be chill about it?!"

"Maybe you *should* chill." Sorel rubbed at the sore spot where he'd hit the dresser. Hopefully, he was using that word right. Adrian had never got around to a proper lesson on modern slang. "There's no need to freak out."

"Well *excuse* me for getting emotional!" Zoomer dropped her remaining fluffy ammo and stomped past Sorel to the door. "I guess I'm just *so* crazy for getting upset!"

Sorel seriously considered just letting her leave. It would certainly be easier to start a new life with one less person from the old one. But again, Adrian's body had its own plans. His mouth opened before he knew what words might come out. "Stop, I didn't mean it like that."

Back to him, Zoomer hung still with her hand on the door. "No?"

Of course, when Sorel *wanted* his mouth to speak for itself, the words fizzled out. He ad-libbed the rest of Adrian's apology as best he could. "It's gonna be hard, I know. But you'll make new friends, go back to school—soon, I bet you won't even miss me."

"Oh my god, it's like you don't even know me!" Zoomer gripped the door-handle like she was trying to crush it in her gasp. "I guess last night was just for show, then. You pretend to patch things up so you can stop feeling bad, then try and ghost me. Is that it?"

"Ghost you?" Repeating the phrase, Sorel wondered if it held some kind of code. Was she trying to tell him she was onto him? "I'm not—"

"I should have known you'd leave one day." Her voice cracked. "Everyone always does." Zoomer moved to leave but Sorel braced the door, blocking her exit.

"Let's not end things this way." This time, he did mean it. He wasn't Zoomer's biggest fan, but she had something special with Adrian. It seemed disrespectful to let it fall apart, so soon. "You're still my best friend, that'll never change."

Glancing over her shoulder, Zoomer hesitated. "Do you really mean that?"

"Would I say it if I didn't?" Adrian's face smiled of its own accord. Sorel went along with it.

Turning slowly, she stared into Sorel's eyes with such intensity, he wondered if she might see him, a tiny driver sitting in a stolen chair. "Fine," she finally decided. "Just promise you'll come back. That's what a *real* best friend would do."

Sorel crossed his heart. "Soon as I'm able."

"Good." She leaped into Sorel's arms, knocking him against the bed. "Because I'm legit gonna miss you!"

"I'll miss you too." Sorel hugged her back. Oddly, he meant that too.

Eyeliner smudged and lipstick smeared into an accidental smirk, Zoomer gave him about five more hugs before she was ready to go. "Alright, already." She shoved him. "Enough with the mushy stuff."

"If you say so." Sorel got off the bed and hopped to his feet. "How's about we get a little fresh air and sunshine in here?" Building on his practice from earlier, he managed to lift the blinds on his first try and began to fiddle with the window frame.

"I didn't even know those opened." Zoomer let out a frail laugh. "Since when did you—" she stopped short. There was a soft thump.

Sorel turned around, finding Zoomer picking up his backpack. She must have knocked it over. For a moment, he could have sworn her hands were shaking. "You alright?" he asked.

"Totes." Zoomer snapped on a toothy grin. "I was just thinking, you've got a point. This road trip thing could be really a blessing or whatever."

"You really mean that?" Sorel braced himself for a sarcastic punchline but Zoomer just nodded with enthusiasm, stray hairs flying from her messy bun.

"Oh yeah," she said. "You know what, though, how about we give you a goodbye dinner? You could come over for some of Granny Z's mac and cheese."

"Ha, good one!" he chuckled. That was one mistake he wouldn't make twice. "The last thing I need is a bad stomach before a long trip."

"Sure. Mhm." Inching backwards, Zoomer pressed against the door. She searched for the handle, not taking her eyes off him. "You'll probably want to have most meals with your folks right now anyway. Lots to talk to about."

"You know it." Sorel turned his attention back towards the window. Even shoving his hardest, the pane only opened a couple inches. That would have to be enough fresh air for now.

"Anyway, I should probably get back to Granny. She really can't be alone for too long." The door clicked and Zoomer squeaked in surprise.

"Whoops!" Dad laughed. "Sorry about that, Z, I was just coming to ask Adrian for his lunch order. We're doing takeout—want in?"

"No thanks!" Zoomer scampered into the hall. "See you later—or not!"

"Um, yeah. Okay." Dad glanced at his son, confusion written on his face.

Sorel just shrugged. "What're you thinking for food?" he asked. "I'm game for anything."

TWENTY-NINE

So, what now?" Adrian was draped within the gnarled grasp of the oak. He ran a hand along its bark, unable to distinguish its textured pattern from that of the empty air. The evening was humid but he felt no heat, only pressure. "I can't go get my body back—can't even pass through the front gate. And as soon as you all get going, I'll fall apart. Why'd you even pull me back?"

"Now there's no need to talk like that." Marty sat like a songbird, perched on a brittle branch. "We're not about to go running off without you."

"Not yet." Adrian rolled over to hang by his knees. He scowled at the horizon, the setting sun a smear of white against a sea of charcoal grey. "But you can't stick around forever. And my options are, what, getting stuck haunting this place for all time or letting myself split into a thousand pieces?"

"Probably more than a thousand," Raj mumbled. Ze wound along an invisible ramp and parked along the treetop.

"Not helping!" Marty snipped.

"You pose an excellent question, Adrian." The layers of Niya's robes rippled like a river in sunlight as she joined the rest of the trio, settling on one of the upper branches. "Why did you pull him back?"

"I told you, I had a feeling!" Marty threw their hands into the air, releasing a small yet sparkling cascade. "And I was right, wasn't I? Clearly, it wasn't his time!"

"Isn't it, though?" asked Raj. "How are we supposed to know if this isn't how the kid is supposed to go?"

Marty pushed a finger to their lips and shushed. "Are you *trying* to panic him?"

"No, ze's right though." Adrian was getting dizzy, though he knew no blood could be rushing to his head. "I screwed up everything, so much. And not just with Sorel. Maybe things really would be better if I called it quits, here and now." He eyed the apartments down the road. Had anyone even noticed he was missing yet? No one had come looking.

"Don't talk like that!" said Marty. "You can't just let go of your life without a fight!"

"I don't know, seems as good a plan as any." Reclining in a leafy bough, Raj rested zir hands behind zir head.

Before Niya could add in her opinion, a shriek cut across the cemetery. "Adrian!" the voice cried out. "I looked everywhere else for you, you gotta be here—please!"

"Who's the fleshy?" Marty cocked their head. Adrian turned to get a better look himself.

A figure passed under the front archway and, in doing so, burst into colour: a black T-shirt almost long enough to be a dress, bright green leggings and a messy bun. A silver pentacle dangled around her neck. Something in Adrian's ghostly gut told him he was supposed to recognize her.

"Wait a second." He twisted upright. "That's my best friend!"

"Hello, Adrian?" Zoomer stumbled onto the cemetery grass, voice already ragged from shouting. "Anybody?!"

Adrian kicked himself loose and scrambled to the ground. "I'm here." He raced towards her, waving his arms. "I'm right here!"

For a moment, it almost seemed like she heard him. Zoomer stopped short and stared in Adrian's direction. Her eyes fell to the ground, on two parts of a broken sneaker. "No." She keeled over, lips quivering. "Please, no." She clasped his broken sole to her chest. "You can't be gone."

"I'm not, I'm right here!" Adrian turned back to the trio, asking, "Why can't she see me?"

"You're too weak." Swooping from the tree, Raj landed beside Adrian. "You're hardly holding together as it is. Revealing yourself to a living person takes way more stamina."

"I'm not crazy." Zoomer was chattering to herself. Her breath was shaky. "He might have your folks fooled but I knew that wasn't you. It couldn't be."

"My folks—?" Adrian gasped. "Sorel must be back at

my place, he's posing as me!"

"Well, at least we know his location now," said Raj.

Niya's dress floated around her like wings. She landed at Adrian's side and put two hands on his shoulders. "Allow me," she whispered. Without needing to explain, Adrian sensed she could help him turn visible.

He stepped out of her grasp. "Maybe I shouldn't."

"You *want* her to think you're dead?" Balanced on pointe, Marty leaped down to join the group. "Seems a bit harsh."

"Of course not," Adrian said quickly. "It's just—I don't know. Once she knows, she'll fully, fully freak."

"What's the alternative, let your ex gaslight her indefinitely?" Raj let out a throaty laugh. "Real pal you are."

Tears ran down Zoomer's cheeks as she cradled his broken shoe. Adrian paced around her in circles. "Okay, but. Just let me think. If I tell her, she'll probably want to try a full-on exorcism on him. Or worse, she'll tell my parents."

Marty walked beside him. "If she wants to help get you back, isn't that a good thing?" they asked.

"I don't know." Adrian shrugged, and for that, he caught a heap of side-eye from Marty. "Part of me thinks I should give Sorel what he wants. Let him live a little while."

"Sorel had his chance at life." Niya said it without a trace of sympathy or of judgement, the way one might mention it's supposed to rain later in the day. "It is time for him to move on."

Zoomer had gone from silent tears to full-on wailing. Adrian threw up his hands. "But what about second chances?" he asked. "I'm not gonna kill a guy twice just for me to get my crappy old body back."

"Jaiden!" Marty called out.

Adrian stomped off towards Sorel's grave. Did this count as his headstone now, since they had switched places? Adrian stared down at the engraving. *Beloved Son.* He kicked it, sock passing clean through the stone like it wasn't even there. Throat dry, he spat the hollow truth. "If Sorel wants my life so bad, he can have it. I was barely using it anyway."

"Oh, hell no!" Marty rushed after him. "We didn't just spend all that time helping you manifest just to have you give up!"

"That is not our decision, Marty." Niya passed through a gap in the breeze and stood behind Sorel's grave. "Adrian, you must make your own choice on whether you wish to live or die. Only know, there are people who would miss and mourn you."

"Except, they wouldn't," Adrian pointed out. "I would still be there, just as Sorel. Or, him as me."

"I'm not so sure it'll be an easy swap for everyone." Raj rolled from behind a nearby tree. Ze nodded back at Zoomer's crumpled form. Lying in the long grass, her shoulders shuddered.

Adrian stared at her in silence. "All the more reason not to tell her," he decided. "If she knows for sure I'm gone, she'll never accept him. And that wouldn't be fair."

"Fair to *whom*, pumpkin?" Marty frowned. Their dangly earrings glinted in the day's fading light. "I know your life might feel like it's in the dumper right now but you're still so young—it gets so much better from here on out!"

"Or it doesn't," said Raj, adjusting zir fingerless gloves. "Hey, if these guys aren't gonna tell you the truth, I'll level with you. Living sucks."

"Rajam," Niya whispered sharply. "What are you doing?"

"You got to give your advice. I get to give mine," ze said, shrugging back in zir chair. "As somebody who was alive for a good long time, I'll be honest, I like being dead way better. Problem here is, this isn't actually about you."

"It's—it's not?" Adrian glanced towards the others.

Marty twisted their lips into an asterisk. "I don't know about this, Raj. Don't we gotta let him choose to live for himself and all that?"

"Agreed," Niya answered with a short nod. "His motivation should be hope, not fear."

"Hope's a cheap bet on a bad horse." Raj hocked a loogie. "Fact is, Sorel's dead and he's only getting deader. That body he's running around in—it's dying too, way faster than if you were at the wheel."

Adrian furrowed his brow, looking to Marty. "Ze is right," they admitted, avoiding a stern look from Niya. "It could last him a couple years, maybe a lot less."

"But, he—?" Ground and sky starting to blur again, Adrian tried to brace himself on Sorel's headstone. He passed through it but managed to keep his footing. "Fine. Okay. Even if he gets just a few years of life, isn't that better than nothing?"

"Unfortunately, it is not." Niya released a long-held

breath. "We have seen a handful of cases like this before. By the time he realizes what is happening, Sorel will have become so reliant on that body that he will not be able to sustain himself as a spirit anymore. He will inevitably occupy another vessel, then another." She hung her head. "It becomes a brutal cycle."

For a while, the only sound was the rustling of leaves and Zoomer's broken sobs. "Sorel wouldn't do that," said Adrian. He pushed aside nagging doubts about their fight, their bitter break-up—none of that mattered now. There was no way he'd ever go so far as to willfully steal another body. This was all just a big misunderstanding. "He wouldn't. I know him."

"Yeah, sure you do." Raj popped a wheelie. "But once that domino effect gets going, it's a real shitshow. Eventually, even body-hopping won't work. He's bound to shred himself to pieces either way, it's just a question of how many living folks he takes down with him." Turning in a circle, ze slammed back down again. "We call it going hashbrowns."

"We do?" Marty snickered.

"Okay, okay," Raj admitted with a huff, "that's what *I* call it."

Marty covered their mouth to laugh as they stepped aside. "All that's to say, this whole situation—it's not just your life on the line." Casting glitter through the air, Marty drew their attention back towards the weeping Zoomer. "From what we've seen, spirits in Sorel's condition go for friends and family next."

"He wouldn't." But Adrian knew that was a lie. If Sorel

was desperate enough, he would take what he needed—
who he needed.

"Would it help if we said 'pretty please'?" asked Raj, a
sneer in zir throat. "Won't you save us the trouble of track-
ing down your boyfriend *after* he becomes a serial killer?"

"Yeah, what ze said," said Marty. "I won't lie, things
are bad right now, but you can stop them from getting any
worse."

Face-down, Zoomer mumbled something into her
closed fists. Was it a spell? Maybe a prayer? Whatever it
was, Adrian could see it coming off her in waves, the way
heat looked on pavement. He held back, still uncertain.
"But, what can I *do*?"

"That is a tricky part," Marty tutted their tongue. "And
sorta why we *didn't* want to tell you *quite* so much." They
cast a brief but withering look towards Raj.

"No use in withholding now," Niya murmured across
the graveyard. "The truth is both complex and simple. You
will need to *want* your body back. Only then may you
receive it." Adrian looked at her for more but Niya stayed
quiet; even the movements of her dress were silent.

"Think of it this way, kid," said Raj. "You don't want to
live, go ahead and kill yourself. But bring your skin sack
down with you, capisce?"

Adrian shifted his weight from one leg to the other.
"None of this seems very fair."

"That's life," Marty answered with a glittery shrug.
"Did you really expect death to be any different?"

THIRTY

Despite the setting sun, Adrian did not cast a shadow. Each step towards Zoomer was its own lifetime, a march towards an ending he both feared and craved. Her hair had fallen over her face and she was whimpering, holding on to his lost sneaker.

"Adrian, please," she murmured, "you can't leave me here."

"I'm sorry." Though clear to his own ears, Adrian's voice could not travel to her. He could sense that now. "I should have listened to you in the first place."

The breeze picked up and rustled the grass. Sniffling, Zoomer wiped a string of snot on the sleeve of her T-shirt. "Adrian, is that you?" she asked the empty graveyard. "Are you here?"

She was answered by an eerie silence, the distant hum of passing cars. The gravestones stood stoic and even the wind had gone still. The cemetery itself was holding its breath.

Niya rested her hand on Adrian's shoulder and Zoomer let out a bloodcurdling scream. "Oh my god, I knew it!" She scrambled to her feet.

"Hey." Adrian waved.

After a second of shock, Zoomer's eyes hardened. "You asshole!" She threw Adrian's busted sneaker at his head and it sailed through him. "You had me so goddamn scared!" She lunged towards him and Adrian stepped out of her path, losing touch with Niya as he did so. Zoomer landed face-first in the dirt.

"Sorry!" Adrian cried out, but in their disconnection, his voice was lost once more. "One sec!"

"Let's try this again, shall we?" Marty appeared at his side, offering a limp wrist. "Easy does it."

A round of electricity shot through Adrian's body, enough of an extra boost to let him remain visible on his own terms for at least a short while. He nodded thanks to Marty. "Zoomer?"

"Jesus, there you are." She whipped around and loudly cursed. Stomping towards him in her platform boots, she left a path of crushed weeds in her wake. "What the hell is wrong with you—and who the hell is that?!" She pointed over his shoulder, where Marty hovered back a step.

"I like this one." Raj manifested with ease, resting an elbow against zir knee. Zoomer yelped. "Any chance she'll die soon? Our crew could use a little fire."

"Please, do not joke about such things." Niya rippled

like a stone across smooth water.

"Wha— How?" Zoomer stumbled back to Adrian. "Dude, you've been dead for like a day, did you join a god-damn ghost-gang?"

"Not exactly," said Niya.

Raj grinned. "Yes, exactly."

"I'd rather stick with 'gay guardian angels,' if that's still on the table," said Marty as they coifed their hair.

Hand over her mouth, Zoomer squealed. "That's exactly what a ghost-gang *would* call themselves!"

Adrian gave a half-hearted shrug. "I made friends?"

Zoomer opened her mouth, only to shut it again. After a few false starts, she decided, "Whatever, tell me later. There's more important stuff to debrief." She nod-ded towards the apartment complex. "Do you know Sorel's back at your place? He's living your freaking life, dude!"

Even though Adrian had suspected, even braced for it, the truth still stung. From the corner of his eye, he could tell Raj was giving him an I-told-you-so look. He refused to entertain it.

"Would you believe it was an accident?" he shrugged.

"How'd I know you'd say that?" Zoomer groaned. "What's the plan then, you go ask politely for your life back? Because let me tell you, I don't think he's gonna love that idea. Last I saw, he was packing for your freaking fam-ily trip!"

"I hope he remembers to bring my good sweater," Adrian muttered. "I hear it gets chilly out east."

Unamused, Zoomer set her sights towards the trio.

"Okay, ghosty dudes. Just give it to me straight—"

"Not possible," Marty winked.

"Also, not dudes," said Raj. "Just to be clear on that."

"You." Zoomer looked to Niya. "Is Adrian, like, dead-dead? Or what?"

"Not quite," Niya explained, neither smiling nor frowning. "However, should Sorel not return his body, the both of them would be in a most unfavourable state."

"Great. That's just great." Zoomer sneered at Adrian, "You know, I told you this would happen. Didn't I say, 'He's too dangerous'?!"

"Did she really?" Flipping their fan back into existence, Marty whispered to Niya, "Maybe Raj is right—we should at least keep an eye on her. Could use a smartie like that on our side."

Raj snapped zir fingers. "That's what I'm saying!"

"Focus." Niya shushed them both. "And yes, I will make a note to follow up."

Adrian hovered a few unsteady inches off the ground. He felt a tad heavier while visible, just enough that it shifted his centre of balance. "You did totally warn me," he admitted. "And you're really not gonna like this next part, but I'm gonna really need your help to make things right."

"I *don't* like the sound of that." Zoomer clenched her teeth.

"Adrian is correct." Niya motioned towards the graveyard's arch. "Even with our help, he would have quite a challenge passing through the iron fence. However, if he were able to receive some corporeal assistance..."

It took a few seconds before Zoomer could grasp the request at hand. "Oh no." She took a long step backwards. "I am so not doing that."

"It's asking a lot, I know." Adrian drifted after her but she was too close to the arch now. Even getting near it was taking all his strength. "But you're my only chance."

"What about your dads or something?" Zoomer eyed the exit. "Hell, I bet I could lure a bus driver here if I had to."

"Zoomer, it has to be you." The further Adrian moved from the trio, the harder it became to maintain his solidity. "It has to be *now*."

◆◆◆

Adrian hadn't gotten his driver's licence. City transit robust as it was, Pop always said there was no rush to learn to drive. But Adrian had meant to do it. He'd been looking into student lessons. Dad even said he'd pay for them, next time he got the chance. At night, when sleep wouldn't come, Adrian would close his eyes and picture his life as a highway, open road merging with the horizon. Foot steady, he'd keep his speed even. All that mattered was that he keep moving.

Sometimes he liked to think about what life would be like after high school. Adrian had never been a stellar student, but he liked shop class and English lit. He'd entertained the idea of enrolling at a local college, even if it meant taking on debt. Zoomer was smart enough, she'd probably get a scholarship. They'd live on credit cards and

Dollarama ramen in a two-bedroom apartment, maybe adopt a grumpy old cat.

He'd always wanted to try couch surfing for a summer. There was a stash of change under his bed, savings for a road trip with no start or end in sight. He'd been planning to get on the wait-list for top surgery, too. After that was done, maybe he'd try moving to a different city, even another country. He'd heard about people who went abroad and worked odd jobs, making a name for themselves as travel bloggers. He could do that.

Peanut butter cookies, baked from scratch. A cozy pile of blankets still warm from the dryer. Cuddling up with his fathers for movie night. There were so many things Adrian still had left to do. If one day he truly grew tired of it all, he would leave on his own terms. But not like this. Never like this.

◆ ◆ ◆

Zoomer was at the gate. She was running.

"Well, that's a fail." Raj looked around the cemetery. "We could try to kick a squirrel soul out of its body. You wanna be a little squirrel?"

"Zoomer!" Adrian swam into the hazy feedback of the gate, willing his way forward. She wasn't through just yet. "I swear, I'll make it up to you," he promised. "And if you never want to talk to me again after all this, I will so get it!" Could she even hear him? He couldn't tell. Voice starting to waver, his materiality was breaking down. "Please, don't just leave me here like this—I don't want to be dead!"

"Gah!" Beneath the iron archway, Zoomer stomped her platform boot. "Crap. Shit. Fine." She stuck out her arm. "You seriously owe me for this, though."

"Thank you, thank you!" Adrian grasped at her. "I swear, I'll try and make this quick." He stepped closer but the earth slipped from his feet. It was like trying to walk on an ice rink without skates. The more he flailed, the harder it was to regain balance. He started kicking, pumping his arms. Every tiny movement took his full concentration. With the last traces of his fingertips, he brushed against her skin.

"Yuck," Raj retched. "It's like watching someone trying to shove toothpaste back in the tube."

Marty tapped the tips of their fingers, a miniature round of applause. "You're doing great, hon!"

"Steady now." Niya's guiding words were a whisper in his ear. "Remember, you have to want your life to retrieve it."

He blinked, and suddenly, his face was aching. Adrian's eyes felt puffy and inflamed, his cheeks sticky from tears he could not remember crying. His throat was impossibly sore. He pressed a hand to his chest and found it warm. The steady rise of breathing lungs and a quivering, beating heart.

"Really, the first thing you do is feel me up?" Zoomer snatched her hands away. "Ugh," she groused. "This is the literal worst."

The pair wiggled themselves together, stomping on one another's toes. With Adrian's first step, he almost tumbled—Zoomer was already taller than him, why did she insist on always wearing platform boots too? Still, he was in a living body again, and that itself was exhilarating. For a moment, he could empathize with Sorel. He never wanted to give this up.

None of the trio remained in sight. Niya's voice could easily be mistaken for the rustling of the trees. "You are doing us a service, taking on this task."

"Try not to die twice!" Raj laughed like grinding gravel.

"Yeah, whatever," Zoomer sneered. "Let's get this shit-show on the road."

"Get out there and get that body back!" said Marty, their words twinkling, indistinguishable from the glint of nearby street lights.

THIRTY-ONE

Sorel had never thought he could love a vegetable so much. He speared another crispy forkful of buttery brussels sprouts and shovelled them in with delight. "These are incredible!" He grinned with bulging cheeks. "How did you even get them to taste so good?"

"Oh, it's just a trick I saw online." Dad sat up a little straighter. "I figured it was time we get rid of all those half-eaten veggie bags sitting in the back of the freezer."

"Good thinking." Pop nodded. He moved to clear the plates, but Sorel sprang up first.

"I can do it!" He flashed a cheery smile. "Please, let *me* do the dishes."

Pop shrugged, sharing with Dad a quiet look of approval. "Well, if you insist!"

Skipping around the coffee table, Sorel balanced their

plates, cups, and cutlery. Arms full, he hurried to the kitchen. Meanwhile Dad and Pop retreated into their phones, muttering about potential road stops and when to set alarms.

The dishwater steamed as Sorel soaked his tired hands—they had been oddly chilly all day. As he filled the sink, he hummed an old tune. One his mother used to sing when she tidied up the house. The soap in this era was gloriously viscous, the water always arriving hot and smooth. Cleaning was a breeze in comparison to the drippy, freezing tap he'd had to use in his last life.

His mother had often struggled to pay the heating bill on time. Sorel could recall that clearly now. She had figured electricity and water were more important. If cold, they could always boil a kettle. He'd gone to bed many nights wearing several pairs of pants and sweaters.

Even remembering was easier in this body. What once had been a hazy half dream now came clearly to his mind. It was as if, just hours ago, Sorel had stood on those chilly kitchen tiles while waiting for water to boil.

In a blink, he was back in the present. The cutlery and plates were washed and stacked. Drying his hands on a dish-towel, his skin was wrinkled and beet red.

Leaning on the counter, Sorel took stock of the apartment. The walls were now bare, traced with white squares where frames used to sit. The family's clothes and favoured possessions were all packed tightly into bags, stacked by the door. They were ready to be hauled off in the morning. Dad had spent the better part of the day bragging about the price he'd gotten for a storage unit. "First month is only a dollar!" Even Pop couldn't say no to that price.

Things were hectic but Sorel didn't mind keeping busy. There were carpets to vacuum, floors to scrub, cabinets and drawers that needed sorting. Dad and Pop had grown tense with one another by noon but that was solved by a meal-break, and soon enough, they were collaborating on to-do lists without so much as a cruel jab. By evening they were simply too tired for nitpicking or petty disagreement.

Dinner had been only slightly burnt. Dad had tried his darndest to whip up a proper homecooked meal. Pop was openly grateful, kissing his compliments to the chef. Happy bellies, happy hearts—that was something Sorel's mother used to say.

Well-fed and worn out, Dad and Pop cuddled together on the couch. How peaceful it was to be alive and well, in the company of a loving family. Were they even aware of how bountiful this life was, how lucky they were to live it so openly? Why Adrian had ever wanted to leave this behind, Sorel could not fathom.

Not that he had much of a choice, Sorel's guilty conscious reminded him. Adrian had hinted that he was unhappy, listless, but he certainly hadn't taken leave of his own accord. What was there to do now though? Sorel reminded himself, the best way to honour Adrian's life was to live it well. If that meant Sorel himself got a second chance for his own happiness, that was just serendipity.

Just as he thought the dishes were done, Sorel spied a stray water glass and hurried over to collect it. "Hey kiddo," Pop said, waving, "what do you think, should we try to drive twelve hours on the first day or take an early pit stop, and make up for it later in the trip?"

"You're asking my opinion?" asked Sorel.

"Of course!" Dad grinned. "It's a family trip, that means all of us get a say." He prodded at a map on his phone. "I'm thinking we grab some camping gear and whenever we get tired, we can pull over and pop tents. Can't you just see it?" Lifting both arms towards the ceiling, he looked up and sighed, "Sleeping under a big open sky, all those twinkling stars!"

"Waking up with back pain," Pop grumbled. "Trying to fit all that extra stuff in the car." He was working up to a good rant but seemed to catch himself. "Though, I suppose there could be benefits. I could finally teach you two how to recognize simple constellations." He turned to Sorel. "So, what's your vote?"

"I like the sound of camping," Sorel decided, taking the last glass to the sink. "There's a yoga mat in my closet. You could sleep on that, to help your back?"

"Smart thinking!" Dad clapped with excitement. Sorel blushed. Thoughtful parents, ones who actually asked for his perspective? Maybe he'd died again and made it to heaven this time.

"Well, that's that then," said Pop. "Let's sort the details in the morning. Adrian, why don't you go lie down—you look like you could use some rest."

The first knock didn't catch anyone's attention. It was drowned by the sound of running water and Pop's boisterous suggestions for a road-trip playlist. The second was more urgent, followed by a series of hard bangs that would not be ignored. "Okay, okay, we hear you!" Dad stood up. Sorel listened with mild curiosity, running the sponge in small circles around the sink. "Oh, hey Zoomer. You forget something?"

"Kind of, yeah. Yes."

Sorel bristled at the sound of Zoomer's voice. What was she doing back here?

There was the stumbling of heavy boots, feet tripping over the welcome mat. "Is—is Adrian still here?" she asked. "We're not too late?"

Playing her off earlier had been tricky enough. He was hardly in the mood to do it twice. But Sorel reminded himself that Adrian would never turn her away. Even when he should. He wrung out the sponge and leaned over with a wide smile. "Hey, pal! Just give me one sec!"

Pop eyed Zoomer's muddy bootprints across the freshly mopped floor. "We were just having a family dinner," he explained. "We've got a long drive in the morning, so now isn't the best time for company."

"Yep, no worries!" Zoomer gave a double thumbs up and hurried towards Adrian's bedroom. "We'll be quick." She waved at Sorel. "Just meet me when you're ready, pal!"

"She's always so busy, isn't she?" Dad glanced towards Pop, who grunted in reply.

"Give me just a minute," Sorel told them. "I'm sure this won't take long."

THIRTY-TWO

Taking in his bedroom through Zoomer's eyes, Adrian was alarmed. One could hardly call it *his* anymore. She had warned him everything would be boxed up and ready to go, but it was another thing entirely to see it in person. His dresser had been cleared out and wiped down, drawers left open and laid bare. The stickers were pried off his bed-frame, leaving tacky residue. No more zines or cards pinned on the walls or hung up by bits of twine. His closet had been completely reorganized, all his favourite items either missing or pushed to the back. His shelves were cleared of the odd knick-knacks he'd picked up at local garage sales, including his model of a spaceship that lit up when one tapped the top. The rug on the floor even seemed to be missing its lint. Pressure welled in Adrian's throat. Nothing was where it was supposed to be.

There was no time to dwell on it now. Footsteps were approaching. Zoomer stood up taller, shoulders squared to the door.

"Hey Z!" Sorel wore Adrian's mouth in a lopsided grin. "I thought we agreed I wasn't coming to Gran's for dinner?"

It was impossible not to stare at his own imposter-self as it strode across the room and bounced onto his bed. Adrian tasted the hint of vomit in the back of Zoomer's mouth. "Newsflash, freak," she hissed. "I wasn't actually inviting you over."

"Uh, yeah," Sorel feebly laughed. "I totally knew that."

Adrian's body was not in a good way. His skin had lost colour, lips vaguely blue and grey. His eyes were bloodshot and turning yellow at the edges. Sorel didn't even seem to notice as he reached up and scratched the back of his neck, coming away with far too much dead skin beneath his nails. "So, what's up then?" he asked with Adrian's voice. His cadence was slightly off, like he wasn't certain of where the emphasis was supposed to lie.

Zoomer pulled the bedroom door shut. Adrian's hand slipped down her arm to catch it before it slammed. There was no need to draw his fathers' attention. The latch shut with a click and Adrian was sure to turn the lock. "Maybe we should try and talk—"

"Not a chance." Zoomer shoved him aside and resumed full control. "You wanna know what's up?" She marched towards Sorel, mimicking his tone. "How about this—I know who you are. I figured out what you've done. And if you want any mercy, drop the act. Now."

"Are you feeling okay?" Sorel patted at a spot beside him on the bed. "Maybe you should have a sit-down."

"You don't have to pretend." Adrian fished his voice out of Zoomer's throat. "Sorel, we want to help you. But I need my body back, first."

"Oh." His facsimile of a smile fell away entirely. "You're here."

"Yeah," Zoomer sneered. "I found him in the graveyard, where *you* ditched him after your little body-snatching trick."

"I hardly recognized you in there, Adrian." Sorel carefully peered at Zoomer's face. "I didn't know you two were so ... close."

"Ugh. Don't make me think about it." Zoomer retched. "Just swap back already so we can get this over with."

"Right now?" Sorel sucked air through his teeth. "This isn't the best time. Could we do a rain check?"

Riding inside Zoomer, Adrian was jostled by her growing rage. "Stop messing around, Sorel!" She balled up her fists. "Adrian's here to get his life back, and you're gonna give it back!"

Once he found his footing, Adrian took over the voice again. "She's right, Sorel," he managed. "I'm sorry, but it's over."

"Is it, though?" Sorel slipped to the edge of the bed. "I don't think it has to be." His gaze strayed downwards, out the window. Adrian just knew he was looking at the graveyard.

Cautiously, Adrian stepped towards him. "I get that it's hard but—"

"Ha!" Sorel snapped his head around. "If you're here, then you know that's one hell of an understatement." He motioned to the empty bedroom walls. "You didn't even want your life! This amazing, rich, beautiful life—I would do so much more with it, if you just let me."

A breeze sneaked through the open window. The hum of the city after dusk drifted outside. In the living room, music was playing—electric guitar and heavy drums, Dad's choice for sure. Pop must be in a good mood because he was singing along to the chorus. It had the added benefit of drowning out their argument.

"I know," said Adrian. "You're right. But this isn't right. It's not fair."

"You want to talk about fair?" Sorel shut the blinds. "You think it's *fair* for me to get stuck in some back lot, floating around while my body rots right under my feet? Is it *fair* to send me back to that place where I can't touch, can't taste, can't do anything but wait for someone to maybe remember I used to matter?" Teeth clenched, Sorel's jaw was set so tight that Adrian himself could feel its ache. "You're so quick to judge. Meanwhile, you've been dead for less than a week and already possessing people—did you even think about that?"

"It's not like that..." Adrian tried to explain, but all the excuses he'd had before seemed too shallow now.

"Isn't it, though?" Sorel saw through Zoomer, right into Adrian. As their eyes met on the ethereal realm, a flicker ran across his face. His sharp lines softened as he released a sigh. "I'm sorry. I never wanted things to go this way."

Winding back control from Adrian, Zoomer offered her arm. "Then do what's right."

Sorel slunk back against the wall. "I want to. Really, I do. But what if it doesn't work?"

"What do you mean?" Adrian looked at him, confused. "We've done this plenty of times."

"But never like this," Sorel pointed out. "Never out here. What if I leave this body and get stuck in this apartment? Or worse, what if you can't get back in and we're just two ghosts stuck with a corpse?" His eyes flitted towards the living room and its blaring music. "Bet those two would be pretty upset about that."

Adrian could feel Zoomer's heartbeat pick up. "He's got a point," she whispered. "I don't even know what I'd say to your folks if you just dropped dead like that."

"But, the others, they—we—" Adrian stammered. It was getting hard to parse Zoomer's feelings from his own. At least one of them was getting seriously nervous. "Sorel, I met three spirits. Ones like you, who haven't passed on. They told me I could get my body back, that I *had* to."

"To be fair though," said Zoomer, "you know those randos even less than this dude."

"Whose side are you on?" asked Adrian.

"You really met other ghosts?" Sorel stood, slack-jawed. Adrian was once again struck with the bizarre nature of their entanglement—his body still had its own memories, told through worn-in details. The thin, almost-imperceptible scar from the time Zoomer had tried to shave a slit in his eyebrows and managed to nick off some skin instead. A slight dip in one shoulder told the story of a learned slouch. Sorel had all the pieces of Adrian's embodied history, yet he wore them differently. It was like standing in front of a funhouse mirror. But so far, the way they wore surprise was exactly the same.

"I really did." Adrian nodded.

Sorel laughed through his nose. "I swear, you got more done in one day of being dead than I did in decades." He shook his head. "Let's say I believe you that swapping back could work—can't you let me live for just a little while, would that be so bad?"

"I'm sorry." Adrian drew closer to Sorel, despite Zoomer dragging her feet. "The ghosts also told me that body you're in, *my* body, it's dying. You'll only get a couple years out of it, more or less."

Zoomer wrinkled her nose. "By the looks of it, you're racing into the *less* category."

The spirit wearing Adrian's face fell silent. Hand braced against the wall, Sorel stared at the pattern of Adrian's comforter. It was folded neatly, likely for the first time in a decade. He stayed lost there for a moment among the simple swirls and abstract shapes. "A lot can happen in a couple years," he spoke under his breath. "Even that would be more than I ever thought I'd have again. But I doubt you'll even let me have that."

When Sorel turned to meet his eyes, Adrian could

hardly bear it. "You know I can't."

Through the layers of corporeality, they witnessed one another. "Irony is," said Sorel, "you're the only person in the world who can understand how I feel right now." He drifted one step closer. "Things are so different now, so much more possible. I want another chance, to see the world the way it is now." He asked with that lopsided smile, "I know that isn't fair, but can't I want it anyway?"

"Of course you can." Adrian blinked back tears. "I would love that for you." He reached with Zoomer's hand and Sorel paused briefly, then took it.

They embraced. Adrian did not rush into his old body nor did Sorel make room. It was deeply strange to be held by his own arms, yet Adrian treasured every second of it. Though neither wore their original skin, they had finally managed to connect in the flesh. Sorel's tears rolled down Adrian's cheeks, staining Zoomer's shoulders. They held even tighter.

With Zoomer's lips, Adrian met his own mouth. Adrian's lips were clammy, like someone who had been swimming in deep water. But his breath, Adrian couldn't explain it—it *tasted* like Sorel. Dusty and sharp, just a little too sweet. They wrapped their arms around each other, and Adrian pushed Sorel onto the bed. He straddled his own hips, Sorel's fingers running through Zoomer's hair. He traced them along her neck, knowing it was Adrian causing those baby hairs to stand on end.

A moan escaped from Adrian. The moment he parted those borrowed lips, Zoomer's voice grabbed its chance.

"Now!" She flattened herself against Sorel, pinning him down; he yelped and squirmed in surprise. "Adrian—go!"

Adrian's consciousness was knocked loose as Zoomer retook control. She forced him from her body, squeezing him into Sorel along the crackling connection of their skin-on-skin contact. When he passed the event horizon of Zoomer's flesh, Adrian met something of an undertow. It dragged him into his own body.

Halfway into himself, Adrian clawed desperately for control. But the shock of Zoomer's maneuver had worn off and Sorel was fighting back. Wriggling and prying himself away, Sorel staunchly refused any entry. Adrian was losing his grip, but Zoomer was not about to welcome him back. With nowhere left to hold, Adrian's hands unravelled.

The memory of his natural shape began to fray into a loose web. Uncertain of all except his own undoing, Adrian clung to the broken pieces of himself. They radiated in all directions. A bending, squeezing numbness snaked through him. There was nothing he could do to stop his ongoing disintegration.

Adrian gasped for air but only managed to fill someone else's lungs. A scream. Raised voices. A loud thud. A twisting mass that fell to the floor. Reality came to him in an array of shattered mirrors, all bent and out of order. He tried to cry out, but the words were garbled before they could even reach his lips. Which mouth was his? He couldn't remember.

"Get! In! There!" Zoomer was shouting. Sorel was lashing back. In the midst of it all, Adrian was floating, rising towards the ceiling and passing through it. He looked down at the grappling duo in dazed curiosity. They were leaking: Zoomer straddling Adrian's body, she dug her arm into Sorel's neck, smoke stealing through the corners of both their noses and mouths. Adrian ran his fingers through it and found it thick, like tangled rope or the tendrils of a jellyfish. He gave a tug and it grew taut, only to then unspool even faster. He noticed, too, that he was made of the material. And it was wisping away. The more he tried to catch it, the quicker he became undone.

Sorel thrashed. Zoomer's eyes burned with a deep, unyielding flame as she snarled, "Get out! Of my! Best friend!" Her words took on a commanding tone unlike anything Adrian had ever heard, her smoke was accumulating, dense as thunder-clouds. Whatever she said next, something inside of Adrian knew that Sorel would have to obey.

"Give him back. Now."

Stolen fingernails dug into Zoomer's fleshy arm. Sorel gnashed at her with what had been Adrian's teeth. He tried desperately to shove her off. It was no use. He fell limp. "Fine," he hissed. "You win. I'll go."

"Good." Zoomer pulled away.

It was only for a split second but that was more than enough. Once she let down her guard, Sorel grabbed at her neck. "I'd rather take yours anyway!"

Amid their struggle, a howling filled the whole apartment. Someone was banging on the bedroom door. His fathers' voices, shouts of panic and concern. They were separated from the commotion by only a strip of plywood, yet—to the many pieces of Adrian that floated across the ceiling—they were an ocean away.

With a forceful twist, Sorel shoved himself on top of Zoomer. She scratched at him, nails digging under dying skin. The fumes of his spirit billowed all around her and began to close in. "It'll be so much easier this way," Sorel spoke within the raging storm. "The grieving Zoomer, distraught by the death of her one and only friend. She could disappear into the woodwork, move away and invent a new life for herself. Would anyone even think to ask why?"

"You can't—you wouldn't!" The sparks of her own essence were starting to scatter. Zoomer's spirit crackled and burned like a bonfire running low on oxygen.

"That's it. Just let go." Sorel's presence grew larger with every word, riding along gales of heavy smoke. "There are so many people waiting for you on the other side, Zoomer. Can't you hear them calling?" He didn't sound anything like himself, at least not as Adrian had known him. But the voice itself was not wholly unfamiliar. Adrian had heard it last at the graveyard. Right before Sorel lost control.

Was this who he was, when in touch with his own power? This could be Sorel's true self, all the rest a great mirage. That funny, strange, beautiful human Adrian thought he knew—was he a kind of luminescent buoy, designed to draw in unsuspecting prey? If so, Adrian had fallen for it. He wondered, when a fish gets snagged, does it recognize the lure as part of the hook? Does it even matter?

The light in Zoomer's eyes threatened to flicker out.

Sorel's hands were on her throat. She grasped at his arms and failed to break his grip. "Adrian," she croaked, reaching for the empty air, "do something!"

A stabbing jolt shot through Adrian. Zoomer had grabbed their connective thread and, like a fistful of balloons, she yanked at his many strings. The pieces of himself knocked together. It was a brief contact but it was enough—Adrian clambered back towards Zoomer, swimming upstream. He touched the very top of her head, the tip of her curls. That was all it took.

He ran through Zoomer's throat, into the clenched hand around her neck. He snapped between them like a spark. Sorel had no time to react. Twisting himself around, Adrian landed back into his own feet. He instantly let go of Zoomer's neck and she panted for breath. Sorel struggled to regain himself but Adrian rushed to occupy every bit of space inside his body. There was nowhere left. He sputtered and coughed up a wad of sludge, excising the last of the unruly ghost.

All was quiet. Adrian stared up at the bedroom ceiling. His arms were wide open, like he was waiting for a hug. He held his palms together and found them clammy, growing warmer. The colour was seeping back into his skin.

Zoomer lay on the ground, dry heaving. There was no sign of the storm that had been Sorel. The bedroom showed little of what had happened, save for the deep red scratches down his arms and bruises forming on her neck.

Someone was still banging on the bedroom door. Dad was screaming in panic. Pop shouted something about getting a screwdriver. He was going to take the hinges off.

"Quick." Adrian knelt at Zoomer's side and helped her up. "Granny Z's mac and cheese."

"No—" She gave a raspy cough. "No thank you. Please."

"Good," he murmured. "I thought for a second..."

"Same, dude." Zoomer rolled onto her stomach and flinched. Fishing out the string around her neck, she held up her crystal pendant. "Woah. Look at this." What once had a been a clear stone was now fogged and riddled with cracks. "I guess the protection worked after all."

Adrian shrank from the broken crystal. "Is he in there?"

Peering close at the shattered lines, Zoomer shook her head. "I don't think so. Seems like he's gone, for real this time." Adrian could feel it too, a distinct absence of a presence. Their spectral battleground had morphed back into the mundanity of his bedroom.

The door burst open and Adrian's fathers tumbled through. "What the hell is going on in here?!" Pop was sweating, a screwdriver in his fist. "Why was the door blocked?!"

"What were all those noises?" Dad glanced around. "Are you okay?!"

Propped up against the bed-frame, Adrian looked to Zoomer. She still held the cracked crystal in her hand. He smirked and sputtered until they both began to giggle. They fell and held on to each other, shivering with shock and relief. In a few moments they had broken into raucous laughter. They didn't stop until tears began to roll down their cheeks and their lungs burned for air.

Epilogue

The 7-Eleven doors chimed and slipped shut at Adrian's back. Zoomer was already a few paces ahead on the sidewalk. She chewed on a neon-green plastic straw jutting from her side of the Slurpee cup. "Do you think your dads will ever let me come over again?"

A breeze ran past, carrying dry leaves and cigarette butts. Adrian thoughtfully twirled his purple straw between his fingers. "I'll ask again once we get properly unpacked. I don't think Pop even wants me and Dad around that much until he gets those boxes all sorted out."

"Whatever," said Zoomer. "Granny's place is more fun anyway." She passed the drink to Adrian. "Just wait til you come over next—I found this sewing machine on eBay for, like, way cheap and now I can make, like, anything!"

Adrian took a sip and winced, hit with the sudden rush

of ice and sugar. Once the initial brain freeze wore off, he went back in for more. "I'm away for like a second and you get so bored you hop on that seamstress grind?"

"I had to do *something* while you were off on the road trip from hell!" Zoomer wrinkled her nose at him, septum glittering. "What, was I supposed to just hang around and wait for you to text me?"

"Obviously." Adrian pushed aside his bangs. His hair had grown a surprising amount in a month and a half. He went in for another sip of their shared Slurpee. Zoomer shoved his shoulder, making the sharp edge of his straw snap against the back of his throat. Adrian gagged and started coughing. Zoomer nearly died of laughter.

The pair made their way around back of the convenience store, into the maze of side streets. They passed below archways of overlapping graffiti, avoiding piss-stained gutters. They wound around piles of forgotten furniture, a mattress left out to go mouldy, and several broken garbage bags. In the backyards of duplexes and square apartment blocks, yard-side trees leaned into the alleyways and shed their summer coats for robes of red and yellow.

From the pocket of her patch-ridden sweater, Zoomer fished out a palm-size package of ten-cent candies. She dropped several sour cherries and Fuzzy Peaches into their melted Slurpee and swirled the sugary mass. Adrian made a face, but if Zoomer caught it, she didn't seem to care. "For real though," she asked, "you coming back to school soon?"

"Yep." Adrian shuffled to one side of the back lane,

making room for a passing car. Puddle water crept under the duct tape that held the sole of his left sneaker in place. "Dad and I both hated the whole home-schooling set-up. Plus, ever since he got that latest draft to his publisher, he's been way busy with revisions."

"So he actually did the thing!" Zoomer dipped her fingers into the cup and fished out one of her syrup-soaked candies. She offered it to Adrian but he politely declined. "Guess that stint out east was good for something after all."

"Guess so." Adrian shrugged. "Dad says he writes best on the road but I think he got most of it done while we were staying with my grandparents—after a couple days of playing nice, he was locked inside the guest bedroom for the rest of our trip."

Across the sky, pink streaks of sunset hinted through the clouds. "Guess everyone gets sick of their folks sometimes." Zoomer threw back the Slurpee and gulped down its grainy syrup. She smacked her lips. "I'm still surprised your parents didn't split on the car ride there."

"Me too," chuckled Adrian. "Even though some stuff was stressful as hell, the drive out was actually kind of fun? Pop gets kinda goofy when he's on the road for a long time. He made this whole playlist of Broadway music and knew the lyrics to every single song."

"That's so gay!" Zoomer stuck out her tongue at Adrian, showing off its bright blue stain. She shoved the empty cup into the overflowing mouth of a back-lane garbage can. "Oh, and I never asked—did you really get to snatch a piece off Canada's largest cheese wheel?"

"Sorry, what?" Adrian chuckled.

"Oh. Right." Zoomer rubbed the back of her neck. She sported a fresh undercut. "Guess that was a conversation with you-know-who."

"You can say his name." Adrian rolled his eyes. "He's not Bloody Mary."

"You don't know that," Zoomer flatly replied.

Adrian tried to shrug off her comment, but the ease between them had shifted. It always happened that way, whenever Sorel came up in conversation. Whether or not they spoke his name aloud, a part of him was still there with them. A shadow hanging at the corners of their time together. Some days, the memories burned hot and fresh. They would arrive like a stab to Adrian's stomach, enough force for him to keel over. Other times, it was more like a bad bruise. A twisted ankle that hadn't had time to heal. He only found it painful when prodded at the wrong angle.

The peak of their shared complex crested into view. With a hop, Zoomer cleared the low fence of a half-empty parking lot. "Still no sign of him?"

"No. Nothing." It took Adrian far more effort to clamber over the lot's wooden barrier. He straddled it briefly, legs swinging on either side. "Do you think it's messed up if I still kinda miss him?"

"Yeah. Probably." Zoomer offered her arm and helped him land on his feet. "But we're both pretty messed up already, so who really cares?"

They approached a busy road. Zoomer leaned back on her heels, staring down the blinking red hand at the crosswalk. "Hey, did those stains ever come out of your couch?"

"Nope!" A truck roared past, and Adrian had to shout to be heard. "Pop has scrubbed it like twenty times!"

"Nasty. And super sketchy." Zoomer dug into her pocket and fished out a few more Fuzzy Peach candies. She popped three in her mouth at once, chewing loudly. "Guess it's kind of a good thing your neighbour narked on you?"

The light changed and they scurried across the street. "Pop's still pretty pissed," said Adrian. "He keeps saying it wasn't *technically* against the apartment's rules. Not that it matters anymore. Looks like the superintendent believed Dad's story about hosting 'out-of-town cousins,' so we're probably not getting evicted." He wiggled a loose rendition of spirit fingers. "So, yay for that."

"Good!" Zoomer kicked at a stray pop bottle along the sidewalk. "You're not allowed to get kicked out, got it? This place was a total snore without you."

Adrian smiled back at her. "I missed you too, Zoomie."

"You are *so* not calling me that." She picked up the pace, making Adrian hurry after.

"What? I thought we were extra-special best-friends-forever!" He spun around to walk backwards, making faces at her. Zoomer pursed her lips, poised to retaliate. But as they rounded the sidewalk's bend, she fell silent. He felt it too, a weight creeping into his stomach.

He didn't have to turn around. He knew exactly where they were.

The outline of an iron archway cut through the pink

and orange sky. "Crap," Zoomer hissed. "I didn't mean to— we can go a different way next time."

"It's okay." Adrian stepped off the curb and crossed towards the graveyard's fence. "Let's go over."

The cemetery grounds were silent, empty as ever. Adrian rested a hand on the entrance, the metal cool on his palm. The rosebush was rich with crimson flowers, a late-season bloom.

A touch on his back made Adrian's heart flutter for an instant, even though he knew it was just Zoomer checking in. "You alright?" She gently squeezed his shoulder.

Adrian sighed. "I keep waiting for things to get better. But every time I look down from my window, it's happening all over again."

"I know the feeling." Zoomer gently nodded. The two of them stood in silence for a while, watching the slow reach of shadows as the sun put itself to bed. The street lights flickered to life and cast down their golden halos.

"Hey." Adrian broke their mutual contemplation. "Still got some of those Fuzzy Peaches?"

The gummies had a few flecks of lint. Adrian brushed them off before kneeling beside the cemetery gate. Zoomer glanced at a pair of passing pedestrians. "What're you doing?"

"Making an offering." Pushing aside a few stray leaves, Adrian nestled the candies into the grass. Zoomer briefly opened her mouth but shut it again without a word.

Something darted in the shadows. Adrian stumbled back into Zoomer's arms, patting himself down. Even once certain there was no ghost trying to worm its way into his body, it took a few moments for his racing heart to calm.

A pair of yellow eyes appeared towards the back of the graveyard. They were paired with short, fuzzy ears and whiskers that twitched with curiosity. Zoomer peered at the creature. "Is that...?"

"A cat." Adrian gripped his chest, catching his breath. "It's just a cat."

The stray tabby was no larger than a loaf of bread. A speckled, orange tail raised high, it slipped from behind a gravestone and held still, staring at Adrian and Zoomer. With a blink, it darted down the cemetery's shallow path and slipped through the fence-posts. A second later, it disappeared into the growing night.

A breeze rushed along the back of Adrian's neck, along the cemetery path, and into the trees. Leaves rustled and began to scatter, a chorus of burgundy and golden yellow. They painted the ground, danced into the air, and were lost among the city's grand autumn tapestry. As the two friends watched the dazzling show, Zoomer took Adrian's hand in her own. They stood there a long while with nothing more needing to be said.

◆◆◆

"I don't know what to say."

Whoever was speaking, Adrian couldn't see them. The words drifted towards him from no place in particular, brushed past his cheek and slipped away again. A grey mist hung low in the air, trickling along the city's narrow sidewalks. The streets were empty, no cars or electric scooters. Grey skyscrapers bent inwards like a gathering of giants, their rows of windows flickering like many winking eyes.

How long had Adrian been away from home? His fathers didn't like him to stay out too late anymore, especially on a school night. He tried to check the time on his phone but the numbers were all jumbled up together.

"You don't have to say anything if you don't want to, darlin'." Another voice. This time, Adrian could vaguely sense its direction. It was coming from the cemetery.

The fog pooled, nearly high enough to envelop the graveyard's crooked oak tree. From deep within its recesses, four shapes slowly began to appear. Adrian lingered on the outside of the gate, unwilling to tread upon that dangerous ground. He peered into the mist, trying to make out their faces, but he couldn't hold the details. Just trying made him dizzy.

"Careful you don't wake him up. Are you sure you are ready?"

"As I'll ever be."

Adrian's heart skipped a beat. He recognized the speaker now. At first a hazy outline, Sorel stepped out of the fog. With each movement, he grew more solid. He was coming closer.

Adrian stumbled backwards, slipping from the sidewalk curb. The world shifted with him, and suddenly, he was upright again. Sorel's arm was under him, bracing his fall. They stood still in the middle of the road, staring at one another.

"Is it really you?" asked Adrian. Sorel replied with a nod and pushed Adrian back to his feet. Where they'd touched, a tingling sensation remained. "Where have you been?" Adrian glanced towards the graveyard. "I went to look for you."

"You won't find me back there, if I can help it." Sorel chuckled and walked past Adrian. He lifted one hand, beckoning him to follow.

When Adrian turned, he was standing in a meadow. Sorel was a few paces ahead. It was dusk, and the valley below was lit by an array of string lights. Empty picnic tables sat scattered around an oblong, single-storey building. On its roof was a massive circular structure; bright orange, flecked with white; it had brown rind and was missing a triangular wedge on one side.

"You seeing this?" Sorel skipped and raised his arms in triumph. "It's Canada's largest cheese wheel!"

Adrian gawked. As he approached, he realized the wheel's surrounding grounds were not empty after all. Shadows flickered on the picnic benches, formed lines at a small concession stand. The amorphous figures danced like firelight. Tiny sparks played together, dodging through the invisible crowd. Groups gathered into collective bonfires. "Why are we here?"

"Oh, well." Sorel tucked his hands into his pockets. "I never got to see it myself, so this way is kind of the next best thing."

They passed a pale, broad flame that was handing out the memory of cotton candy. One of the silhouettes brushed against Adrian's shoulder. Even through his shirt, it prickled his skin. He shivered. "And this way is what exactly?"

"Not important." Sorel led him towards a narrow staircase. "Well, kind of important but hard to explain. And we only have a little while."

A gentle breeze picked up across the meadow, rustling the leaves of nearby trees. It carried the scent of cotton candy and popcorn from the shadow families picnicking nearby. The silhouettes conversed among themselves, the specifics of their conversations imperceptible. Some unseen speaker played a faint melody, its tune blending seamlessly with the general chatter.

For the first time, Adrian noticed the cheese was slowly rotating. Small gondolas were built right into the wheel. Shadow figures were taking turns loading in for rides. Sorel flagged down a lift and held open its door. "Care for a go-around?"

Adrian crossed his arms. "You brought me all the way here to try and score another date?"

The easy smile fell from Sorel's face. "No." He spoke softly. "I know better than to ask for that. I was sorta hoping we could just talk about, you know, what happened?"

"Talk? About what?!" Adrian clenched his fists. He wondered what might happen if he tried to punch a ghost—probably wasn't worth it to find out. "Are we gonna debrief the part where you tried to body-snatch me, or when you tried to murder my best friend?"

Sorel looked down at his shoes. "I was thinking, all of it?"

Everything in Adrian wanted to walk away, to march back up the hill and get out of this weird limbo place. Well, but maybe not *everything* in him. "Fine." Adrian shoved past Sorel, stepping into the gondola. "Let's just get this over with."

The seat's cushions were pungent, like aging cheddar. A safety bar was locked down by an unseen hand. Adrian gripped it and found the texture oddly spongy. He scooted over, putting as much distance as possible between himself and Sorel.

They began to lift, pausing occasionally for the next riders to load in. "Well, I'm here now," said Adrian. "What did you wanna say?"

"Well, so after I..." Sorel's words trailed off. He inhaled deeply, exhaled through his nose and tried again. "After I tried to steal your life, I met up with some other spirits. They were already in the know about everything—apparently, you met?"

"Oh." The tension in Adrian's jaw softened. "The trio. You found them."

"Yeah." Sorel tucked a lock of hair behind his ear. "Um, everybody says hi. Especially Marty."

"Sounds about right." Adrian fought back a rising smirk.

The wheel hummed as it turned, their gondola rocking lightly. Strangely, Adrian wasn't getting seasick. The grounds spread open below them, string lights twinkling like tiny stars. "So, they got you to come and see me," he speculated. "Trying to give you a shot at redemption or something?"

"Or something." Sorel's hair tousled in the breeze. "It was my idea, though. I wanted to tell you that I know how wrong it was to try and take, well, everything from you."

"Mhm?" Adrian channelled his best impression of Pop's disappointed grimace. "Better late than never, I guess."

Sorel turned to face the wind. The ground below shrank further away, shadow people dancing in the setting sunlight. "I know it'll never be enough, but I really am sorry. There's no reason for you to trust me, but I promise, I'll never come near you or Zoomer ever again."

The wheel stopped again. Their seat wavered in place. "Like, *never* never?" asked Adrian.

Nodding, Sorel spoke under his breath. "The trio's leaving soon, and I'm going with them. I don't understand where we're going, but I know you can't follow."

"So, this really is goodbye." All the rage and resentment inside Adrian washed off like city dirt after a storm. If this was really their last chance, he wasn't going to waste it being angry. "Sorel, what you did—it's okay. Well, not okay, but I know it wasn't you."

"But it was." Sorel scowled. He gripped the safety bar, knuckles turning white. "That's the worst part. Everything I did, there was a part of me that wanted to do it. I was so desperate and scared, I was willing to hurt people. Even those I..."—he sniffled and wiped his nose with his shirtsleeve—"...that I loved."

"Fine, then it was you." Adrian scooted closer. "But I wasn't perfect either. I never should have let things go that far."

"Don't say that." When he blinked, Sorel's cheeks were wet with tears. "I'm the only one to blame."

Adrian reached for him but Sorel shrank back. "That makes me, what," he chuckled, "some hapless victim of your evil machinations—that the story we're going with?"

"I would never say that." Gathering himself, Sorel cleared his throat. "You're a survivor. You saved all of us!"

"Don't even start with that." Adrian poked at Sorel's shoulder. It was surprisingly solid. "I'm not a hero, and you're not a monster. At least, not *most* of the time." That last part coaxed out a shared, tentative smile. "You were scared," said Adrian. "We both were. If I was in your shoes, I might have tried the same thing—sort of did, if you think about it." Gingerly, he moved closer once again. This time, Sorel didn't pull away. Adrian ran his fingertips over those freckles that glittered like dust in a sunbeam.

"God, I've missed you," Sorel whimpered. He leaned into the warmth of Adrian's open palm. "It feels so good to just have you hold me."

"You're hot," smirked Adrian. "Like, physically."

"Ditto," Sorel winked. Warmth rose to Adrian's cheeks.

They snuggled, watching the sunset drift from gold to pink. After some silence, Sorel spoke again. "You've always been so good to me. Even though I didn't mean to, I still kinda took advantage of that."

Adrian squeezed Sorel's knee. "And I took advantage of you back. Every time we left the cemetery, I was playing with your life—or, your death. We both knew what we were doing was risky, and that it couldn't last forever."

Folding his hand atop Adrian's, Sorel murmured, "I guess we did, yeah."

The day's light was running long. As the cheese wheel hummed to life again, Adrian and Sorel rose a few more feet. They were at the very peak of its summit, able to see beyond the clearing now. Iridescent hills arched out in all directions, speckled with dark forest and glittering streams. Mist snaked along the furthest edges. A wine-dark sky hung above, early starlight twinkling between drifting clouds. In the distance, city lights sparkled.

An arm over his shoulder, Adrian lay against Sorel's chest. He basked in the novel joy of listening to the rhythm of his heartbeat. "I keep trying not to think about you. I try and talk to Zoomer about it and she acts like she understands, but she doesn't really get it. The only one who ever could was—"

"You." Sorel nuzzled him, lips pressed to the top of Adrian's head. "I know."

The fog grew thicker. It looked like cottonwood seeds, drifting out of the trees and rolling down the hills. It began to fill the valley like a lake. The shadow people were gone. Adrian's eyes were growing heavy; he fought back a yawn.

"Will I see you again?"

Sorel's eyes sparkled, even in the absence of light.

"Probably not."

The rise of a full moon cast them both as pale blue silhouettes. Sorel tucked a hand under Adrian's chin and lifted his face. "I want you to know, you are the most amazing thing that has ever happened to me."

Adrian sighed into Sorel's lips. "Same."

Sorel had a new taste, tangy like a raspberry that still needed time to ripen. Hands grasping, Adrian ran his fingers through those silky, ginger curls. They fell into one another and sent the gondola rocking. Sorel laughed into Adrian's mouth, his breath warm.

The wheel started turning but it didn't feel like they were descending. Rather, they were climbing higher, impossibly so, rising into to the night sky like they were in a hot air balloon. Adrian kept his eyes shut.

He woke to tears on his cheeks. Adrian clutched his eyelids together, tugging on the thread of his fading dream. Silently, he begged it to stay, but there was no use bargaining. All things had their own end.

Sunrise danced across his bedroom walls. Adrian clutched his pillow, deeply exhausted. All those sleepless months, midnight wanderings, and odd-hour adventures, they had caught up with him at last. He didn't try to fight it. Something told him, when next he woke, he would finally be well rested. Adrian drifted, soothed by a lullaby of birdsongs mixed with early morning traffic. The city was readying itself for the start of a new day.

ACKNOWLEDGEMENTS

Storytelling is rarely an easy task, and it is never done alone. Though a single author's name may sit below the title, those of us drawn to this work know it is never that simple. We are a compilation of all the tellers who have come before us, those who grace us with their own stories each day, and all those with yarns still yearning for the spinning wheel. It is an honour and a responsibility to participate in such an act of collective weaving. For this reason, I would like to pause here and express my gratitude.

Firstly, I offer my sincere thanks to the Canada Council for the Arts and the Ontario Arts Council. This book would not have been possible without their funding and support. If any of those on the review committee so happen to be reading this book, thank you for taking a chance on this queer little project.

There is so much thanks to be given to all the editors and collaborators who helped this story come to life. Ronan Sadler, thank you for reading this story in its earliest drafts and seeing its potential. Felix Chau Bradley, thank you for your thoughtful editorial guidance and ongoing support. Thank you to Myriad Augustine for all your feedback on this and so many other projects. Keet Geniza, your graphic design brought my characters to life and the final product is just magnificent! To the co-founders of Metonymy Press,

Oliver Fugler and Ashley Fortier, I am so grateful for all the love and care you have given to this work. Without all of you, this story would never have made it out into the big, wide world.

I've also been so fortunate to have the support of my family and dear friends. Thank you to Andrew McAllister, for loving me so fully; every day is a date with you. Thank you to Hannah Dees, for all the late-night bad-TV marathons and early morning chats over tea and coffee. Thank you to River Nason Harwood-Dees, for being absolutely you. Thank you to Shane Forrest, Mackenzie Stewart, Michiko Bown-Kai, McKenzie Grey, Lauren Munro, Caitlin and John Chee, Tamar Brannigan, Jasbina S. Misir, Frances O'Shaughnessy, Sebastian DeLine, and Adria Kurchina-Tyson: your dedicated enthusiasm for this project kept me going through even the toughest of times. Special thanks to Christine Hsu, who helped spark the idea for this story. And thank you to my grandparents, Bill and Cheryl Telford and Tony Harwood-Jones and Heather Dixon, for always taking my calls.

This book is also in dedication to those who will never get a chance to read it, including Pina Newman, Emet Tauber, Kerri O'Kee, and Ara Jo. Each of you was such a gift to the world; your sparks were bright, your minds were brilliant, and your hearts were full of love for all those you met. You deserved so much more. Thank you for sharing your stories with me, when you did. You are so missed.

Last but not least, thank you to Dunkin. For jumping on the bed in the morning, for cuddling at my feet during long writing days, for getting me out of the house even when I really didn't want to go; I wish you could have lived forever, but you lived well and I guess that's all we can really ask for. Run free and sleep in warm sunbeams, my friend.

Photo by Katia Taylor

ABOUT THE AUTHOR

Markus Harwood-Jones (he/they) is a proudly queer and trans space-case who has been writing since he can remember. Markus specializes in writing young-adult fiction and has a soft spot for sappy love stories. He lives in downtown Toronto with his husband, their platonic co-parent, and their extra-cute kiddo. Markus is an aspiring TikTokker and can be found on social media under the handle @MarkusBones.

ALSO AVAILABLE FROM METONYMY PRESS

LOTE by Shola von Reinhold

Personal Attention Roleplay by H Felix Chau Bradley

The Good Arabs by Eli Tareq El Bechelany-Lynch

A Natural History of Transition by Callum Angus

Dear Black Girls by Shanice Nicole and Kezna Dalz

ZOM-FAM by Kama La Mackerel

Dear Twin by Addie Tsai

Little Blue Encyclopedia (for Vivian) by Hazel Jane Plante

nîtisânak by Jas M. Morgan

Lyric Sexology Vol. 1 by Trish Salah

Fierce Femmes and Notorious Liars:
A Dangerous Trans Girl's Confabulous Memoir
by Kai Cheng Thom

Small Beauty by jiaqing wilson-yang

She Is Sitting in the Night: Re-visioning Thea's Tarot
by Oliver Pickle and Ruth West